MURDER
KNOCKS
TWICE

ALSO BY SUSANNA CALKINS

A Murder at Rosamund's Gate

From the Charred Remains

The Masque of a Murderer

A Death Along the River Fleet

MURDER KNOCKS TWICE

A SPEAKEASY MURDER

SUSANNA CALKINS

MINOTAUR BOOKS

NEW YORK

MURDER KNOCKS TWICE. Copyright © 2019 by Susanna Calkins. All rights reserved. Printed in the United States of America. For information, address St. Martin's Press, 175 Fifth Avenue, New York, N.Y. 10010.

www.minotaurbooks.com

Designed by Omar Chapa

The Library of Congress Cataloging-in-Publication Data is available upon request.

ISBN 978-1-250-19083-3 (trade paperback)
ISBN 978-1-250-19084-0 (e-book)

First Edition: April 2019

10 9 8 7 6 5 4 3 2 1

For Matt, Quentin, and Alex

MURDER KNOCKS TWICE

CHAPTER 1

Turning off Halsted, Gina Ricci made her way down the long alley, picking her way through dumped-over rubbish bins, old tin cans, sodden newspapers, and dirty puddles of melted snow. The late afternoon sun made it easy enough for her to see, at least, and when she reached the third door—weather-beaten green with an eye-level metal grille—she knocked.

Two short raps, followed by a third, just as she'd been told.

"Hullo, darling," a man called out behind her. "Looking for someone?"

She turned around, chewing her spearmint gum a bit faster. A blond man, maybe in his late twenties and dressed in rumpled evening clothes, was stumbling toward her. *"I can't give you anything . . ."* he called to her, his voice half singing, half slurring the words of the popular song. His blue eyes were bloodshot, though his smile was wide. Hiccupping, he continued with the lyrics. *". . . but love, baby!"*

"Aw, go on," Gina snapped back. "New Year's ended two days ago."

"Is that right?" he asked, pulling a silver flask from the inside of his short tuxedo jacket. "I hadn't noticed." After he took a swig, he held it up to her. "Come on, let's get fried."

"It's four thirty in the afternoon," she said, pulling her winter coat around her more tightly, feeling like an old schoolteacher. Lulu would laugh if she saw her.

Still, it was getting cold, and she didn't like being forced to wait outside, especially only steps away from a boob on a bender. Besides, the alley smelled vaguely of vomit.

Gina looked up and down the alley. This was definitely the third door on the right, directly off Halsted.

She frowned. Or was it supposed to be three doors down from the *other* direction—off Morgan Street? No, Lulu had assured her it was this way. Besides, the door was green, exactly as Lulu had described. This had to be it.

Pulling back her coat sleeve, Gina checked her watch. She was on time. Why hadn't anyone opened the door?

Had Lulu been having a bit of fun at her expense? She'd been surprised when Lulu had approached her at their local market a few days ago, greeting her with a warm hug. She'd seen her around the neighborhood, of course, but they hadn't talked in years, at least not since Lulu was still Louise Smith and long before both women had bobbed their hair. Lulu had asked Gina about her papa, and Gina had shared some of her worries. One thing had led to the other, and suddenly Lulu was telling her about a position that had opened where she worked.

It's darb, Lulu had said, striking a glamorous pose. Then she'd dropped the affectation, adding more earnestly, *Tips are great, I swear.* There had been a weariness behind Lulu's eyes when she'd spoken, and the memory of the redhead's sly smile now gave Gina pause.

Almost as if reading her thoughts, the man spoke again. "Sure you're in the right place?" Then he waved his flask at her.

Gina rolled her eyes at his blatant defiance of the Volstead Act. Drinking inside, hidden from the prying eyes of Prohibition agents, was one thing, but it was quite another to drink out in the open. Cops were supposed to enforce public intoxication laws. "Better watch it," she warned him. "Or you'll be getting comfy in a caboose in no time."

"Ah, don't sweat it, kid." He took another guzzle but returned the flask to his inner jacket pocket. The lining was probably cushioned to keep the vial from being discovered by prying eyes. He gestured toward the still-closed door. "Big Mike has the police in his pocket. Where do you suppose the cops go for a nip when they're off duty?"

Gina was not altogether surprised. She didn't know Mike Castallazzo, the owner of the establishment she was trying to enter, but it stood to reason that he had a few cops on his payroll. Chicago police were notoriously corrupt. Had been as long as she could remember.

Knocking at the door again, Gina repeated the same cadence as before, but a little louder.

This time, she heard a scrabbling sound from behind the grille and someone slid open a small slot in the door. She could see two dark brown eyes peering out at her. Lulu had told her the doorkeeper's name was Gucciani. Gooch for short.

"Hey there, Mr. Gucciani?" she called. "Lulu sent me. It's me, Gina."

"And me! Ned!" the man called out with a half hiccup.

The eyes disappeared when a piece of wood was slid back over the hole.

"What the——?" Gina exclaimed. Where had the man gone? She banged her fists against the door in frustration, immediately wishing she hadn't when pain shot through both hands.

She heard the man who'd called himself Ned laugh. "That could have gone better, you think?"

Whirling around to face him, she put up her fists the way her brother had taught her when she was a kid. "Why don't you mind your own apples?"

"Hey, settle down there, missy!" he said. "How's your hand? Looks like that hurt. Knocking me around won't do much to make it better, either."

She chomped on her gum, trying to regain her cool. His self-assurance was really starting to bug her. "My hand's fine. How about you beat it?" She frowned. "I bet he'd have let me in, if you hadn't been hanging around."

"Not my fault, sweetheart. You didn't say the right word," he said. "Can't crack this joint without it. They're mighty particular in that regard. Besides, they have to let *me* in."

"What?" Gina asked, thoroughly confused. "Why's that?"

Ned snickered. "Watch and see." He leaned past her, knocking on the door as she had just done.

"I just tried that," she said.

To her surprise, though, the little slot behind the grille opened again. Ned put his mouth close to the metal and whispered something that sounded like "purple berries."

"What did you say?" Gina asked, but before he could answer, the door swung open, revealing a huge, portly man dressed in a tailored pinstripe suit. The man was clean-shaven, with olive-toned skin and thick black hair, and he loomed over her by at least a foot. A cigar dangled from his lips.

"Hey, Gooch," he said to the man, stepping inside. He turned back to Gina. "Coming?" he asked.

Gina scrambled after him, only to be stopped by Gooch once she was three steps into the building.

"Stay here," the man warned, as he relocked the door behind her. Ned, who was a few steps ahead of her, paused.

Gina looked around. They had entered a small room with a single lightbulb swinging above the entranceway, casting shadows on the cracked and peeling walls. As her eyes adjusted to the light, she could make out a closed door marked TEA ROOM ENTRANCE to her right, and another doorway at the far end of the room. A tall stool was in the corner by the green alley door, and at eye level there was a peephole from which a faint line of sunlight flowed. Evidently the doorkeeper maintained a perch by the door, allowing him to keep watch over the alley unseen, without having to slide open the panel behind the grille.

Gooch must have known I was there the whole time, Gina thought, feeling a bit annoyed. *And here I was, freezing!*

Her indignant feelings fled, though, when Gooch turned back to her. As he moved, his suit coat swung open to reveal a handgun strapped to his waist.

"What's your business here?" he demanded.

Gina swallowed. Of course, she'd seen guns before, but still she felt rattled. *What kind of dumb sap am I anyway, letting Lulu talk me into this gig? Gotta be an easier way to make some bucks.*

Yet there really wasn't. Her father was depending on her, and now that the restaurant she'd been working at had closed, they were in a pickle.

Gooch was still staring down at her, waiting for her to reply, his thoughts hidden behind an untwitching mask. She tried to squeak something, but no actual words came out of her mouth. Behind him, Ned raised an eyebrow but didn't say anything. *Get a grip, Gina,* she thought to herself.

"Lulu said Signora Castallazzo needed some help. In the *tea room?*" she added, with a meaningful look at the little sign, to show she was in on the scheme.

"Is that so?" he asked. "Then why did you come this way? Could have walked in the front door. Tea room's open till seven p.m."

A bit late for a tea room to be open, but Gina didn't think she should say that. "Lulu told me to come in through the back way," she said instead, trying to keep her voice from cracking.

Gooch grunted. Without taking his eyes off her, he leaned over and tugged on a long cord that ran down the length of the wall and disappeared into a small hole in the floor.

What was happening? She glanced back at Ned, who didn't seem too concerned.

"Uh, Mr. Gooch. I'm sure that I—" Gina broke off as the door at the end of the room opened and another heavyset man appeared. Like Gooch, he was also dressed in a pinstripe suit and wore a white tie. He was balder than Gooch, though, and his face was distinctly pockmarked. Right now, he was scowling at Gina.

"You Gina?" he asked. His words were heavy. *Russian,* Gina thought. *Or perhaps Serbian.* Their neighborhood was full of recent immigrants from Eastern and Central Europe, and sometimes their accents were hard to tell apart.

She nodded, her heart beating quickly. How many guns did he have under *his* jacket? Probably at least two.

The man looked at Gooch. "*Ja*, she checks out. Signora said a new girl would be coming by."

Gina breathed a small sigh of relief. The sound surprised her. She hadn't even realized that she had been holding her breath.

"Well, that's settled, then," Ned said. He clapped the man on the shoulder. "This here's Lesky. We call him Little Johnny. Ain't he bonny?"

Little Johnny crossed his arms, ignoring Ned.

Ned wasn't done. He pointed at Gooch. "You've met Gooch. He watches the hooch."

Gooch looked at his watch, not responding to Ned's banter. "Break's over, piano man."

"How about I take Gina here to the Signora first," Ned offered. "Show her around?"

"Easy there, Neddy Fingers," Gooch said, for the first time cracking the slightest of grins. To Gina he added, "Better stay away from this one. He's a first-rate swinger."

When Little Johnny grinned, Gina could see his mouth was full of gold teeth. With a slight shudder, she wondered if his teeth had come out all at once. She knew a man who'd taken a hammer to the face, after getting on the wrong side of the law. She put the thought aside when Gooch opened the unmarked door at the end of the room and gestured for her to follow.

Little Johnny stayed behind, positioning himself on the stool by the door. Evidently it was his turn to keep watch on the alley.

"So you work here," she whispered to Ned as they walked after Gooch down a long dark corridor. "You couldn't just have told me that? When I was knocking at the door?"

"Now what fun would that have been?" Ned replied, stretching his long fingers. "I'm the piano man, didn't you get that?"

"I also got 'Neddy Fingers.'"

"Hey, I'm a swell fella."

At the end of the corridor, they reached another old wooden door. Gina thought she could hear the faint sound of music coming from just beyond.

To her surprise, Ned put his hand on the doorknob. "Allow me," he said to Gooch and swung open the door with a great flourish. After giving a little bow, he stepped aside so she could enter first. "Welcome to the Third Door," he said. "Greatest speakeasy in Chicago."

Ned led Gina down three steps, turned to the right, and stopped. Following him, Gina was about to make a cutting remark about booze in a basement, but the words died on her lips when she found herself on a balcony of sorts, overlooking a vast and unexpectedly beautiful room. "Oh" was all she could muster, as she gaped in amazement.

Lulu had not done the Third Door justice when she had described the establishment to Gina. Clearly connecting the basements of several buildings, the speakeasy was far larger than she'd expected. This was no dime-store dump, either. The place was *gorgeous*.

Great chandeliers hung from a patterned tin ceiling, casting enough light for Gina to easily see the world below. About fifteen mostly empty oak tables were arranged around a wooden dance floor, a grand piano toward the back of the room. A long ornately paneled bar with dozens of colored bottles and glasses ran the length of the room, with five framed mirrors catching and reflecting the light. Two red upholstered love seats were positioned against a richly paneled wall, and a set of plush purple chairs was in another corner, where the original brick of the basement foundations could still be seen. A portrait of Mussolini was mounted on one end of the bar, and a framed painting of a nude woman stepping from a bath was positioned at the other.

Throughout the room, Gina noted only a handful of people. A white-haired bartender was pouring a drink for a patron sitting at the bar. Two or three couples were seated at tables, sipping brightly colored cocktails in fancy glasses. The dance floor itself was empty except for one couple dancing lazily to Al Jolson crooning from a gramophone. Small candles flickered in glasses on every table, adding a sense of magic and allure to the smoky haze. This was a secret place. A forbidden place.

Gina felt a thrill run through her.

Beyond the main area, she could see a few closed doors. Signora Castallazzo was likely behind one of them, she thought. Eagerly she started forward.

To her surprise, Ned put his hand on her arm. "You know there are other exits," he whispered, so that Gooch wouldn't hear him. "Want me to take you? One leads to the gangway. No one else ever needs to know you were here. You could just go home."

Gina looked up at him. His earlier demeanor as a drunk playboy seemed to have dissipated, and she didn't like his change in tone. "Why? I need the work."

"There's other work."

His comment made Gina pause. She'd never even been in a place like the Third Door before. She'd had her share of bootlegged alcohol, of course, usually in the form of moonshine and bathtub gin concocted by her neighbors. Sometimes a dollop added to her tea in a restaurant, back when she and her papa had a bit of money to spare. Unless a gal had a fancy man taking her around—which Gina didn't—places like this got real expensive, real quick. It wasn't like she was out prowling for a man, either.

Nor, she suspected, would her mother have been particularly pleased to see her employed at the Third Door, given its rather scandalous reputation. Though her mother—sweet Molly O'Brien—had passed away when she was ten, Gina felt deep inside that her mother would not have approved. She thought about taking Ned's advice, finding the other exit, and walking right out.

As she stood there, Jolson's chipper voice continued to float from the gramophone below. *I'm sitting on top of the world,* he sang. *I'm singing a song . . .*

She'd seen Jolson's talkie the year before—*The Singing Fool,* it was called—with her father at the Uptown Theatre, before the palsy had slowed him down.

She straightened her back. She couldn't give up now. "Take me to Signora Castallazzo," Gina said to Gooch. "I'm ready."

Gina followed the men down the remainder of the stairs, stuffing her hat in her handbag and laying her coat over her arm as she descended.

"The Signora will be in her salon," Gooch said, pointing to a door on the other side of the speakeasy floor. "Over there."

Seeing the gleaming exuberance around her, she suddenly felt quite dumpy in her new flannel velour polka-dot dress. *Don't be too fussy,* Lulu had told her. *The Signora prefers her girls to look smart and sophisticated.*

When she had stood before the department store mirrors yesterday, though, Gina had been quite entranced by the dress, running her fingers along the green polka dots that flowed over the collar, cuffs, and belt loops. She'd traced the pearl buttons that ran above the belt, and twirled about on the dressing room pedestal, watching the drop-waist skirt swish with her movements. How splendid she had felt, laying the five and a half dollars down on the counter.

It's for my new job, she had informed the sales clerk, full of her own self-importance.

Secretary? the woman had guessed.

No, Gina had replied, taken aback by the clerk's appraisal. She'd then swept out of the store in a fit of pique, miffed that she'd been taken for an office worker. She'd thought the dress was elegant, suitable to meet her new employer.

Now she wished she had heeded the clerk's reaction. The dress was clearly more appropriate for an office than a night-club, and to make matters worse, the heat of the room was making the wool feel overly warm and scratchy. She wished she could tear it off.

The feeling was amplified when Ned turned back toward her and, seeing her fuss at her skirt, pursed his lips to deliver a low unappreciative whistle. "Tea room's upstairs," he reminded her. "Some grannies need their crumpets."

She scowled at him. "Aren't you supposed to be working?" She cocked her head toward the couple dancing slowly to the record. "Better hurry. You seem to have been replaced."

"Indeed," he replied. He hesitated, and she wondered whether he was going to warn her again. Instead, he just gave her a cocky grin and headed over to the gramophone, where he removed the arm from the record and shut the cabinet cover with some force. Stretching his fingers, he sat down at the piano and began to play.

"Hullo, love," he called to a waitress as she passed by the piano, carrying a tray of brightly hued cocktails and wearing a short dress that no secretary would have been caught dead in. Catching Gina's eye again, he winked. *"I want to be loved by you,"* he sang, now with a surprisingly pleasant tenor. *"By you and nobody else but you."*

Rolling her eyes at his antics, Gina walked toward the Signora's salon. She was almost halfway there when she heard a woman's sultry voice call out her name.

Gina turned around to discover a stylish woman dressed in a tailored gray dress standing by the bar, regarding her critically. Immediately she knew, from the woman's stern bearing and authoritative air, that this was Signora Castallazzo. Lulu had called her "the lady of stone and steel," and that seemed exactly right.

The Signora's black hair was bobbed right to her chin, straight and sleek without a single finger wave. Though it was nearing evening, long sleeves still covered her arms, and she had knotted several strands of white pearls at her diaphragm. Her lips were bright red, and her dark gray eyes scrutinized Gina from top to bottom, lingering at her unadorned neckline. Once again, Gina wished she had not left all her costume jewelry in a wooden box on her dresser at home.

"I am Signora Castallazzo," the woman declared in her richly accented voice.

"Pleased to meet you," Gina said, sticking out her hand as she remembered her mother teaching her.

The Signora ignored the gesture, still studying her. "You seem sweet."

Gina started to thank her and then realized that she wasn't being paid a compliment. *Don't be a rube,* she thought. *You gotta show the Signora that you can handle yourself. That you're not looking for a swell to take care of you.*

Putting her hand on her hip, Gina struck a pose like Clara Bow in *It.* "I'm no dumbbell," she said. "No one's gonna sweet-talk me."

Even though Gina felt like an idiot, the Signora seemed to approve, for she gave the slightest smile. "Come with me," she said. "Let's find you something more *appropriate* to wear."

Gina followed the Signora into a back room that had a long counter that ran the length of the wall, messily displaying oval mirrors, hair-filled brushes, opened tubes of lipstick, and jars full of powder and blush. A cloying aroma of perfumes and other scents tickled her nose and caused her to sneeze.

"Er, pardon me," she said hastily, when the Signora handed her a Kleenex with suspicion.

Gina continued to look around. On the other side of the room there were several racks of sequined dresses, sparkling headdresses and fluffy feather boas. She'd never had occasion to wear such glittery attire, let alone had the funds to purchase them.

"Keen," she breathed, running her fingers over the silver beaded fringe of one of the dresses.

The Signora's next words felt like a slap. "Those outfits are for our *entertainers.* Cigarette girls wear something different." She looked Gina up and down as she began to rummage through the rack. "You look like you've stayed off the sweets, at least."

Slipping a silky piece off its hanger, the Signora regarded it for a moment before handing it to her. "This one." She pointed one elegant finger at a beautifully embroidered screen at the end of the room, emblazoned with brightly colored birds and butterflies. "Change. There."

A few minutes later, Gina found herself in a short black dress with a plunging neckline, black pumps, and a white se-quined headband holding back her short brown waves. Only her undergarments and hosiery were her own, and she was grateful that she'd splurged on black rayon stockings instead of the gray woolens she usually wore.

As she contemplated her image in the mirror, the Signora handed her a tube of red lipstick. "Brighten up a bit."

Gina did as she was told. The Signora surveyed her criti-cally. "You'll do. You'll need to be here every day except Sun-day by five thirty, ready to start at six p.m., unless I tell you otherwise. Most nights we go until one or two a.m., although if business is slow, we may send you home at midnight."

Papa will be fine without me, she thought, trying again to sup-press another faint qualm. *I'll be fine without him, too.*

The Signora was not done. "The dress you came in will never do, I hope you understand. You may wear this dress for the next few days, but then I expect you to purchase at least two more." She took a calling card out of a small silk bag that was tied to her waist and wrote something on it. "If you take this to Madame Laupin—she's above us, over on Polk—she will charge the dresses to my account. That charge will be subtracted from your pay."

Accepting the card, Gina gulped. She hadn't anticipated

the extra costs, but there was nothing she could do about that now. She could already tell that disagreements with the Signora would be unlikely to end in her favor.

Just then a tall redheaded woman with a white feather in her hair bounced into the dressing room. It was Lulu.

As she sat down at the counter, Lulu did a double take. "Gina!" she exclaimed in surprise. "You got the gig! I wasn't sure—" She broke off when she caught sight of the Signora's raised eyebrow in the mirror. She continued to appraise Gina's silk gown and headpiece, a peculiar look on her face. "I mean, you look swell!"

"Thanks," Gina replied, trying not to feel annoyed. Lulu didn't have to seem *that* surprised by her improved appearance.

"Good evening, Lulu," the Signora said, her cool tone effectively cutting off all conversation between the two women. She glanced pointedly down at her watch, a delicate affair that probably cost more than Gina could make in a year. "A little late, aren't we?"

Gina could not remember ever seeing Lulu look so meek. "I'm sorry, Signora. It won't happen again."

"I should hope not." The Signora touched her hair in the mirror, brushing back a single errant strand. "I need to dress for evening. Lulu, why don't you go ahead and show Gina where everything is. Introduce her to Billy. He'll fill up her tray." She fixed Lulu with a meaningful look. "I want you to train Gina *properly*."

"Yes, Signora." Lulu said. Had her cheeks flushed slightly? It was hard to tell. "Come on, Gina, I'll show you around." She pulled a sparkling purple dress off the rack as the Signora left. "Let me just slip this on."

Without bothering to step behind the screen, Lulu pulled

off her day dress and sat down in front of the mirror, wearing only her undergarments, to adjust her hair and reapply her makeup. She didn't seem overly concerned about being late, now that the Signora was no longer around.

"Ain't this place grand?" Lulu asked, tweezing one of her eyebrows. "Big Mike's thinking of getting a second joint established, but I like it here, don't you?"

"Yeah," Gina agreed, sitting on the stool next to Lulu. The black dress slipped a little farther down her front, and she tugged it back into place. Her knees were completely uncovered as well. She glanced at her watch. "Doesn't the Signora expect us to start soon?"

"Ah, relax. Kick back a little." A mascara wand still in her hand, Lulu reached into her handbag and held a silver flask out to Gina. "A little cocktail to get us started? You look like you could use it, doll."

Glancing at herself in the mirror, Gina could see her face looked drawn, and her mouth was puckered unbecomingly. "Sure, why not?" she said, taking a small sip from the flask. The gin burned the inside of her mouth but warmed her throat and stomach when she swallowed. With a shudder, she handed it back.

Lulu smirked. "You'll get used to it." She continued chattering, mostly about why she was late, telling Gina all about how one of her gentleman friends had taken her to the movies and then out for a lemon ice. "I couldn't very well refuse him a little more of my company, now could I?" she asked, her question punctuated by a little trilling laugh. "Who'da thought you'd be such a dish!" She caught Gina's eyes in the mirror. "You'll be turning some heads tonight."

Finally she stood up and pulled up the thigh-length purple dress, which crisscrossed in a daring way across the front and in the back. For a finishing touch, she wrapped a long strand of costume pearls around her neck and looped another strand around her wrist. She gave a little swirl, and her dress flared seductively around her slim form. "All right, Gina," she said. "Time to learn the ropes!"

CHAPTER 2

As Lulu showed her around, a little bob to her step, Gina sought to look cool and nonchalant, as if she strolled about a speakeasy every night. The Third Door, though large, only had a few rooms, plus a number of dark passageways that led out in all directions. There was a common salon for the performers and staff, with separate dressing areas for the men and women. The Signora had a small salon where she conducted business. The Signor, it seemed, had his own office as well, on the other side. Toward the back there was a storage area where barrels of whiskey and rye were kept. On the other side there was a gambling den, where mostly men but the occasional woman played cards.

"Faye serves them," Lulu said, sounding spiteful. "A shame, too, because they tip real good, and some of them are awful sweet."

"Why is Faye the only one who serves them?"

"The Signora says they ask for her. Heaven knows why," she said, giving her red hair a flip. "Besides, you don't want to mess with Faye. Come on, let me introduce you to Billy Bottles, our barkeep. Billy, yoo-hoo!" she called out to the older man sporting a long white apron and a crisp yellow bow tie. "This is Gina, our new ciggie seller." To Gina she added, "Billy's real knowledgeable about smokes and drinks."

The barkeep, who looked to be in his fifties, glanced at Gina while still wiping out glasses with a white towel. "Lucky Strikes will do for the regular gents. A few will show off by getting a Sobranie or two," he said in a gruff voice while pointing to fancy metal box behind the counter.

"My Papa likes those," she ventured. Although he usually couldn't afford them and just bought the cheaper American brands.

Ignoring her, Billy continued. "Marlboros for the ladies. *Mild as May,* you can tell them. *Ivory tips to protect the lips.* Got it?"

Gina nodded. She'd seen the advertisements in the newspapers. Besides, what woman would want yellow-stained lips and fingers when she smoked? That had to be an easy sell.

"All you really need to know is the puffers and the smokers," Lulu went on. "Puffers take the short pulls, blow out in gusts, take any brand you offer."

"Oh yeah? Then what's a smoker?"

"They're the ones who really enjoy a good smoke. Find *pleasure* in it." She drawled out the word "pleasure" with a giggle.

"You don't say?" Gina asked, checking out the room to see if she could pick out those different types.

Ignoring them both, Billy continued, carefully arranging her tray with a colorful box full of cigars on one side and different containers of cigarettes on the other side. There was some gum there, too—Wrigley's Spearmint, her favorite, as well as Juicy Fruit and Doublemint. "Here's your lighter, and here's your cigar cutter. Saturday nights you switch out with roses for the one-timers."

"One-timers?" Gina asked, hearing Billy snort softly behind her.

"Yeah, that's right. One-timers. Guys and gals who don't come here, except on a lark. In their glad rags, slumming it in the city. Debs, College Joes. You know the type. Those gents will buy their ladies a flower," Lulu explained, sounding almost wistful. "The regulars, well, they're all pikers about it. Won't put up the scratch to buy their dame any more than they have to. Except their dames don't expect it either, so I guess it evens out. Still, I think it's sweet."

"Sure, real sweet," Billy added, holding the black strap of the tray. "Ready?"

Gina bowed her head and, with Lulu's help, managed to place the strap around her neck and position the tray so that it hung easily at her waist. The weight wasn't overly much, but it was strange. "Ugh," she said.

"I remember Dorrie would get a neck strain something awful," Lulu said, sounding sympathetic. "Don't let that happen to you."

Billy carefully counted out some bills and some change. "Here's what you start with. Any losses, clams or stock, will come out of your wages. *Capiche?*"

Gina nodded. "I understand."

As she moved across the floor, the strap yanked at the small hairs on her neck and pulled her low-cut dress down to even more indecent levels. Resting the tray on the piano, Gina fumbled at the strap. "Gee, these gaspers are heavier than they look," she said to Ned, who was looking on in interest.

"Better get used to it," Lulu teased, coming behind her. "The Signora won't take too kindly to a girl who can't manage her tray."

"Oh, is that what happened to the other girl?" Gina asked. "What did you say her name was? Dorrie?"

She was still adjusting the tray, and it took her a moment to realize that neither Lulu nor Ned had answered her question. At the unexpected silence, she looked up.

To her surprise, Lulu's eyes had filled with tears, and Ned was staring intently down at the piano keys. He played three notes in quick succession with his right hand without looking up.

"What is it?" Gina asked.

"Dorrie's gone," Lulu whispered, darting a quick glance around.

"Gone?" Gina asked.

Ned cleared his throat but didn't say anything.

"Well, where did she go?" Gina asked, trying to sound lighthearted. The manner of the other two was decidedly odd. "Run off to get married or something?"

"No." Lulu said. Her tone grew flat. "If you must know, she died. Just before Christmas."

"What? That's terrible! I'm so sorry!" Gina exclaimed, looking from one face to the other.

Lulu surveyed herself in the mirrored panel behind the bar. "Yeah. That's why the Signora needed a new girl," she said, wiping a smudge of black liner from her lower lid with her index finger. Gina could see she was trembling, even though she seemed to be trying to hide it. "That's why they hired *you*."

"What happened to her?"

"She was killed," Ned said, rubbing his forehead. He sounded weary. "Stabbed."

"My God! Who killed her?" Gina asked, feeling a bit breathless. "A customer?"

"Of course not!" Lulu gave Ned a frightened look. "It happened on the L. In the Loop." Straightening up, she pursed her lips. "Dorrie just never showed up again after Christmas Eve. I thought at first maybe she'd gone to Hollywood. She was a real peach, a doll. She could have lit up the silver screen. Or performed at the Moulin Rouge. That's in Paris, you know."

Gina nodded, feeling like she was supposed to do something. Ned made a sound that resembled a smothered cough.

"It's true!" Lulu insisted. "I thought maybe she had done it, just packed her bags and blew this joint! She was always talking about it." She gave Ned another nervous look. "Then we heard later . . . what had happened. It was in the papers."

"Still doesn't make sense," Ned said, idly playing a few discordant notes. "Where was she going?"

"You know we're not supposed to talk about it," Lulu whispered.

"Why not?" Gina asked, echoing Lulu's secretive tone.

"The Signora, Big Mike—well, they don't like it. Dorrie was a particular pet of theirs." Lulu unexpectedly slung one slender arm around Gina's shoulders and gave her a little squeeze. "Enough of that sad tale. It's time for us to get back to work."

With that, Ned began playing again, a mechanical and spiritless tune. It was clear that the girl's death had affected him deeply.

Taking a deep breath, Gina turned her attention back to fixing the strap on her tray so that it would not pinch her neck.

Lulu leaned over to help her. "Just keep the strap here, a bit more around your shoulders. I started on cigarettes, you know. I know everything about it." She gave her hair one last pat, her earlier distress tucked back away. She tossed her head in a saucy way. "Let's get 'em, sister!"

Before long, Gina's neck and feet were starting to ache. Tripping along after Lulu was not easy. After showing her how to keep her money, Lulu explained how to make a little extra in tips. "Smile. Bend over a little if he's standing. A little wiggle when you walk away won't hurt much, either. Get you some more dough."

"Can't I just say nice things about his tie?" Gina wanted to know, not quite sure if she could pull off these tricks. Although the cut of the dress and inches on her heels seemed to be taking care of that for her, given the general smiles she was getting from the male patrons.

"If he's with his wife, don't even bother," Lulu said with a laugh. "Just sell him whatever smokes he needs."

Gina also learned what to do if a customer got too fresh. "That's an easy one," Lulu explained. "Gooch or one of the others will throw him out. The Signora don't like when they get too handy with us." She elbowed Gina in the ribs. "Whatever you do, don't slap him. Let the guys take care of it." She paused. "Mind you don't get too handy with the customers, either. Flirt enough to keep them buying, but the Signora will throw *you* out if people start thinking they can have their way with you."

"They're all hoods, heels, and bums. Got it!" Gina replied. "Besides, it won't be a problem."

Lulu raised an eyebrow. "Don't tell me you've got a sheik now? I guarantee, you won't for long, if you keep working here. Men like coming to these places, but no one wants their girl working at one." She laughed again, sounding a little bitter.

When Gina didn't share any more details of her love life, Lulu went on. "Some of the other girls here, they're gold diggers." She laughed again, as two cocktail waitresses sauntered toward them. "Speak of the devil, here are two of them now. Jade and Faye. Hello gals!"

Faye was a silvery blonde with an equally silvery laugh. When she extended her hand in greeting, her art deco bracelets slipped about on her slim arm. "Charmed," she said with an easy smile that betrayed an endearing dimple.

Jade, a light-skinned black woman with green eyes, was a little more watchful, touching hands with Gina only briefly. She twirled the long white pearls that wrapped around her neck and plunged down the front of her chic green gown. "I guess it didn't take too long to replace Dorrie, did it?" she asked, sounding bitter. "I see you're even wearing her dress and headband."

Gina put her hand to her headband. "I am?" she asked, startled. She noticed that Lulu didn't meet her eyes.

"I don't remember you auditioning," Faye said, crossing her arms over her chest. Jade echoed the gesture.

"Audition?" Gina asked, looking back and forth between the two women.

"Didn't have to," Lulu said, tensing. "The Signora must have just taken my word about how good she'd be."

"*Your* word?" Faye said, raising a delicately arched eyebrow. "How *unusual*."

"I suppose you sing," Jade commented, looking Gina up and down. "Because you don't have a dancer's form. No offense, darling."

"No, I don't dance. Or sing," Gina said, standing a little

straighter. "I thought I was just selling cigarettes and serving cocktails. You all sing and dance?"

"Yes indeed," Lulu replied, puffing out her chest a bit. "On evenings when we don't have a regular act in the house, we girls perform. Why, just last week a man told me I should be working in Hollywood!"

"Oh, I hear that every day," Jade said, patting her hair. "In fact, I had a photographer in last week. From *Variety*. Marty told him about me."

"The Signora didn't tell you that we all perform, too?" Faye asked Gina, clearly still focusing on the earlier part of the conversation. Her eyes narrowed a bit. "How odd."

"No one mentioned it to me," Gina said, looking meaningfully at Lulu. She smiled through gritted teeth. "I can do a passable Charleston, but that's about it."

All three women looked a bit relieved. "Well, maybe the Signora didn't need another performer," Faye said, smiling brightly.

"Or maybe she forgot to tell me. Maybe I still need to audition," Gina said, feeling disappointed. She couldn't afford to lose this job already, and it looked like it was all slipping away.

"Oh, she wouldn't have forgotten," Jade assured her. "The Signora doesn't forget anything, ever. We do need someone to serve drinks while we're out there." She smiled at Gina again, this time looking more sincere.

"Yes," Faye added. "Just remember the back room's mine."

At their first break, Lulu told Gina about what to do in of a police raid or, even less likely, a visit from Pro' agents. She pointed at the stairs Gina had come down when she had first arrived. "If the Drys come—and we'll know because Big Mike and the Signora have lookouts and contacts—you're to go up either to the drugstore or the tea shop, button on a sweater, and tie an apron over your dress. Just start wiping a table, or bring someone a soda or tea. Gooch will turn out the lights on both ends of the alley, warning people away. Over the next few days, you'll work in both places so you look like you know your way around."

Gina looked up at the balcony above, trying to imagine a bunch of burly Prohibition agents busting their way down the stairs, breaking up the place. Papa would not be very happy if she were arrested. "There *are* other ways out, aren't there?" she asked, remembering what Ned had told her earlier. "Other exits?"

"Sure, for the patrons. There's a tunnel beyond that back exit," Lulu pointed behind her, toward the ladies' dressing room. "You'll see a ladder that leads up to the gangway between the buildings. The gangway leads you onto Harrison or the alley. Go out that way and you might run right into the Drys." She paused. "There's another tunnel, too, although I don't know exactly where it leads. Most will go that way. Really dirty passage, though. Hasn't been used in a while."

"What about us? Seems easier for us to run, too."

Lulu grabbed her by the shoulders. "Gina, you *can't* run," she said, giving her a little shake. "Promise me that. You could get caught. Even worse, if you run, the Signora and Big Mike—they might think you're disloyal. You understand?"

"*Capiche,*" Gina replied, trying to sound like Billy Bottles.

"Jeepers creepers, Gina, I'm serious."

"All right, yes, I get you. Don't run. Don't hide. Business as usual. Got it."

Privately, Gina thought Lulu was being dramatic. *I'll bet that's why she's looking to be a stage actress or movie star. Drama suits her.* She was curious, though. "Do raids happen often?"

"Nah," Lulu said, laughing as she nodded. "Only when the chief of police is hankering for a Rum Runner."

Gina laughed, too. "You're handing me a line!"

"All I know for sure is, we've come close, but we've never been closed down. Not like Nicky the Greek's place, which was raided just after Thanksgiving, and"—she lowered her voice—"you heard what went down *there.*"

Gina nodded. Nicky the Greek ran several restaurants in Greektown, just a few streets over from the Third Door. She'd heard that the Prohibition agents had closed all of his places in one day, rounding up Nicky and his men in a single huge raid—the bum's rush. Two days later, Nicky's men were all found dead in a construction zone in the Loop. There were whispers that a rival gang had ordered the hit, but no one wanted to point a finger.

Lulu's mascara-framed eyes grew wide as the drama in her voice increased. "I heard Big Mike saying that with Nicky outta the picture, Capone and his mugs are gonna take over *everything.*"

Gina breathed in sharply. She'd grown up hearing about Johnny Torrio, Big Jim Colosimo, and of course the famed bootlegger, brothel bouncer, and boxing promoter, Alphonse Capone. Just a few years older than herself, he was building an empire on the South and West Sides of Chicago. It wasn't surprising that Big Mike and the Signora might have reservations

about Capone being so near their turf. She shivered. What
if the same thing happened here?

"Hey, don't worry, though," Lulu said, evidently having
correctly followed Gina's thoughts. Playfully, she chucked
Gina under the chin. "We get all sorts here. Bob Hope was even
here a few times, when he was in town. After he'd done his act
at the Stratford, some nights he'd pop by for a few drinks."

"No kidding . . . Bob Hope?" Gina and her dad had listened to the vaudevillian a few times on the radio, although
had never seen him in person.

"Yeah, real swell guy. Good tipper, too." Looking smug,
Lulu adjusted the cigarettes in Gina's tray while she continued
to check off names of famous people who had set foot in the
place. "Lou Gehrig's been here, when they're playing the White
Sox. Babe Ruth, too. The Bambino, now he could drink everyone under the table." She named a few more famous baseball
players, and some starlets, too, before touching Gina's elbow.
"Just don't get too chummy with the patrons. *That* won't sit
well with the Signora."

As the evening grew later, more and more patrons entered the
Third Door. Gina learned she was expected to greet new arrivals if she was near the steps and direct them toward a table
if one was available. She wondered if Little Johnny was mon-
itoring the arrivals, because they rarely descended in large
groups, almost always in twos and threes. Certainly no more
than six appeared at once.

Most patrons were clearly familiar with the layout and
each other, twirling their fingers at acquaintances as they descended, affecting the languid air of the rich and sophisticated.
Some of them slipped into the back room for the nightly card

game; others stayed out at the tables, drinking Rum Runners and whiskey sours, generally getting bent. A few were obviously new to the establishment: the ladies giggling and clutching each other in amazement, the young men—College Joes mostly—pounding each other on the back for having the nerve to crack the joint.

The music continued to play loudly, and couples danced the Lindy and the Charleston, not caring about the small dance floor or the frequent jostling with other couples. Sometimes the dance music came from the gramophone, which Ned cranked up between sets. Mostly, though, Ned was on the piano. From time to time, Gina saw the piano player take a little quaff from his flask, causing her to raise an eyebrow. She would never march with the Women's Temperance League, that was for certain, but there was something unfortunate about a man who seemed to live his life in the cups. Throughout it all, Gooch and Little Johnny seemed to be keeping a careful eye on the goings-on of all the patrons, tossing out rabble-rousers, dewdroppers looking for free drinks, and the occasional backroom cheat.

Gina had made a few rounds with her cigarettes before Billy Bottles called her over around nine o'clock, when there was finally a break in the music. "I'll need you to bring some drinks to customers while the cocktail waitresses are getting ready to dance," he said. He handed her a tray with two martinis. "Take your cigarette tray off and bring these drinks to the couple over there. Hurry now, there won't be much time once they start to really move."

Just then, Ned began to play a ragtime tune, and Lulu, Faye, and Jade emerged from the dressing room in skimpy halter tops and flowing skirts and began to shimmy across the wooden dance floor. Energized by the sight of the girls stomping and high-kicking, the speakeasy's customers began to whistle and cheer, a few gents making catcalls.

"Get hot! Get hot!" several urged. Hearing them, the women widened their smiles and added more flounce to their steps.

After she dropped off the drinks, Gina leaned against the piano, taking it all in. Nobody was clamoring for service, since nearly all eyes were on the girls. On the other side of the room, Gina noticed a middle-aged man in evening clothes holding a black camera to his chest, taking photographs of the hoofers with their high kicks and shimmying shoulders, as well as the crowd as they cheered the dancers on.

"Gonna take up dancing next?" Ned called up to her, his fingers still flying, never missing a note. "Gotta cozy up to Big Mike first." He looked a bit disgusted. "I gotta warn you, though. They all think they're gonna end up in the movies or over in Gay Paree."

"You don't think they can make it?" Gina asked.

"Not a one. At least not these. Only the real headliners could. Not cocktail waitresses told to take their clothes off." He seemed disappointed. "That your bent, though?"

"No, if you must know, I was watching the photographer. Who is he?"

Ned whistled. "Got a thing for old Marty Doyle? I have to admit, even I didn't see that coming. He's got to be forty at least. Maybe a bit older." Taking one hand off the piano keys, he made a muscle. "How about giving a younger guy a chance?"

"Don't be ridiculous," she said, miming the gesture of flicking off a fly. "I know your sort."

"You don't know anything," he chuckled, and finished the tune with a final flourish. "What's so interesting about Marty?"

"Oh, I'm just interested in photography," she said. "People here don't mind having their pictures taken?" For some reason, that surprised her.

"Some do. Most don't." Ned shut the lid of the piano. "Time for Mr. Coleman now. You don't want to miss him."

With that, Ned seated himself at the bar, where Billy poured him a drink. He began to applaud loudly when a black man in a dark suit sauntered into the room. Putting his trumpet to his lips, with no other accompaniment, Mr. Coleman began to play a soulful-sounding tune, to the clear enjoyment of the Third Door patrons.

Gina began to circle quietly among the tables, trying not to disturb the performance. As she took drink orders, she noticed Marty taking pictures of couples at different tables, occasionally writing in a small notebook that he kept in his breast pocket. As Ned had said, some waved him away, but most did preen and smile, often mimicking the poses of Hollywood starlets. She noticed, too, that Marty seemed to keep his eye on the main stairs from the Third Door's entrance, probably to keep track of anyone particularly rich or famous who might be stopping by.

At one point, though, Gina looked up from a table only to discover that the photographer was staring at her, from across the empty dance floor. His camera was positioned in her direction. *Was he taking pictures of me?* She gave him an uncertain wave of her hand, but he had already turned away. *Well, that was bonkers,* she thought, turning her attention back to her customers, who were impatiently waiting for their change.

———————

Gina and Lulu didn't leave the Third Door until close to one in the morning. Although the drinking and gambling were still going strong in the back room, when the dancing ceased the Signora told the servers they could go home. Lulu was none too happy that Faye had stayed on, still serving the men in the back.

"I don't know why Big Mike always picks Faye to stay," Lulu complained as soon as they left the premises and were out of earshot. "It used to be Dorrie; now it's always Faye. She's so bossy, thinks she knows everything about the joint. It's not fair, though."

"You wanted to stay longer?" Gina asked. Her own feet were hurting so much from the high heels she couldn't bear the thought of another minute spent upright on the speakeasy's hard floor.

"Of course! That's when all the best tipping happens. Sometimes more." She added the last meaningfully. "I wouldn't go home with just any of them. I got my standards. Of course, if he's a real doll, I might change my mind. You know what I mean?" She nudged Gina companionably.

Gina nodded, but her stomach recoiled at the thought. She'd been used by a man before, and she didn't intend to let that happen again. "I thought the Signora didn't like the girls mixing with the patrons."

"Just don't bring her any trouble, that's the rule." With a shrug, Lulu went on. "It's always Faye or Jade now. You think they're prettier than me?" she asked suddenly, stopping under the streetlight. Indeed, she looked beautiful, despite the petulant twist to her lips.

"No, not at all," Gina said honestly. "You look lovely."

Lulu gave her a delighted smile and took her arm companionably. "I'm so glad that you came to work with me," Lulu squealed softly, squeezing her arm a bit. She squeaked again. "Isn't it all *divine?* You know they change the password every day?"

"Divine," Gina agreed. "Hey, wait! Every day? What's the password for tomorrow?"

"'Oatmeal Cookies,' if you can believe it. Sorry I forgot to tell you. I didn't think—" She broke off, then continued, "I mean, how'd you get in, then? Gooch and Little Johnny, they don't go around the rules, as you might have noticed."

"*Ned* got me in."

Lulu laughed, pulling off her silk-rose-and-feather hairpiece and putting it in her bag. "Ah, that Ned. He's a doll, isn't he? Of course"—she lowered her tone confidentially—"he's dangerous around the ladies. Don't get caught up with *him.*"

"Yeah, I heard about 'Neddy Fingers,'" Gina said, and both women tittered. Then she remembered how the photographer had been staring at her. "What about Marty?" she asked cautiously. "What's *he* like? I never had a chance to talk to him, he was so busy."

"Oh, Marty's all right. Keeps to himself, I suppose. He lives above the pharmacy, you know. That's where he develops his photos. He's taken pictures of me, too. To send to Hollywood. He takes pictures of all the girls, if they want."

"Oh," Gina replied. "That's nice that he does that, I suppose."

Her tone must have conveyed her sense of skepticism, because Lulu quickly added, "Oh, he's not a creeper, or anything like that. There's magazine contests, you see. Auditions, too. For stage. Sometimes even for movies."

Gina's head was still whirling from the day, and she fell silent. The two women kept walking quickly west on Polk, where they both lived, their heels echoing a bit too loudly in the quiet streets. By day, the Near West Side was safe, full of hardworking people tending their kids and shouting at each other in Italian, Greek, Gaelic, and even the Cajun-tinged tongue of the Deep South. At night, though, dangers seemed to lurk everywhere. The stray figures they glimpsed in the alleys and gangways seemed up to no good: women in stilettos vying for a score; men finding their way to vice and sin.

A qualm of uncertainty passed over her. It seemed Lulu might have felt the same. "I used to walk home with Dorrie," she said softly. "Almost every night."

"Oh," Gina said, not sure what else to say. "I'm sorry she died."

Lulu continued, sounding sad. "You know, Dorrie only lived a few doors down from us." Her voice trailed off. "She'd just moved in with a gal pal a few months ago. Couldn't take her mother anymore, I suppose."

They both fell quiet again. Gina cast about to bring Lulu out of her suddenly despondent mood. "Lulu," she said, "I never really thanked you for getting me this job. It sounds like you put in a good word for me."

"Oh, yes. Well, we girls from the neighborhood need to stick together." She seemed about to say something else but then stopped herself. When they reached her stoop, though, she turned back to Gina. "You'll be careful, won't you?"

"Oh, it's just another block. I'll be fine," Gina replied, trying to sound more confident than she felt. It was not often that she spent time walking around in the bitter hours of the morning.

"I mean at the Third Door," Lulu said, a cautious tone still in her voice. "It's different than what you're used to."

She thinks I'm a knucklehead, Gina thought, feeling annoyed. "Pfft. I'll be fine."

The puzzled look on Lulu's face was quickly smoothed away. "I know," she said. "See you tomorrow."

CHAPTER 3

"Hope the furnace didn't go out again," Gina muttered to herself when she woke to a freezing bedroom the next morning. She could even see the faint wisps of her breath, hanging in the air. Though she wanted to stay snuggled beneath the heavy woolen blankets, she forced herself out of her bed with a groan. Her body protested every movement, aching from the late-night hours, high heels, and heavy trays. When she touched the radiator in her room, sure enough, it was cold. With any luck, her father had just forgotten to shovel in more coal. They couldn't afford a new furnace.

She could hear her father now, banging about in the kitchen. Quickly she donned a day dress and sweater, then entered the tiny kitchen to find broken eggs all over the range, their shells and yolks everywhere.

Gina bit her lip. Those were all the eggs they had left, and she wasn't sure they had money to spare to buy more at the market.

"Good morning, Papa," she said, regarding her father with some alarm. His grayish black hair was mussed, and his cheeks were more ruddy than usual. She was relieved, though, to see the stubble on his face; at least he had not attempted to shave himself again. "What are you up to?"

"Didn't want to wake you," her father replied, tightening the belt on his old blue bathrobe. His hands were shaking more than usual. "Just making some breakfast. Or at least trying to." He gave a self-deprecating chuckle.

Gina sighed. Opening the icebox, she took out the carrot soup she had made yesterday afternoon before heading to the Third Door. She had planned to save it for his dinner, but they might as well eat it now.

"Why don't you listen to the radio?" she suggested, opening up the jar. "I'll warm up some soup in a jiffy."

"Soup? Well, all right," Papa replied, sitting down at the small kitchen table and turning on the radio he'd built a few years ago. Fortunately, she'd just tuned it yesterday. When her papa's palsy had grown worse, she'd learned to fix the radio herself, popping off the back panel and tightening the tubes when necessary.

Right now, though, she was very glad to hear her papa humming along to "My Blue Heaven" with Gene Austin. He'd been more down than up ever since he'd lost his job driving the L train eighteen months before, after he had crashed the train at the Randolph Street station. Even though no one had been seriously injured, the Chicago Rapid Transit Company had deemed him physically unfit to safely manage the equipment. Since then he had cobbled together a series of jobs, often fixing small electronics and household items for neighbors, building up a small enterprise in the process. On his good days, he could still complete such tasks, but on his bad days— which seemed to be increasing in number—he could barely handle a broom, let alone rewire a radio. Customers didn't trust a man who couldn't hammer straight, or fix the inside of a lamp or radio. So Gina had taken to fixing them herself, with their neighbors none the wiser.

She set a bowl down in front of him.

"You made carrot stew," he said, sounding delighted. Leaning over the bowl, he breathed in deeply. "Your mother's recipe. Not from a can!"

Gina turned a guilty eye toward the cabinet half-stocked with Campbell's tomato and vegetable soups. Personally, she enjoyed the canned soups, and the convenience of them even more, but she was glad now that she had spent the day before figuring out her mama's old recipe.

"I wish Mama had written down more of these family recipes," she said. "Do you think we might ask my grandmother—?"

Her papa stiffened. Laying his spoon down, he said, "No, Gina. We can't."

"Why not?"

"You know why." Lowering his head so that it was just above the bowl, he carefully brought the spoon to his lips, trying hard to keep the precious liquid from spilling.

Gina sighed. She'd never really understood what had caused the strife with her mother's family; she just knew that they hadn't shown up for her brother's funeral ten years before. Whether they hadn't been invited or hadn't wanted to come, Gina had never known. The crushing misery of those days following her brother's death in northern France had numbed her, and any questions she might have raised seemed pointless. Even when the armistice ended the Great War a few weeks later, nothing felt right in the world.

He looked up at her then. "You were out late."

"I was working, Papa. I started a new job, remember? At the Third Door."

He scowled as his hands began to shake more. "Of course I remember, Gina. There's nothing wrong with my mind, even if I've got these damn shakes." He banged his fists down on the table. "I don't know why you have to work at that *place*."

Gina sat down in the other chair and laid her hands on top of his. That seemed to steady them both. "Papa, it's not so bad, really. And I'll be working in the drugstore and tea room, too." Then her voice grew stern. "We need the money. Tips are good. I promise, I'll be fine."

The memory of the black silk dress and headdress flashed into her mind then. Had Dorrie thought she'd be fine?

Kissing the top of his head, she put the disturbing thought out of her mind. Then she moved the dirty dishes aside, spread his newspaper open on the table, picked up his screwdriver, and began to unscrew part of Mrs. Hayford's lamp. At least this was something she could fix.

Gina stood in front of Madame Laupin's dress shop a few hours later, breathing in a lovely cinnamon aroma from the brightly lit bakery next door. Like the two other stores on this block of Polk Street, it contained two large windows on either side of the front door. Unlike the bakery, with its gleaming windows and pretty display of cakes, the dress store looked a bit drab and dingy. On the glass, she could just make out MADAME LAUPIN'S, LATEST FASHIONS in faded black script. Only an exquisitely clothed dress form suggested the treasures that lay inside.

Gina mounted the two cracked front steps and opened the door. A bell tinkled above her head when she walked inside the store.

"Bonjour!" A woman called from a back room. *"Un moment, merci."*

"Hello!" Gina called out, looking around the dressmaker's shop, which was impeccably clean. Indeed, although the room was dark, it had an unexpectedly sophisticated atmosphere. Two mannequins displayed elegant creations, and a gleaming sewing machine graced a polished wooden table in one corner. One whole wall had shelves of precisely folded materials, from winter wools to printed silks and summer lace. A long table ran nearly the length of the wall. It was bare now, but a small scrap of fabric lying on the floor suggested that the seamstress used it to cut and measure material. By the window was a glass display case, in which jewelry, headpieces, and ivory combs could be seen.

Gina was gazing into the display case when a teeny woman dressed all in black entered the store from a back room.

"Oui, mademoiselle?" the woman said, looking at her in an appraising way. "Is there something I can help you with?"

The unexpected elegance of the shop had overwhelmed her, and Gina no longer felt that such beauty could be meant for her. She opened her mouth to speak but simply gulped instead, unsure what to say.

The woman was still regarding her steadily. "Did someone send you to me, *ma cherie?*"

Without a word, Gina handed the Signora's calling card to Madame Laupin.

"Ah, the Signora!" the dressmaker said, beaming as comprehension dawned. She appraised Gina critically. "You sing, I presume? Surely you do not dance?"

Gina straightened her posture. "I'll be selling cigarettes and flowers." *And booze*, she almost added, stopping herself just in time. "I won't be performing. Madame Laupin said I'm to have two dresses, billed to her account."

"*Oui*, I understand. I know just what you need," the woman replied, ushering her into a back room. "Allow me to take your measurements. After that, we may select the fabrics."

A half hour later, a delicate mixture of silks, georgettes, and voile, all in shimmery greens and matted black, was neatly folded on the dressmaker's table, to be made into two lovely frocks. Gina could not keep from exclaiming over the gorgeousness of it all. "Golly, these are swell!"

Madame Laupin smiled indulgently. "Yes, the Signora does like her girls—even her cigarette sellers—to look . . . how do you say it? . . . . 'swell.'" She pulled out a black ledger to record the sale. Getting a glimpse of the price, Gina stifled a gasp. *How many weeks will it take to pay that charge back?*

Then she touched the beautiful fabrics again. The two dresses cost dearly, to be sure, but she suspected that for the quality of the workmanship she was getting quite a bargain. "Thank you, Madame Laupin. I'll treasure them."

"Wear them in good health, *ma cherie*," Madame Laupin replied, as she held open the door for Gina. Then a funny expression crossed her features, as if she had remembered something.

"Is something wrong, Madame?"

"Just don't go off where you shouldn't, *ma cherie*. Sometimes girls do that." There was something in the dressmaker's tone. A warning.

Gina hazarded a guess. "Like—Dorrie, you mean?"

Madame Laupin just gave a funny click of her tongue. "Best not speak of that, *mademoiselle*." She opened the door a bit wider. "*Au revoir.* Mind your step, if you would."

As Gina stepped away from Madame Laupin's, it was hard not to wonder about the elusive Dorrie. Not that it was her business, of course. It was best to focus on the matters at hand, she decided. She felt guilty thinking it, but Dorrie's loss was certainly her gain, and she was determined to make the most of it.

She had been instructed to stop by the tea room before she began today's shift at the Third Door; it was one street over on Harrison, on the other side of the alley. As Lulu had mentioned, she needed to learn everything she could about working there, and at the drugstore, so she'd be ready in the unlikely case of a raid.

As she passed the pastry shop, Le Polonaise, Gina took a deep breath, enjoying the delicious aromas emerging from within. Maybe one day she'd be bringing in enough extra bucks to feel she could purchase some of the delicate cakes in the window for her papa to enjoy.

Her thoughts were interrupted then by the piercing sound of a whistle blowing on the balcony above the pastry shop entrance. Gazing upward, she took in two runny-nosed, stringy-haired urchins, a boy and a girl, grinning down at her. The girl had her arm slung around a midsized mangy-looking dog who wore a mournful expression on its face.

"Whatcha doing?" the girl called down to her. She seemed to have a slight Polish accent. "You were in Madame Laupin's. For about forty-five minutes. Isn't that so, Emil?" Here she glanced at the boy, who nodded in agreement.

Gina was slightly surprised that they had paid such close attention to her comings and goings. "Buying some dresses," she replied, about to continue onward. "Starting a new job."

"Are you working at the tea room?" Emil asked, bright with curiosity. The girl raised an eyebrow.

"Why, yes," Gina replied, a bit uncomfortable now. She was not sure if she should be declaring that information so openly in the street. Since the children were still looking at her, she asked, "Do you live up there?"

"Oh, yes. Our father owns the pastry shop," the girl replied with pride. "We have the best pastries. Polish mostly. Some French treats, too."

"They smell delicious," Gina replied.

"The Signora sells them in her *tea room*." Both children giggled then, and Gina smiled, too. It seemed like they were all in on the joke. Certainly, if they lived near the Third Door, they'd seen and heard everything.

"You don't say," Gina said. "Well, I must go. Best not be late. It's my first day working there."

"If today's your first day—you must be taking Dorrie's place," the girl said, sounding a bit sad.

"Zosia!" Emil whispered loudly to his sister. "We're not supposed to talk about her."

"Yes, I am filling in for Dorrie," Gina replied, her curiosity about the dead girl once again piqued. "Did you know her?"

"Yeah, she'd bring us hokey-pokey," Zosia said. "Peppermint sticks, my favorite. She'd throw them up to us and we'd catch them. She knew Papa and Mama wouldn't let us have sweets. Sometimes we get to eat cakes if they are burnt. We're not usually allowed candy."

"Lucky you!" Gina replied. "She sounds like she was a very nice person."

"Well . . ." Emil paused.

"We had an agreement," Zosia said.

"Shhh!" Emil said. "Zosia, don't tell her."

"An agreement?" Gina asked. "That sounds interesting."

"Just sometimes we see things that other people don't like us to see," Zosia explained.

"We were supposed to let Big Mike or the Signora know if we saw something," Emil said, evidently giving in. "Sometimes we'd just tell Dorrie."

"I see," Gina replied. It seemed that the entire block was under the Castallazzos' watchful eye. With a faint feeling of unease, she waved good-bye to the children and entered the tea shop.

Full of lace doilies, china figurines, and delicate pastries, the prim tea shop proved to be completely at odds with the exuberant speakeasy below. The place was overseen by Mrs. Metzger, an older woman with plump red cheeks and grayish blond hair pulled back in a bun. Though a bit finicky in decor, the place was also warm and comfortable, like Mrs. Metzger herself, and seemed to attract an elderly, and very chatty, group of women from the community. The tea room tasks were much like those she'd learned when she had worked in the restaurant—sweep the floor, wipe down tables, and take the occasional order.

"I'll take mine with an extra dollop, dear," one of the white-haired women said to Gina, after ordering hot chocolate.

"An extra dollop?" she repeated. "In your chocolate?"

"Just one, please." She winked at her companion. "More

than that, I'll be taking a nap right here on the table." Both
women giggled.

Gina went back behind the counter and started to make
the hot chocolate. An extra dollop of what? Sugar? She'd added
more honey to the other women's tea when they'd made that
request.

As she uncertainly regarded the honey swizzler in her
hand, she heard Mrs. Metzger chuckle from behind her. "Different kind of dollop, dear." The tea shop owner reached inside a sugar canister below the counter and in one swift
movement extracted a small, dark flask from inside. Shield-
ing her actions from the customers, she poured out a measure
of deep brown liquid. Taking a step closer to Gina, she murmured through clenched lips, "Bourbon or rum with chocolate, dear."

Gina placed the spiked drink on the lace-covered table
in front of the customer. "Where are you from?" the woman
asked her. "I think I've seen you around."

Gina was about to answer when she caught the faintest
shake of Mrs. Metzger's head. "Gina, please be a dear and take
care of those crumbs in the corner," the tea shop owner said,
nodding toward a broom. The message was clear. She was not
to engage with the patrons in a personal way. She only spoke
of pastries, hot drinks, and dollops until just before six o'clock,
when it was time to head down to the Third Door.

"Here you go! Two Aviations," Gina said, carefully laying the
light blue drinks down in front of two natty fellows seated at
a corner table. For the last fifteen minutes, the men had been
attempting to convince her that they'd been pilots in the Great
War. Something about their smarmy smiles made her suspect

that they were lying. Probably trying to impress her, which, even if she were in the market for a man, was most certainly the wrong way to go about it.

Out of the corner of her eye, she noticed Marty enter the speakeasy, scouring the room until his eyes locked on hers. He moved toward her then, looking like he had something on his mind. The would-be flyboys were still trying to tell her about one of their supposed exploits.

"Hold on, boys," she said, putting them off. "You can tell me all about it later."

As she moved to meet the photographer, she found her path suddenly blocked by people stopping to watch two rather glamorous-looking couples descend the stairs in what seemed to Gina to be an overly slow and dramatic fashion.

From the excited whispers going on around her, she could tell that these were no ordinary folk.

Both the women were dressed in heavy furs and sported fancy diamond necklaces and bracelets. The men were wearing stylish overcoats and fedoras, glancing surreptitiously about them. Seeing Marty move toward them with his camera, they held up their hands in warning.

"No pictures, mate," Gina heard one of them say to Marty.

The women strode confidently forward, the diamonds in their earrings and tiaras sparkling even in the dim light.

Stepping back against the piano, she heard Ned give a low whistle. "They're hot to trot tonight," he said under his breath.

"Who are they? Performers?" Gina asked, feeling doubtful. Though she hadn't thumbed through *Variety* to the extent that Lulu most certainly had, she didn't recognize either woman. "Stage actresses?"

Ned chuckled. "Doll, you really are a babe. They're with

the O'Banions. Those are their wives. Or maybe their girl-
friends. Sometimes it's hard to keep track."

"Oh," Gina said, then fell silent. The O'Banions she had
heard of. North Side Irish. Her mother's world.

"The question is," Ned said, "what are they doing *here*?"

As if in answer to that question, the Signora emerged from
her salon in a beautiful evening gown and approached the
foursome. Gooch, Gina could see, was keeping a keen eye on
them from across the room. Little Johnny appeared out of nowhere and took a position on the other side of the room, his
right hand casually resting on his hip.

The couples stood up when the Signora arrived at their
table, and she pressed the cheeks of each woman in turn.
"Lottie, Maisy, darlings. So wonderful to see you again. It's
been *ages*."

"Likewise," the taller of the two women said, her voice
nasal.

The Signora beckoned to Faye, who had been respectfully
waiting a half step away.

"Me and Maisy, we'll have highballs," Lottie said.
"With gin."

"The good stuff," added Maisy, speaking in the same
sneering way as her friend.

"Of course," Faye said, and moved toward the bar. The two
women settled down in a self-conscious way, clearly aware that
all eyes were on them.

In a lower voice, the Signora spoke to the men. "Gentlemen, follow me."

The two men followed her out of the room, accompanied
by Little Johnny. Gooch, Gina noticed, stayed out on the main
speakeasy floor. The two women sat back down at the table.

Maisy began poking around in her embroidered handbag, her bright red mouth turned down at the edges as she peered inside.

Hoping that she was interpreting the woman's intention correctly, Gina moved over with her tray. "Ciggies?" she asked.

"Marlboros," Maisy replied. She accepted the pack from Gina and handed her fifteen cents.

A moment later, the Signora returned to the dance floor, coming to stand beside the piano. When she clapped her hands, Ned immediately ended the tune he was playing with a flourish, and everyone turned toward the Signora.

"Ladies and gentlemen," she said, in a commanding way. "I trust you are enjoying your evening. We are quite fortunate that the Sullivan dance team could join us tonight. Please help me welcome Danny and Sheila Sullivan to the floor."

As Ned began to play a lively fox-trot tempo, a man and a woman swept gracefully onto the dance floor, to great applause and catcalls. Danny Sullivan, likely in his midtwenties, was expertly leading his wife around in a series of intricate, well-choreographed steps. The fluid movements of their lean, muscled bodies and their practiced smiles suggested years of hoofing together at a very high level. Tonight, though, the pair looked like they were having fun like everyone else, a graceful flurry of silks and beads. The music was contagious, and other couples began to shimmy about as well.

Gina circled around the room again, smiling. Her shoulders were aching, and so were her feet. The pumps were starting to take their toll, making her feel like she could not take another step. She still didn't really understand when she was allowed to set down her tray, on busy nights like this.

As Gina made her way to the next table, she caught sight of Jade, staring at the Sullivans. There was pure envy there, and anger, too. As if sensing her gaze, Jade looked toward her then, and they caught eyes. Gina gave her a sympathetic smile, which Jade just shrugged off before turning away.

Later that evening Gina stood with her back to the stairs, keeping an eye out for any patron desiring a smoke. She'd left her tray at the bar to give the aching muscles in her neck and shoulders a chance to recover. She was just slipping her feet out of her shoes to wriggle her toes, when a man came stumbling down the steps, nearly falling straight onto the speakeasy floor beside her.

"Already blotto?" Gina asked cheerfully, grabbing the man's arm to help him get righted. Gooch, to her surprise, had rushed over quickly to grab the man's other arm and keep him upright.

"Sure, sweets. I'm blotto on life," the man snapped back. He turned to Gooch. "Hand me my cane, will you?"

To Gina's chagrin, Gooch bent down to withdraw a long wooden cane from underneath a nearby table and handed it to the man. It must have slipped from the man's grasp when he stumbled down the steps.

"Oh, I'm so sorry," Gina said, looking up at the man. His coat was pulled up high around his neck, and his wool cap was pulled down low, obscuring nearly half of his face. She could see now that the cap and cane had deceived her, for he was far younger than she'd first assumed. Probably just a few years older than herself, maybe in his late twenties or early thirties. Handsome. His hazel eyes, sweeping over her, were angry. "I didn't know, and—"

"Game start yet?" the man asked Gooch, shaking Gina's
hand from his arm.

Gooch checked his watch. "Just about." He handed the
man his cane. "Good evening, Mr. Roark."

When Roark accepted the cane, Gina could see that
he was missing his pinky and part of his ring finger on his right
hand. A mortified flush still stinging her cheeks, she watched
as he walked toward the back room, a heavy limp marking
his movements. She wondered if he'd been injured in the Great
War.

With a sigh, Gina took out a small towel and began to
wipe clean a few of the empty tables. She hated thinking about
the war, which had claimed her older brother, Aidan, when
she was only thirteen. She could still remember the day he left.
She and her papa had accompanied him to the train station,
where they had all been caught up in the excitement of waving
flags and pounding drums. How he'd grinned at the pretty
girls blowing kisses and throwing flowers as the train pulled
out to Fort Sheridan, just north of Chicago.

That was, as it had turned out, the last time they would
ever see him. She wished now that they had thought to borrow
a camera that day, but back then so few people owned even the
most basic Brownies. A few months later, they had received a
letter from when he was in Texas, along with the other Illinois recruits, and a month after that, another letter excitedly
detailing his arrival to a tiny town in northern France.

For several long months, they had waited in vain for another letter. Instead, they had received a sharp knock at their
door, which they had opened to find a uniformed soldier
standing stiffly, a yellow paper in his hands and deep sympathy in his eyes. The tersely worded telegram was one she'd

never forget: *"Deeply regret inform you Private Aidan Ricci Infantry officially reported killed in action November 1 1918 France."*

After they had received the telegram, Gina had sewn a gold star atop the blue star hanging in their window, which her father had first proudly placed when Aidan joined the service. It hung there until the armistice was declared soon after, and then her father had carefully folded it away in a box.

"Snap, snap!" Faye called out to her, pulling Gina from her reverie, as she passed by with a perfectly balanced tray of drinks. Most were a warm amber color, tinkling with ice. Whiskey, Gina guessed.

"Get the curtain, will you?" Faye hissed at Gina. "Don't stand there mooning around."

Hastily Gina rushed in front of Faye and pulled back the curtain that kept the back room closed off from curious eyes. She glimpsed a group of men sitting around a large round wooden table, chips and cards strewn all over its dull oak surface. In her haste, though, she accidentally jostled Faye, causing the drinks to slosh on her tray and one to spill outright.

"Numbskull," Faye said under her breath, smiling toward the table as she righted the glass and walked into the room. She set a drink in front of each man, smiling coyly as they tucked bills down the front of her dress. As Gina looked around, she realized that all of the men were disfigured in some way. Some had contorted faces; others were missing appendages. One had a black patch over one eye. Clearly all had served in the Great War.

"Hey, Faye, why don'tcha send in Dorrie?" one of the men called. "I could use a smoke."

"Dorrie's not here, Donny," Faye replied, to a chorus of disappointed howls from the men. Obviously Dorrie had been a favorite. "We got a new girl now. Name's Gina." Through clenched teeth, she said to Gina, "Go get your cigarette tray. Can't you see these dolls need their cigs?"

"Sure, I'll be back in a jiffy," Gina replied.

On her way out, she heard Roark ask Faye what had happened to Dorrie, but she didn't hear the woman's reply.

As Gina checked over her cigarette tray, Faye emerged to put in an order with Billy Bottles. A man lurched up to her then and began speaking to her in a wheedling tone.

"Not now, Milt," Faye said, smiling in her enchanting way.

"Aw, why not, pretty Faye. Pretty please, pretty Faye," the man continued in the same cajoling tone, seeming a bit bamboozled. He was probably in his midtwenties, and Gina thought she'd seen him drinking in the back room moments ago. Maybe an ex-soldier.

"I'm busy," she heard Faye reply, putting a bit of steel in her silvery voice.

"Come on!" The man put his hand on her slim hip.

Oh, brother, Gina thought. She was curious, though, to see how the delicate woman would deal with the unwanted advances. She could see that Gooch was now watching the exchange, too.

"Put a sock in it, Milt," Faye said sweetly, before sashaying away. As she passed Gina she whispered, "Total bozo. Stay away from him."

The man scowled at her and looked like he was about to follow Faye. Instead, he sat down at the bar when Gooch gave him a hard look.

Reentering the back room with her tray refilled, Gina went over to Donny, since he was the one who had first called for a smoke. When she approached him, she could see that the man sitting next to him was missing half his jaw, with a metal plate inserted to fit his face.

"Marlboro?" she asked, trying not to look at his misshapen face. Then she flushed when they all guffawed. Mentally she slapped her head, remembering too late that the brand was mostly smoked by women.

"A few packs of Lucky Strikes will do us, sweetheart," Roark said. He tossed two quarters on her tray. "You can leave this sideshow."

She flinched at his harsh tone and hurriedly set three packs down in the center of the table.

The blond man, Donny, smiled up at her. Though his face was pallid and worn, his blue eyes were bright and friendly. "Don't mind Lieutenant Roark, ma'am. He can be a real bear. Ain't that right, Lieutenant?"

"You were in the Great War?" she asked, smiling back. She ignored Roark, who she could sense was now scowling at her.

"Yes, ma'am, 33rd Infantry Division. In the 130th."

When he said the name of the division, all the men pounded their fists into their hands at once while emitting a deep grunt. Evidently that was the sound of their unit.

"My brother was over there, too," Gina said, swallowing as unexpected emotion came over her. Sometimes she wondered what kind of man her brother would have become. "In the 123rd. Northern France."

"Did he make it back, ma'am?" Donny asked, though his tone was soft and knowing.

She gave a swift shake of her head, willing herself not to cry. "We got a letter from him, saying he was in the Ardennes Forest. Then there was a telegram . . ." Her voice trailed off. There was nothing more to say.

The men exchanged a look, shuffling their feet. No one felt too comfortable thinking about their comrades who didn't make it back. Gina began to stack the dirty glasses on her tray, clinking them so loudly she thought they might break. "I'm sorry," she said, blindly trying to get out of the room.

Unexpectedly, Roark broke the strained silence. "What was his name?" he asked. "Your brother?"

She didn't look at him. "Aidan Ricci."

"To Aidan," Roark said, and raised a glass. The others followed suit, all taking a sip, then banging their glasses down.

Blinking back tears, Gina mustered a smile. "Thank you. My name's Gina." When Roark did not return her smile, she looked toward the others. "I know Faye's your girl, but I'll be back around to see if you need any more cigarettes."

Then she paused, not wanting to leave the room on a sad note. "Say," she said, turning back to them, her smile bright again. "Any of you fellows drink Aviations?"

The men all began to guffaw. "Not even flyboys drink Aviations," Donny said. "That's just a Lindy thing."

Walking back onto the speakeasy floor, she chuckled when she noticed the would-be pilots still trying out their lines on a couple of doe-eyed Doras.

CHAPTER 4

"Hey, Big Mike's here," a balding man with spectacles said to his companion. As she handed the man back his change from the Italian cigar he'd just purchased, she turned around. A large man, dressed impeccably in a white suit, had stepped out of the back office and was now shaking hands with customers as he passed, patting others warmly on their backs. Clearly a gregarious fellow.

"Hello, my friends," he called out to several tables of people. "Are we having a wonderful time?"

A roar of approval followed. "Oh yeah, Big Mike," several shouted back. "And how!"

"Good, good," he said, rubbing his hands together. "Let's keep it that way!" He rapped his knuckles on the grand piano as he walked by. "Let's get this place hopping, Neddy! Ladies, let's make sure these glasses stay full."

"Sure thing, Big Mike," Ned replied, his fingers picking up the pace as he played a hot dance number. A number of couples got up from their seats and began to dance, beads and heels clicking, fringed skirts shaking, and boas twirling.

So this was Big Mike, the owner of the joint. Certainly

he was larger than life, as she'd heard. Gina didn't realize she'd been staring at him, though, until she accidentally caught his eye, and he began to stride straight toward her.

Gina extended her hand. "Good evening, Signor Castallazzo. I'm your new cigarette girl."

"Call me Big Mike," he replied, with an easy grin as he closed his hand around her fingers. He looked like he was only half paying attention. "Everyone else does. My wife told me she'd started a new girl on cigarettes."

"I'm Gina Ricci."

His eyes flickered back, his attention caught. "Ricci?" His eyes traveled over her face.

"Yeah." She wondered at his sudden interest. "The Signora hired me yesterday to replace—I mean, to fill the open position."

"Ah, yes. Poor Dorrie. God rest her soul. She'll be missed." He crossed himself, looking deeply sorrowful. He continued to study her face. "Ricci. You wouldn't be related to Frank Ricci, would you?"

"Frank Ricci? Sure!" Gina replied. "That's my papa! You know him?"

"Do I know your papa?" Big Mike threw his head back and gave a great roaring laugh. He seemed truly delighted. "Frankie the Cat—we ran with the same crowd when we were young knuckleheads. Grew up in Little Italy, on the same block of Maxwell Street. His pop and my pop, they were tight."

He looked back at her, still smiling hugely. "You're Frankie's girl! Imagine that!" he exclaimed. "When my wife mentioned, I didn't realize—hey, Gooch!" he called to the bouncer, interrupting himself. "Didya hear? I got Frankie Ricci's daughter here, working at my establishment."

"Her pop's Frankie the Cat?" Gooch asked, a respectful tone creeping into his voice. "Well, ain't she full of surprises?"

"Frankie the Cat? What do you mean?" Gina asked, looking from one to the other. Out of the corner of her eye, she noticed Marty, who was a step away from Gooch, swivel toward her and set his camera on a table. He looked startled—and angry.

"What's your papa up to these days? Still driving trains?" Big Mike asked.

"No, not anymore. He's a handyman now. Fixes stuff." Pride prevented her from adding anything else about her father's current poor state of health.

Big Mike's eyes traveled again over her face. "You resemble your mother," he said, his smile fading a bit.

"You knew my mama?"

"Molly? Sure, we all did. She was hot to trot. North Sider, though."

A slight silence followed. Even after all these years, Gina hated thinking about her mother. She changed the subject. "I never heard anyone call my papa Frankie the Cat. Why do you call him that?"

Big Mike guffawed and glanced at Gooch, who gave a knowing chuckle. "That's from our early days." Though he seemed ready to explain more, he broke off when his wife approached them with a purposeful glide.

"Gina," the Signora said with exaggerated patience, looking down over her long elegant nose. "My husband has perhaps forgotten that those cigarettes aren't going to sell themselves, but I have not."

"Yes, Signora," Gina replied, straightening her tray, about to move away.

"And Gina," the Signora said, a sudden chill to her tone. "We may sell gum, but you may not chew it in here. You look like a cow chewing its cud."

"Maria, sweetheart, don't be hard on her," Big Mike said to his wife. "Didya know she's Frankie Ricci's little girl?"

"Oh, is that so?" the Signora replied, her face darkening. "I hadn't realized."

Gina's hands began to sweat, and she nearly dropped the tray. She didn't know why, but an uneasy feeling had suddenly swelled up inside her.

Cramming a stick of spearmint gum in her mouth, Gina sank down into one of the sofas in the back salon for a quick break. An hour had passed since she'd spoken to Big Mike, and she was still wondering about what he had told her. Papa never talked about his life before he married her mother, and not once had she ever heard anyone around the neighborhood call him Frankie the Cat.

Pulling off her pumps, Gina began to rub her feet while looking at a copy of *Variety* one of the other girls had left on the table, thumbing through pictures of actresses and descriptions of the latest talkies.

A moment later, Marty Doyle stepped into the salon and, after a darting look around, dropped into a plush blue chair next to her sofa. Gina straightened up, about to greet him, but something about his scowl kept her from saying anything. She slid the *Variety* back onto the table.

Still without speaking, Marty removed the camera from

his neck and placed it on the table in front of them both. He crossed his arms and finally spoke. "What are you doing here?"

"Uh, hello," she replied. "I'm Gina Ricci. The new ciggie girl."

"I know *who* you are," he snapped back. "What I want to know is, what are you doing *here*?"

"Just taking my break," she replied. "The Signora told me to—"

He waved his hand impatiently. "Why are you working *here*, at the Third Door?"

"I don't know what you mean," she said, faltering a bit. He seemed really angry. She started to edge away from him. "Lulu told me about the opening here, and—"

"Your father didn't send you?"

"My father? What—? No. Why would he?" she asked.

"Your father. I heard what Big Mike said. He's Frankie the Cat. Frankie Ricci, right?"

"Yeah, that's right. Did you know him? Do you know why he was called that?"

Marty ignored her questions. "Your mother—" Here the photographer swallowed, his pronounced Adam's apple rising sharply in his throat. "Your mother was Molly O'Brien."

Was. She noted his use of past tense. He knew her mother had passed away. He knew her name.

"Yes," she said, her voice dropping. "What's it to you?"

"You don't know who I am?"

"You're Marty Doyle, the photographer here. In fact, I was keen to know more about what you do. I—"

He held up his hand, once again effectively cutting her off. "You, Gina Aileen Ricci, are my cousin's daughter."

Gina studied his face, taking in his dark features and blue eyes. "I never heard of you."

"It seems your father didn't tell you about me. I can assure you, lass, your mother and I are—were—cousins." He paused, looking up at the exposed pipes in the ceiling. "She could well have been my younger sister. We grew up together, over on the North Side. She was a bit of a favorite of mine."

"Then how come I never met you?" Gina demanded, still not convinced. "All these years, I never heard of you. I certainly never heard *from* you, or any of Mama's kin. If she was such a 'favorite' of yours? Why is that? Why has my father never spoken of you?"

"Bad blood, I suppose. I remember when your mother marched away, on your father's arm," Marty said, his face softening at the memory. "Quite a ruckus, when she left home. Your mother's kin didn't take too kindly to her running off with an Italian from the Near West Side, I can tell you that. Especially not with 'Frankie the Cat.'" He grimaced. "They wanted her to marry into the Daleys."

The Daleys were a well-connected Irish Catholic family on the North Side. More of her mother's people, it seemed. "You're kidding."

"No." Sadness crept into his voice. "I should have stood up for her. But I was busy with my own life, I suppose." He coughed. "You said Lulu told you about the job. You two are good friends, I take it?"

"Well, not exactly," she hedged. Something in his stern gaze reminded Gina of her mother, prompting her to continue. "Honestly, I haven't really spoken to Lulu in years. I ran into her at the market, and we struck up a conversation. I ended up mentioning that I was looking for a job, and then she told me about the opening here."

Gina bit her lip as she reflected back on that conversation with Lulu. Was that how it had occurred? Or had Lulu begun talking about the Third Door, how exciting it was, how much jack she'd made each night, and then she'd mentioned there was an opening? Had they run into each other, or had Lulu sought her out? Maybe the conversation had gone a little differently than she had initially recalled. What did it matter now anyway?

"I don't like it," Marty muttered, more to himself than to her. "Molly's daughter! Working here? Why now?"

"Why not now?" Gina demanded. "I have no choice."

"There's always a choice."

Gina stiffened at the rebuke. "Not for me." She hesitated and then plowed on, her anger making her bold. "If you had ever bothered to get to know us, you'd know that my papa's not well. He can't work. It's up to me to take care of everything, to put food on the table, to pay the rent. So don't tell me there's a choice. Because I don't know what that choice is!"

He grimaced. "I'm sorry to hear your father's not well. And you're right. I should have known. I shouldn't have let all these years go by."

"Well, why did you?" Marty didn't reply, only began to fiddle with his camera case, opening and shutting the latch in a nervous way. "Could you introduce me to the rest of the family?" she pressed. "Maybe they'd want to meet me."

His laugh was bitter. "Not likely. Sorry, kid." Then, before she could ask more questions, he lowered his voice. "Something about this isn't right. I just don't get why they hired you."

"What do you mean?"

"There's something I need to find out first." He looked at her intently. "Keep all of this to yourself, all right?"

Before she could reply, a sound outside the door startled them both. The other girls would be coming in soon to get ready for their song-and-dance number. Giving her a warning look, he picked up his camera and left the salon, leaving Gina with a swirl of questions.

Her break over, Gina went to retrieve her tray, dumbfounded by what she had just learned. To think, after all this time, that she had met a relative. For so long, it had just been her and Papa. And she believed the photographer's claim. The family resemblance couldn't be denied. *I have just met my mother's cousin,* she thought, feeling absurdly pleased.

But what about the other thing Marty had said? About something not being "right" about her hiring. What had he meant by that?

She watched as Lulu and the other waitresses passed by her in a flutter of giggles, changing for their first set of the evening. *Had* Lulu sought her out directly, as Marty seemed to have implied? Though questions burned, there was no time to ask Lulu anything now. Besides, she had promised Marty she would keep everything to herself, at least for the time being. The urgency in his request was hard to ignore.

Moving over to the far end of the bar to see if Billy had any drink orders, Gina ended up next to two men, both hunched over their glasses of whiskey. One was tapping his fingers on the table, keeping the beat with Ned's ragtime melody. The other, an older man who might have been in his seventies, looked lost in thought. He was wearing a white shirt with suspenders connected to gray slacks; his jacket was slung carefully over the back of his chair. He looked familiar somehow. Maybe she'd seen him around the neighborhood.

She approached the man who was keeping tune. "Cigarettes, sir?" she asked. "Or perhaps a cigar?"

Instead of answering, the man gave a mirthless laugh. He put his hands to his high collar, which had a loosened tie wrapped around it.

"Don't do it, Joe," warned the other man.

Billy Bottles wagged a finger at the man from the other end of the bar. "Don't do it, Joe," he echoed.

Curious, Gina couldn't refrain. "Don't do what?" she asked. The next minute she wished she hadn't.

Half fascinated and half repulsed, Gina watched as Joe slowly loosened his tie further and even more slowly unbuttoned the rest of his collar, revealing a deep slash across his throat. A slash that had been meant to kill.

"What in the world—?" Curiosity overcoming her mild sense of nausea, Gina peered at the scar, much to the amusement of the other men. "I guess no smokes for you, then, huh?"

The other men chuckled. The man made a funny sound then that almost sounded like a laugh. It quickly became a harsh wheezing, and Gina backed away.

The old man leaned over and pounded him on the back. "Better watch it, Joe. Don't want this gal feeling guilty if you keel over now."

Joe took a drink but then staggered away toward the restroom, still coughing, leaving half his whiskey in the glass.

"Jeepers!" Gina exclaimed, when he was out of earshot. "What happened to him?"

"Aw, don't mind Joe Lewis," Billy Bottles said. "Hasn't spoken much since Capone got his hands on him."

"Holy cow! What did he do?"

The bartender shrugged. "Not for me to say. However, Mr. Darrow here"—he gestured to the man with suspenders—"well, he might know something of it." With that, he moved away to the other end of the bar, where he began mixing some other cocktails.

Gina looked back at the older man in surprise. No wonder he'd looked so familiar. This was none other than Clarence Darrow, the famous defense attorney. She'd seen him on the front page of the newspaper many times. "You defended the boy murderers."

It was hard not to remember that case of Leopold and Loeb. Several years ago, the strange murder of a teenage boy at the hands of two University of Chicago students had been front-page news. It was the perfect murder, some had said, except that one of the men, Leopold, had accidentally dropped his glasses at the scene. Darrow had been brought in to defend the two men, getting them life in prison rather than the death penalty.

"Successfully," he added, sipping his whiskey. "I'm rather afraid, my dear, that you have me at a disadvantage. You know that I am Clarence Darrow; I only know that you are the new cigarette girl."

"Yeah, that's right," she said. "Gina Ricci." She wondered if he was going to say something about her dad being Frankie the Cat, as others had done when they heard her full name. When he didn't, she gestured in the direction the man named Joe had just gone. "What happened to that guy? Billy said

Capone——?" She mimicked the gesture of someone slitting a throat.

The attorney took another drink, like a man with all the time in the world. "Story goes that Joe Lewis didn't want to renew his contract over at the Green Mill. He was a song-and-dance man, you know. That's one of Capone's establishments."

"Oh yeah?"

"You can probably follow the tale from there. One of Capone's men *allegedly* cut Joe's tongue and throat to keep him from singing somewhere else." He tugged on his suspenders again. "Now how about you let me choose a cigar?"

As she waited for some giggling coeds to pay for their smokes, Gina found herself looking around the speakeasy for Marty. *"My mother's cousin,"* she whispered to herself, then looked around nervously, hoping no one had heard.

She had downed a shot of bourbon a few minutes before, on a patron's quarter, and was now feeling a bit squiffy. She put a hand on the back of a chair to keep herself from swaying. The girls were still pawing through their handbags, trying to find a few more dimes between them.

"These cocktails are expensive! Seventy-five cents each!" she heard one of them mutter to the other. "We need someone to pay for them."

"Exactly, Trixie," the other replied. "I *told* you that before we came."

The woman called Trixie clutched her companion's arm. "Maddie, we're saved! Isn't that Professor Adelson over there? With Professor Rothchild?" Putting a dime on Gina's tray, Trixie pointed to two bearded men in the corner engaged in a very earnest conversation. "You can bring us some gin rickeys in a few minutes, after we've settled in over there." She smirked. "Those gentlemen will be paying." Gina watched them slink their way over to their professors, who looked startled at their approach. After what looked like an awkward exchange, though, the women were invited to sit down.

It was then that Gina spotted Marty standing in that shadowy corner, camera in hand, not moving about the floor the way he usually did. Questions from their earlier conversation still burned inside her. *Was* there something odd about the way she had gotten the job? She thought again about what Marty had said. *Something about this isn't right.*

Time to get some answers, she thought, winding her way toward him, twisting between drunk couples clinging to each other and staggering through the Lindy.

Marty looked toward her then, and it was clear that he'd been tracking her movements as much as she'd been tracking his. When they caught eyes, he shook his head at her almost imperceptibly. The message was clear. *Not yet. Stay away.*

That only made Gina more determined. She pressed forward until someone grabbed her arm. "Say, miss, we'd like some smokes."

A man in his fifties was looking up at her, while his white-haired companion peered onto her tray with dissatisfaction. "This all you have? The other girl, Dorrie, she always made sure she had Palinas on hand."

"I'll check with Billy," she replied absently, still intent on watching Marty. He seemed to have turned his attention to the Signora, following her movements as she circled through the speakeasy, conversing in her sultry way with the patrons. "He'll know what Big Mike keeps in the humidor."

"Well, get to it, then," the man said gruffly. "We'll be here."

Her eyes still on Marty, she watched as he began to thread his way purposefully through the patrons, following the proprietress through the beaded doorway and into the corridor that led to her private salon.

Unhooking her tray from around her neck, Gina called over to Billy. "I need a quick break. Some customers are asking for Palinas. Table five."

Without waiting for the bartender to reply, Gina went through the same doorway that she'd just seen Marty disappear through. She could see that the Signora's salon door was shut. As she edged closer, she could feel the sweat collecting under her arms and on her forehead. Glancing up and down the corridor, she edged over to the door. She didn't want to think about what would happen to her if Gooch or, worse, the Signora caught her eavesdropping. She just *had* to know what Marty and the Signora were talking about.

Luckily, Marty's angry words carried easily. "You brought the lass here, and I want to know why!"

The Signora murmured something inaudible, although Marty's shouted reply was perfectly clear. "Baloney!"

The Signora continued speaking, this time in a calm and chilly way that was more audible. "Frankly, I'm a bit puzzled as to why you are so put out. I understand now that she's a relative. Do you suppose we'll treat her badly?" Even through the door, Gina could hear the menacing quality that underlay the Signora's silken tone.

Without thinking, Gina crossed her arms around her own body, as if to ward off the sudden chill. *Stop talking, Marty,* she wanted to shout through the wooden door.

The Signora had continued. "Perhaps you are dissatisfied with how we treat *you*?"

Almost as if he had heard Gina's plea, Marty's tone became more conciliatory. "No, no, Signora. Forget I brought it up. I was wrong to do so. Forgive me, Signora."

His voice seemed to be closer to the door, and Gina leapt out of the way as it opened. Though she tried to feign innocence, there could be no doubt as to what she'd been doing in the otherwise empty corridor. Seeing her, Marty scowled and put his finger to his lips, indicating that she should stay silent. He passed her by without another word.

"Marty?" she called, racing after him. "What did the Signora tell you?"

"The Signora said she had no idea who you were, or that you had any connection to me."

"You don't believe that?"

"Time to get back to work."

She started to protest. "But—"

He grabbed her arm. "This is not a coincidence," he whispered harshly in her ear. "You're a fool to think it is. Talk to your father."

"Papa? Why?"

"Gina!" he said. "You know where you work, and who you work for. Maybe it doesn't matter why." He stalked off.

Gina leaned back against the wall, trembling a bit from the unexpected vehemence of their encounter. What could Papa know about any of this? She had to speak to him as soon as possible.

CHAPTER 5

Gina watched her father take his last bite of toast, chewing slowly and carefully. She knew he'd had a bad night the night before, the medicine working on the shakes only some of the time. But she could no longer put off the questions that had been raging inside her since she first heard them. "Papa?"

"Yeah?"

"Why were you called Frankie the Cat?"

He pushed the plate aside, a spasm crossing his face. "Where'd you hear that? I haven't been called that in years."

"Mike Castallazzo. He owns the Third Door."

"Castallazzo!" He spat out the name. "That double-dealer! Didn't know Big Mike owned that joint. I'd never have let you work there."

Though startled by his outburst, Gina pressed on. "His wife, the Signora—she's the one who hired me. He hadn't re-alized who I was until we met." She paused. "He said you were friends. That you ran together in the old days."

"Yeah. The old days, sure. We were pals. Back when he was still *Little* Mike." He said the last with a snort. "*Big* Mike came later, after I was already out."

"They said you were Frankie the Cat. What did that mean? Why did they call you that?"

"It's just a name from around the neighborhood," he said. "It's on account of my nine lives. Like a cat. Got myself in and out of a lot of scrapes when I was a youth."

"Scrapes?" Gina asked, taking a seat across from him with a bowl of her own. She pulled at a chunk of the Italian bread that Mrs. Angelo sold at her corner market. "What sort of scrapes?"

"Back in the orphanage. Stupid stuff. Came in handy though when I started boxing. Name stuck."

"Oh!" Her father rarely talked about his days in the ring. Suddenly there was a gleam in her father's eyes, one she hadn't seen in years. "That chest on my dresser. Bring it here," he commanded. "I'll tell you all about it."

After retrieving the chest, Gina set it on the table. With shaking hands, her father lifted the lid. There were several yellowed photographs of him as a young man, striking a fighting pose, along with some newspaper clippings mentioning his time in the ring. On one, which had a picture of him knocking out his opponent, someone had written, "Frankie the Cat, jabbing a good one."

Gina inspected the picture. Seeing her father as a young man, full of muscles and a stunning vitality, was a stark reminder of all he'd come to lose. "How many years did you box?" she asked, fighting the sudden lump in her throat.

"Oh, probably as soon as I could walk and swing my arms at the same time. Then I started working for Big Mike's father. His pop heard about my boxing, came out to see a bout. Saw me take down my opponent in one blow. Offered me a job on the spot."

"What kind of job?" Gina asked.

Her papa hesitated. "Let's just say I made sure things went the way Big Mike's pop wanted them to go."

Gina's mind flashed to men who worked at the Third Door. "Like Gooch? Mr. Gucciani, I mean."

"Gooch?" Her papa frowned. "He's not so bad. At least he wasn't back when I knew him. If I'd have known, though, that you were working for Big Mike—"

"Papa, I'm just selling cigarettes and serving drinks," Gina interrupted. "Besides, we need the money."

She regretted her bluntness immediately when she caught the wounded expression on his face. Hastily she sought to change his mood. "Is that when you met Mama? When you worked for Big Mike's pop?"

"Ah, Molly," he said, a fondness coming over his face as he launched into the beloved story she hadn't heard in years. Sweet Molly O'Brien, charmed away from her Irish neighborhood along the lake by the smooth-talking young boxer she'd met by chance on the Metropolitan West Side Elevated Railroad. As her father would tell the story later, he skipped his stop on the L, entranced by the young woman whom he would come to woo and marry within six months' time.

"Was that why you stopped boxing? Mama didn't like it?"

"Oh, no, not at all. Your mother, sweetheart that she was, had the fight of the Irish in her. I don't think she liked when I got knocked out, of course, but fortunately I didn't do that so often." He paused. "What she didn't like was me working for Big Mike's pop. She got me the job driving the L instead. Told me it would remind me every day of how we met. And you know what, it did."

Gina smiled in return. Then her papa's tone changed a bit.

He shook his head. "I want you to know, Gina, I'm not proud of that life, when I worked for Big Mike's father. Your mother changed everything. She changed *me*." He paused. "You're starting to be just like her. Beautiful, kind, and with some of that same temper I admired in your mother."

Gina took a deep breath. "Papa," she said, "there's a man who works at the Third Door. Name's Marty. He's the photographer. He said..." She hesitated. "He said he's Mama's cousin."

"Marty Doyle." His tone was flat.

"Yes, that's right." She watched her father's hand begin to tremble more than before.

"He turned against her, like the rest of her uppity family. Just about broke her heart."

"What happened?"

"Your grandparents didn't like Molly taking up with me. Disowned her on the spot. Even her dearest cousin couldn't find a way to defend her. Willy-willed, that's what your *Marty* was." He practically spat out his name. "I'll never forgive him for that."

"Is that why we never met her family? Didn't they want to meet us?" Unexpectedly a tear came to her eye. "Not even when she died?"

"They didn't want to know us, your mother always said. That's why I didn't tell them when she passed. Or when we lost Aidan." He swallowed and looked away. It was clear that the conversation was over.

A few days later, when Gina arrived at the Third Door, she found everyone in a strained mood.

"Hurry, Gina," Faye said through a clenched smile. A

single strand of her silvery hair had slipped free of her head-piece. It would have looked charming on someone else, but on Faye it looked like an icicle on her chiseled cheek. "Get dressed. The Signora wants you to shake a leg. Lulu's not here yet."

"What's going on?" she asked Ned when he sauntered over to the bar to have Billy Bottles refill his flask with gin.

"A bunch of rumrunners got caught on Lake Michigan in a boat bound for Chicago," he whispered, cracking his knuckles. "Big Mike and the Signora are boiling mad."

"It was one of their shipments, I take it."

"You bet. Apparently the poor suckers were stranded out there in the cold for eleven days, bouncing about on the waves. With only a single gas torch for heat. It's a wonder they survived!"

"What will happen to the bootleggers?" Gina asked.

Overhearing her, Mr. Darrow chuckled. "No question about that. They'll spend the rest of their days in prison." He took a puff of his cigar. "Unless, of course, Congress finally votes to repeal Prohibition. Figures out that it's causing more damage than good."

"I suppose," Gina said. *Keeps me employed, though. Pays well enough.* However, she didn't want to offend Mr. Darrow, who seemed to feel strongly about it. She returned to the situation with the rumrunners. "What will they do about the missed shipment?"

Ned shrugged. "Probably what they always do. Buy some rotgut at half the price and slap some fake labels on the bottles. The booze-swillers here will never know the difference."

"If they don't know the difference, why do they bother with bootlegged liquor from Canada?" Gina asked.

"Sometimes our customers know their liquor," Billy explained, frowning at Ned. "Some of them come from *your* part of the world. Society folks."

Gina glanced at Ned, who had reddened slightly. "Not my world. At least not anymore."

Faye walked over again. "The Signora doesn't pay you sots to stand around yapping at the bar, now does she?"

Billy tightened his lips but moved to the other end of the bar. Ned stalked back to his piano and began to bang something out on the keys. With a smile, Gina recognized the words to the popular tune. *"Ha-ha-ha!"* he sang. *"Pardon me while I laugh."*

Over the next hour, Gina worked the room, getting better at reading the needs of customers. Light a cigarette here, crack a joke there. Always pushing gin drinks and beer, since they were running low on rum. Right now, she was on her own. The cocktail waitresses were getting ready for their next set, and she was taking care of the floor alone.

"You're a natural, doll," Ned said to her once when she walked by the piano.

She shrugged and passed the order on to Billy Bottles. She didn't feel like a natural, though, a few minutes later when a tipsy young woman pulling a friend along by the elbow pushed past her, causing three drinks to spill into her cocktail tray. When she glanced around, she found that the Signora was staring straight at her, her face a mask, no indication of what she was thinking. She knew for sure she couldn't set half-empty glasses in front of this crowd, not with the prices they were paying. She returned to Billy.

"Could you top these gin rickeys off?" she asked, as she set the glasses on the counter and wiped the tray.

"Not tippling off the customer's drinks, are you?" he said with a wink before regarding the drinks with a professional eye. She watched as the barkeep added a bit of foam from whatever he'd been concocting in his shaker and a dollop more gin to each glass. "Should be good to go. We'll call these the Billy Bottles Rickey."

After she delivered the newly doctored drinks to the customers, who didn't seem to have noticed either the wait or the change in recipe, she stood quietly by the stairs, keeping an eye on the room. The Signora had at last returned to her salon, and Gina felt she could relax. Ned had stopped playing and put a record on the spinner. She saw Marty moving about the room, but she hadn't interacted with him since their exchange outside the Signora's salon. He hadn't worked the last few nights, and she got the feeling now that he might be avoiding her. Every time she had moved in his direction, he seemed to be moving the other way.

Sensing a large presence next to her, she looked up to find the ever-stoic Gooch looking out over the room. Seizing the moment, she spoke to him. "So, Gooch. Mr. Gucciani. You knew my papa from the old days?" she asked.

Gooch grunted.

Not deterred, Gina continued. "He said he got in a bunch of scrapes. That's why you called him Frankie the Cat, right?"

Still no response.

"You must have known my mama?"

At last a flicker. "Sure, kid. We all knew Molly. Real sweet girl." He seemed like he was about to say something else, but instead he glanced first at his watch and then at the beaded entrance to the main room. His tone changed. "Where are those girls? Where's Fingers?"

The floor was still full of customers dancing and hanging on to each other, doing their high-spirited drunken best to dance the Charleston. Usually, Gina had learned, the customers knew to clear the dance floor for the girls and other performers when Ned tinkled a delightful little overture. However, Ned was not at his customary place at the piano, and indeed was nowhere to be seen.

The girls had appeared in the beaded doorway, dressed in their fabulous feathers and beads. In their hands, they were carrying bananas, of all things. Bananas?

Then Gina realized what they were planning. "If you clear the floor, I'll put the record on," she said to Gooch.

Hoping she had guessed correctly, Gina laid down her tray on the bar and, with a quick review of the wax records stacked inside the gramophone, found the disc she was looking for. She held it up to Jade, who nodded curtly. She waved to Gooch, who gave a piercing whistle. "Make room for the dancers," he said in a tone that was both loud and menacing.

Startled, everyone cleared the dance floor immediately, standing around the room, sitting on the bar stools, or taking chairs by the tables along the wall. His command was not one to be ignored. Giggling a little to herself, Gina quickly removed the other record, replacing it with "Yes, We Have No Bananas."

The girls flounced through their routine, which contained a number of suggestive gestures that made the audience roar and clamor for more drinks. When they were done, the girls raced off to change, not wanting to miss out on all the good tipping that was sure to follow.

Gina was left alone again. Seeing that Ned had still not returned, Gina placed another record on the gramophone, and "Flapper Walk" began to play, to great squeals from the women in the audience, who jumped up and began to dance together in pairs.

"Good choice," Billy Bottles said. "This crowd's ready to stay hopping—oh, no!"

Gina turned around to see one of those hopping coeds fall violently against the gramophone. The next moment the record began to skip, to a collective groan from the others. Gooch came over and, with a strong arm, escorted the woman and her companion out of the Third Door, Jade following behind them.

Faye had gone over to inspect the gramophone. "Needle's broken," she said. "Spare me these simpleton Bettys."

"Is there another needle?" Gina asked. "Maybe I can fix it."

"Hey, girls, how about some drinks first?" a customer called out.

Gina waved Faye and Lulu away. "Go, take care of their drink orders. I'll see if there's another needle."

"If not, there's always the Radiola. Get some dance music out of New York," Lulu said.

"Do it quick," Faye ordered. "Before we lose *all* our customers." Indeed, a few patrons had already started to walk up the stairs, murmuring about heading over to the dance emporium on Walnut.

"Good luck getting a stiff drink there," Billy Bottles muttered. "Everyone knows that place waters down their drinks. It's *all* rotgut there."

Gina looked around. Where was Ned, anyway? Well, no time to worry about that now. The most important thing was to get the music playing again. She was surprised that the Signora had not come to find out what was going on by now.

Unable to find a second needle inside the gramophone

cabinet, Gina pushed it back into the corner, while Billy Bottles mopped up the offending vomit. "Where's the Radiola?" she asked.

Billy pointed behind to the door behind the bar. "Back there. I'll roll it out. I think it's busted, though."

"Oh yeah? What's the matter with it?"

Billy shrugged and went into the back room to push out the Radiola. A moment later, they had it plugged in. When they turned it on, though, a harsh buzzing sound filled the air. Gina listened to it for a second, then turned the dial. "Let's try a different channel."

She twiddled with the dial again, and they heard the same harsh sound. "Sounds like a capacitor needs to be fixed." She pulled the radio away from the wall and looked for the release that would allow the back panel to swing open.

The patrons' thirst momentarily quenched, Lulu and Faye had returned to hover anxiously over her.

"Do you even know how to fix it?" Faye asked, tapping her foot in annoyance. "What's the holdup?"

"Just gimme a sec," Gina said, still fiddling with the dials, trying not to feel irked by Faye's bossy manner.

"Oh yeah, your dad fixes radios," Lulu said. "I remember."

"Yeah, he did." She stopped, not wanting to say anything else about her papa. "I need needle-nose pliers."

The women looked uncomprehending.

"A tool kit?" Gina asked a bit more impatiently.

"I know where one is," Lulu said, retrieving a small box of tools from behind the bar and handing it to Gina.

"Hurry up," Faye said. "This crowd wants their tunes."

Gina didn't hesitate, applying the tools to the vacuum tubes and other parts of the Radiola.

"Sure hope you know what you're doing," a man said from behind her. She looked up to see Roark scowling down at her.

Although she ignored him, he continued. "Hope you don't go electrifying yourself."

To her chagrin, she found herself double-checking that she had indeed unplugged the cord from the electric outlet on the wall. He chuckled.

"You're in my light," she told him.

"Alright bearcat, I'm just here to help." Unexpectedly, he pulled out a flashlight from the toolbox and swung the light so that she could see. "What's the diagnosis, Doctor?" he asked, crouching awkwardly down beside her. His tone seemed to be more interested than mocking now.

"Could be a filter, could be a blown tube. I can't tell right now if it's the loudspeaker or the radio itself." She glanced at him, registering the change in his expression. "Shine the light to the left, would you?"

He stayed silent as she carefully twisted the wire by the capacitor back into place. "Big Mike needs to get those capacitors changed," she muttered to herself.

Awkwardly he stood back up. "Learn that trade during the Great War, did you? When all of us men were off fighting?"

Gina could hear the bitterness in his voice, and she knew exactly why he was angry. So many men were. They had fought hard for their country, often getting injured and maimed, to return to what? Scorn, poverty, humiliation, and unemployment. Her brother could easily have been one of the thousands of disillusioned and bitter men. If, of course, he had returned.

Ignoring Roark, she shut the panel and plugged the radio back in. Fiddling with the dials, within a few seconds she had dance music broadcasting from New York City.

Only then did she look back up at Roark. "I've learned my father's trade because he has no son to support him, and he no longer has the capacity to fend for himself. I've done what I need to do. If you'll excuse me, I gotta get back to work."

She handed the toolbox to Billy Bottles. "Nice work, doll," he said.

"Nothing to it," she said, giving him a little wink. As she slipped the straps of her tray around her neck, she glanced back at Roark. He was still standing by the radio, looking thoughtful.

CHAPTER 6

Gina yanked impatiently at her stocking as she hurried to the drugstore for her shift, hoping to keep the bandages covering her blisters intact. Her feet were still aching from the long night before. Eventually Ned had returned to his piano, bleary-eyed and looking dismal. Lulu had whispered to her that he'd been found by Little Johnny asleep in the alley, having tossed back one too many before he went on break. Whether he'd gotten in trouble for his wrongdoing was difficult to say. Even blotto, Ned was still a fine piano player.

The sky was already darkening a bit as the late afternoon sun went behind a cloud. It was only four in the afternoon, but as the Signora had instructed, she was to work at the drugstore for two hours before heading down to the Third Door for her shift.

As she opened the door to Rosenstein's Drugs, she noted a bold sign in the window. RUBBING ALCOHOL ONLY. She chuckled and went inside, a bell above the door jangling as she entered the store. An odd mix of aromas tickled her nose, sweet scents of vanilla and malt alongside the more pungent smells of ground-up herbs and medicines.

The store was bigger than she expected, with a soda counter and stools to her left. The center held wooden shelves full of canned foods, soaps, talcs, and other sundries. At the right she saw the pharmacy counter, with rows of bottles and jars containing medicines and remedies.

Evidently having heard the bell, a stout and balding man, wearing spectacles, a neatly pressed white coat, and an equally neat bow tie stepped into view, grinding something with a mortar and pestle.

"Mr. Rosenstein?" Gina asked. "I'm Gina Ricci."

"What may I do for you?" Like nearly everyone else's on the near West Side, Mr. Rosenstein's speech contained a trace of an accent, although his English was impeccable. Yiddish, she guessed. He held out his hand. "You have a prescription to be filled?"

"I'm *working* here today." She gave him a meaningful wink. "The Signora sent me."

"The Signora . . . ?" His brow cleared. "Benny will show you around. *Benny!*"

A young black man stepped out from one of the aisles, brushing his hands on his white apron. He was perhaps in his early twenties. "Yes, sir?" he said to the pharmacist.

"Show this young lady around the store. *The Signora,*" he said, pointing meaningfully at the floor and the speakeasy below, "wants her to learn what we do here. Show her how to stack the shelves and make a fizzy drink, would you?"

"Sure thing, Mr. Rosenstein." Benny smiled at her. "This way, miss."

"Name's Gina," she ventured, looking around. She wondered about how the Castallazzos had come to control the pharmacy. Had they taken the establishment over when they set up the Third Door, or had they invited Mr. Rosenstein to set up his pharmacy as a front? Did it even matter?

Over the next hour, Benny showed her how to scoop ice cream, stack cans on shelves, and check boxes of goods against an inventory. Throughout he kept up a running commentary about baseball. Cubs, White Sox, Red Sox, Yankees—who was expected to be traded, who had a big year ahead of him, whose career was over. "I did get to meet Bobby Williams, shortstop, though." His eyes gleamed. "Plays for the Chicago American Giants. They won the Negro League World Series in '26 and '27. He even signed a ball for me after a game!"

Gina smiled in response to his excitement, though she didn't care so much about the sport herself. When she was growing up, her papa had mainly followed boxing. Although it was Aidan who'd shown her a few basic boxing moves, before he'd gone and gotten himself killed in France.

As they stacked cans, she noted other advertisements and warnings. On the one end, there were clear POISON signs, complete with skulls and crossbones. COMPLETELY DENATURED ALCOHOL, one sign proclaimed above a row of dark and slightly dusty bottles. TO BE USED FOR ART, MECHANICAL, AND BURNING PURPOSES ONLY.

She pointed to the sign. "People really drink that stuff?"

"That's why the antidote is just below. Emetics of mustard."

Peering at the sign, Gina read the smaller print out loud. *"Completely denatured alcohol is a violent poison. It cannot be applied externally to human or animal tissue without seriously injurious results. It cannot be taken internally without inducing blindness and general physical decay—* Goodness!—*ultimately resulting in death."*

Benny nodded a bit mournfully. "Some people just see the

word 'alcohol.' So when they bring up a vial of this stuff for purchase, we usually direct them to the other shelf. In case what they really need is 'medicinal alcohol.'" He waved to the signs that hung above the next row, over bottles of Aspironal and Sani-Tone. BETTER THAN WHISKEY FOR COLDS AND FLU, one sign read. Another proclaimed itself a "health-protecting" tonic.

Gina shook a bottle of Sani-Tone, the thick syrupy substance causing her stomach to lurch at the sight. The vodka and gin she'd had at the Third Door had been hard enough to swill on its own. The medicinal liquor looked positively lethal. She put it back on the shelf.

Benny headed over to the soda counter. "Want some Coca-Cola?" Benny asked, pouring himself a glass from the tap. "Mr. Rosenstein don't mind if we have one glass when we work."

Grateful for the refreshment, she took the proffered glass. "Did you see Babe Ruth when he was here?" she asked. She remembered that Lulu had said that the home run king had visited the Third Door. "What was he like?"

Benny chuckled. "Girl, I've seen him. At the *ballpark*, when I could spare a buck for the ticket. Other than that, believe it or not, the Babe and I have never met."

"Oh, I thought—" Then she stopped, confused.

He nodded at the back door that led down to the speak-easy. "You thought I work down there?"

"Well, yes."

"Nah, this is a real job." He waved at the pharmacy counter. "At least it is for me."

"How long have you been working here?" Gina asked.

"Almost a year now. A bit of a story about how I ended

up here." Benny began to rinse out the two soda glasses in the small sink affixed to the back wall. "Originally, I tried to apply at Vincenzo's Market. You know that place, over on Halsted?"

Gina nodded. She'd frequently bought meat and vegetables from them. That market had been around as long as she could remember, the Italian family who owned it having been there at least three generations. She knew guys from the neighborhood who had worked there. "They're always hiring young men, aren't they? I've seen the Help Wanted sign in their window."

"Yeah, that's what I thought, too." He began to towel dry the glasses. "When I asked about the position, they made it clear that they didn't want to hire the likes of me."

"Oh," Gina said, lost for words.

Benny continued. "Then the next day, a funny thing happened. My mom, she got an advertisement from Vincenzo's, inviting us to shop at their market. She said to me, 'Benny, there's no way in tarnation that we're spending even one penny in a store that don't see fit to hire you.'" He smiled at the recollection. "My mama and me, and some of our neighbors, too, we all walked right into Vincenzo's and told that to the man himself. You should have seen his face when we walked in! He probably thought we were gonna bust up the place."

"Your mama sounds tough," Gina said.

"Yeah, she sure is. 'Don't mess with Mama,' we always say. There she was, talking to Mr. Vincenzo, telling him how I was real smart and was just trying to make some money for the family. That I wasn't some criminal." He began to wipe the soda well down, with quick vigorous strokes. "You know what the best part is? We'd barely walked two steps out the door when Mr. Rosenstein came up to us and offered me a job—this job—on the spot."

"Golly! Why'd he do that?"

"Because I am a Jew," Mr. Rosenstein said, appearing suddenly beside them. He'd evidently overheard at least the last part of Benny's story. There was a slight quaver to his voice as he continued. "In my homeland, too often have men like me been held back. In Benny, I saw myself."

"I'm gonna be a doctor," Benny said, puffing out his chest. "Mr. Rosenstein's already taught me all kinds of stuff about pharmacy."

"Oh yeah?" Gina asked, trying not to sound skeptical in the face of his enthusiasm. She'd never heard of a black doctor.

"Yeah. The thing is, black folks can't get much service from white doctors, at least not around here. Believe it or not, there are medical schools that educate black men to be doctors." He smiled broadly. "I'm saving up now to attend Howard University Medical School. Mr. Rosenstein gave me some books to study. Chemistry. Math. Anatomy." For a second, the brightness in his eyes dimmed. "Just gotta make enough dough to get me there."

"You will, so long as you get back to work." Despite his scolding tone, there was a fondness there as well. The pharmacist glanced at Gina. "Speaking of which, it's nearly six o'clock. You'd better run along. You *don't* want to keep the Signora waiting, of that I am certain."

"Two Rum Runners," Lulu called to Billy, a few hours later.

Hearing the order, Gina smiled to herself. It was at least the eleventh call for the same drink since she'd started her shift. Big Mike had made Rum Runners the drink of the evening. One of his little jokes, since they'd learned that the bootleggers who'd seen their shipment seized had been mysteriously released from jail overnight. Mysterious indeed. From Big Mike's pleased smile, she suspected he knew something about whose palms had been greased to make that escape possible. Regardless, at twenty cents, the drink was a bargain, bringing extra cheer to the evening.

As she waited for Billy to make the cocktails, Lulu put her elbows behind her on the counter. "Must be nice," she said, bouncing a bit to Ned's piano playing.

"What?" Gina asked, following her gaze. A beautiful woman with a shimmering headdress and a white fur coat with spotted trim flung about her shoulders had sauntered down the stairs. Behind her a much taller, immaculately dressed older woman followed, a pinched expression upon her face. The younger woman moved as if she were ready to dance the evening away, while the other looked like someone had pushed her down the stairs with a pitchfork at her back.

"That's Genevieve Beering," Lulu whispered to her, indicating the woman who had slipped out of the fur coat to disclose a shimmering gossamer gown. "One of Chicago's finest."

Everyone had heard of the Beerings. Like the McCormicks, the Wrigleys, and the Searles, they were Chicago royalty; their social and philanthropic doings regularly filled the society pages. Even here at the speakeasy, there was some bowing and scraping going on as if she owned the place.

"Who's her companion?"

Lulu squinted, obviously less interested in the other woman. "Oh, that's Greta Van der Veer," she said. "I think."

"What a beautiful necklace Miss Beering is wearing," Gina said, returning her gaze to the heiress. "I wonder what it cost."

"You could probably sell ciggies for the next ten years and still not be able to afford it," Faye said, overhearing their exchange.

"Oh, no, surely not *that* long, Faye." Jade jumped in. "Maybe just nine years. Nine and a half, tops."

Gina laughed along with the other women, although she had the feeling that the laugh might be at her own expense. Jade and Faye sashayed off, back to their respective tables.

Miss Beering seated herself grandly in her chair, nodding her head graciously and accepting accolades as a princess might receive her subjects. "To the manor born," she had heard a character described in a talkie once, and it reminded her of the heiress now. Miss Van der Veer, on the other hand, looked decidedly uncomfortable with all the attention. Her back was straight and her face wrinkled and pallid, as if she wanted to be anywhere but the speakeasy.

Nor was she drinking, Gina noticed, although the heiress had already downed two red-hued cocktails in rapid succession. No cheap drink of the evening, not for this woman. Mary Pickfords, from the looks of it. Gina wholeheartedly approved of that tasty concoction, appreciating the light fruity flavors of the pineapple juice mixed in with rum and grenadine.

When Gina stopped to sell some Chesterfields to a couple of college boys at a nearby table, she heard the Signora glide over to greet Miss Beering in a gracious but not overly solicitous way.

"Take me to your darling husband, would you?" Miss Beering asked, more a command than a question. She touched her necklace. "There's something I'd like to discuss with him."

Although the Signora's expression did not change, she straightened to her full height. "I'm afraid the Signor is busy," she said, with a gracious and well-trained smile.

"Oh, but Big Mike will see *me*," Miss Beering replied. She smoothed her hair, causing a silver and amethyst bracelet to slip down along her slender arm.

Her smile never wavering, the Signora inclined her head. "I shall see if he's available. Please, follow me."

With a graceful gesture, the Signora moved toward the back room. As Gina moved over to collect the women's empty glasses, she saw Miss Van der Veer clutch the heiress's arm before she walked away. "What are you doing?" Gina heard her hiss.

Miss Beering shook off her companion's hand. "I know what I'm doing, Greta," she hissed back. "Now leave me be. Have a drink, for God's sake. Loosen up." With that Miss Beering easily caught up with the Signora, without a backward glance at her companion.

Not missing a beat, Gina walked up to Miss Van der Veer, who had moved over to the bar, still staring in the direction that Miss Beering had just gone. "Can I get you something?" she asked, indicating an empty stool at the end of the bar. The table that the two women had vacated had already been taken by another couple.

"A fizzy lemonade and a pack of Marlboros," Miss Van der Veer replied, sliding stiffly onto the stool. She continued to look around, her nose wrinkled.

Billy Bottles slipped the drink in front of her, and the woman tapped the glass impatiently with one long fingernail.

"Does she come here a lot?" Gina whispered to Lulu, with a nod in the direction that Genevieve Beering had gone.

"Sure. A few times. I've seen her play cards," Lulu said, as she placed the drinks on her tray.

"She's come for a game? With the servicemen?" Gina asked, surprised. It was hard to imagine that elegant woman, dripping with jewels, sitting at the same table as those disfigured men with their injured bodies and patched-up faces. Hardly the usual companions of a wealthy heiress.

Lulu laughed. "Hardly. Twice a month or so Big Mike organizes a high-stakes game. Real dough gets passed out there, from what I understand." She gestured toward Miss Van der Veer, who was still scowling down at her lemonade. "That one, not so much. A real sourpuss, she is."

"Tell Billy to slip some gin in that drink," Faye whispered, evidently catching the last bit of conversation as she whirled by, tray in hand. "She's souring the whole room."

Sure enough, as Miss Van der Veer continued to look anxiously toward the beaded doorway where the heiress had disappeared, Billy added a dollop of sweet sherry to her drink.

About half an hour later, Gina leaned over to light some smokes for some men who'd been talking nonstop about stock prices and market shares since they had first strolled in. The men kept chuckling about the gains they'd made for their clients, and by extension for themselves. She didn't know much about the stock market and speculation, but it was clear that the rich were getting richer while the poor got even poorer, and that's how the rich people liked it.

Out of the corner of her eye she caught sight of the heiress stalking out of the back room, directly toward Miss Van
der Veer. Her companion had already hopped off the bar stool,
and met her halfway across the floor. "Time to go, Genevieve,"
she said, almost as a mother would speak to her wayward
child.

The heiress gave a terse nod and allowed Miss Van der
Veer to escort her out. As they passed, Gina watched the heiress's dark expression slip away, to be replaced by her usual
gracious and beautiful mask.

"Here you go, Mrs. Dugan," Gina said, carefully placing a cup
of steaming and spiked cider in front of an elderly woman
seated in Mrs. Metzger's tea shop.

This was her third day working in the tea shop, and she
was getting the hang of serving hot drinks, pastries, and other
light fare to customers. Despite the prim lace curtains and
delicate teacups, the place was not nearly as stuffy as she had
expected it to be when she had first walked in a few days before. With very few men on the premises, the women tended
to joke around with each other more. It probably helped that
most took the "extra dollop" in their teacups. For those in on
the secret, Mrs. Metzger's tea room offered a reputable place
for married women and widows to have a quiet drink, without being bothered by their husbands, handsy gin-swillers, or
the Drys.

Some of the women had fascinating stories, and Gina
found herself lingering as two women discussed their time
driving ambulances during the Great War. It was hard not to
think about Aidan then. Had he even made it to an ambu-
lance? Or had he just died on the spot? *Killed in action* was all

the telegram had said. She shook her head, trying not to think about it.

She was adding hot water to a teapot when a ruckus out on the street caused all of the patrons to fall silent. It sounded like someone banging on drums and shouting.

"What in heaven's name is that?" Mrs. Dugan asked.

Mrs. Dugan's companion, another elderly woman with bright blue eyes, tugged on Gina's sleeve. "Don't just stand there gawking, girl. Take a peek."

Seeing Mrs. Metzger give her a nod, Gina opened the door of the tea shop to find out what was happening out on the street. There she saw five women in gray and white dresses, all with starched white aprons and white caps, walking down the street toward the shop. One woman was banging on an enormous drum that had been strapped to her neck and waist. Another was tooting discordantly into a small tin horn. The other three were chanting something that was hard to discern.

When they reached the tea shop entrance they stopped, the drummer still pounding away. "No more alcohol," one of the women shouted, pumping her first in the air.

The shouts continued.

"Alcohol ruins families!"

"Alcohol kills!"

"Alcohol is the devil's drink!"

Gina recognized them. They were temperance workers—those humorless women who had helped bring about Prohibition ten years ago, and who still sought to bring about absolute sobriety and temperance. She didn't know if they were part of the Anti-Saloon League or Woman's Christian Temperance movement or some offshoot thereof, but it didn't really matter. She stepped back inside the tea room, shutting the door behind her.

Undeterred, the temperance workers just shouted more loudly, clearly audible even through the closed door. One of the women slammed her hand on the tea room window, staring directly at Mrs. Dugan. "There is sin here!"

Though initially startled, Mrs. Dugan recovered quickly. "To think I was just about to ask for another nip," she stage-whispered to her companion. "I suppose we'll need to hold off now. Given the *sinful* nature of this establishment."

Both women giggled. "It does take the chill off, now don't it?" her companion replied, reaching up to the sash that held the lace curtain back. "How about we just close the curtain?"

The smiles slipped from their faces, though, when the door opened and the temperance workers pushed their way inside. They renewed their chants and drumming. In loud and grating voices, they called, "Pour out your devil's drink! Alcohol kills!"

One of them began to lay pamphlets on the tables. Gina expected the patrons to get up and leave, but they continued to look on with interest, as if about to take in a show. She looked to the proprietress for guidance.

Mrs. Metzger just looked annoyed. "Gina," she said, jerking her head toward the back door. The implication was clear. *Get some help.*

Gina exited the tea room through the back door and called to Little Johnny, who was sitting behind the green door, keeping watch on the alley. He didn't seem surprised to see her.

"What's the ruckus?" he asked, his Russian accent thick.

"Some temperance workers are mucking about in the tea room."

Little Johnny pulled the cord three sharp times. She heard faraway bells chime in the Signora's office.

A moment later, the Signora and Gooch appeared at the top of the stairs with purpose and strode into the tea room. The intruders stopped midchant and fell silent.

"Good evening, ladies," the Signora said. "If you are here for coffee or tea, pray seat yourselves." She gestured to two empty tables in the corner. "Miss Ricci will take your order."

The temperance workers looked scandalized and began to sputter. "We would never patronize this establishment," one said, smoothing back a strand of hair that had escaped her tight bun. "Not where the devil's drink is poured."

"Is that so?" the Signora inquired, looking around at her patrons. "Any 'devil's drink' here?"

One lady held up her teacup and gave the temperance workers an arch smile. "Just Darjeeling, I can assure you."

"Thank you," the Signora said with an approving nod. Turning back to the temperance workers, she said in an icy voice, "You have harassed my patrons enough. I must ask you to leave my establishment at once."

Little Johnny entered the tea shop then, as if on cue. Gina wondered if he'd been listening behind the closed door. Like Gooch, he flanked the Signora. Now the patrons began to pull on their wraps and take their leave. Propriety clearly took precedence over curiosity, and they most certainly did not want to be part of the unseemly scuffle that was sure to follow.

One of the temperance workers planted her hands on her hips. "We're not leaving!" she declared. "Not until I know what happened to my daughter!"

Her companions seemed surprised, and Gina felt the Signora stiffen beside her.

"Your daughter, madam?" the Signora asked, her voice silky and dangerous. "I have no idea what you are talking about."

"I am speaking about my daughter, Dorrie Edwards. She worked here, my Dorrie did, in this gateway to sin!" The woman fairly spat out the words. "Now she's *dead!*"

"Ah, Mrs. Edwards," the Signora said, her voice tight but controlled. "I am indeed sorry for your daughter's passing. That she could be struck down in such a way, at such a young age, well, that was most certainly cruel. Her murder, as you well know, happened while she was on the L train, down in the Loop. Nowhere near here."

"This place, with its liquid abominations, brought my daughter to sin," Mrs. Edwards shouted, hysteria rising in her voice.

The other temperance workers shouted their agreement. "Do tell!"

The Signora drew herself up then, standing almost six feet tall. "I am indeed most sorry for your loss. However, what Dorrie did on her own time—and with *whom*—was no concern of mine."

Tears were flowing down Dorrie's mother's face. "I know you know something about it!" The desperate conviction underlying her anger and desperation was hard to miss. The other temperance workers were now looking at her with concern in their eyes—she seemed to be going in a direction they had not expected.

"We live in Murder City," the Signora said coldly. "I cannot possibly account for all the murders that happen here." She waved at Little Johnny and Gooch, who each grabbed one of the woman's arms to forcibly lead her out of the establishment. The other temperance workers filed out meekly behind them.

Before Gooch had shut the door, Dorrie's mother shouted one more thing at the Signora. "Then why did you ask her to do it?"

The Signora turned away without replying, and Gooch locked the door. Little Johnny began closing the curtains and shuttering the windows. This was the first time that Gina had seen the tea room get locked up, and she realized how protected they were from the outside. *Or locked in.* She pushed the thought away.

Distantly they could still hear Mrs. Edwards screaming out on the street, but everything was muffled behind the heavy wooden panels. The Signora turned to Little Johnny. "Take care of that." She then looked at Mrs. Metzger, who seemed unfazed by everything that had occurred. "You may close up now," she said. "Gina, head downstairs for your shift."

"Yes, Signora," Gina replied, feeling a bit shaken.

"And Gina," she said, her words coated in steel, "I expect all my employees to be discreet."

Gooch stood beside the Signora in silent enforcement of her words. His knuckles rested on his hips now in such a way that his jacket was opened up, exposing his handgun.

"Yes, Signora," she repeated, a chill washing over her. Trying to hide her sudden alarm, she gave a nonchalant fluff to her curls. "I get it."

As she scurried down the stairs, questions surged through her mind. What had Dorrie's mother meant? What was it that the Signora had asked Dorrie to do?

CHAPTER 7

Gina was still distracted by the encounter in the tea room when Ned called her over to the piano. He seemed to be in an unexpectedly jovial mood, even telling her a few jokes that he had overheard from a bunch of smartly dressed College Joes in the corner. All the while he easily played one of his regular quick-stepping tunes.

Despite her fear of Gooch and the Signora, she just *had* to get some answers about what Mrs. Edwards could have meant. After a quick look around to make sure neither Gooch nor the Signora was watching, she took a deep breath and said, "Say, Ned. Do you think there was something *funny* about Dorrie's death?"

He stopped playing abruptly. "Funny? Got sliced on the L, doll. A short journey on a long train. Nothing funny about that." He then began to bang out a jazzy tune.

"I mean, Dorrie's mother was just here and—"

He glanced up at her, his expression changing. "Park it, doll," he said, patting the end of his piano bench. His playing was still loud but less showy than before, as if he didn't want to draw any attention in their direction.

She sat down beside him, keeping time with her foot, trying to look lighthearted.

"Tell me all about it," he said. His words seemed to come out of the side of his mouth, and he didn't look at her.

"She stopped by the tea shop, with some other temperance workers. They were giving the Signora an earful, but she was having none of it."

"Yeah, yeah," he said, grimacing when he hit a wrong note. "What did Mrs. Edwards say to her?"

"She said that—" Gina hesitated, thinking about the Signora's warning. Regardless, she pushed on, hoping she could trust Ned. "Just that she didn't believe that Dorrie was murdered by some random stranger. That someone here might know more about it."

"You don't say," he said. He didn't seem too impressed. "I only met her mother once. It was pretty clear that she was a bit mad. Hated that Dorrie worked here. Guess Dorrie's pop was a vicious drunk. Her mom thought for sure Dorrie would turn out the same. Or come home knocked up."

"Yet her mother seemed convinced that Dorrie was doing something that got her killed."

"Talking to a stranger at the wrong time." He scratched his jaw. "I'm sure her mother is just looking for answers that she'll never find."

"Did you know Dorrie well?" Gina persisted. Something in Ned's manner just didn't seem right. Faye, who happened to be passing by at that moment, gave Gina a curious look but didn't stop.

Still playing with one hand, he pulled his ever-present flask from his inside jacket pocket and took a quick swig. "Not so well. I know she didn't deserve what happened to her." He looked blankly at the music in front of him. "Nothing more to say about it, toots," he said, playing a little faster. "The Signora likes my music up-tempo, dance music. I don't want to talk about some dumb girl who got herself killed."

Clearly dismissed, Gina got up and walked back to the bar, to keep an eye on her tables.

"He was keen on her," Faye said to her, over her shoulder. "Took her out a few times. Practically engaged."

"What?" Gina asked.

"Dorrie. I heard you asking about her." She lowered her voice. "Not for me to say, of course, but you have to wonder where she was going so late that night. She was killed in the Loop. Ned lives in Old Town." Her implication was obvious. Dorrie had another guy.

"Oh. Did she and Ned have a fight?"

Faye shrugged her delicate shoulders. "Who can say? He's been blotto since she died, anyone can tell you that.."

"He's not the only man to drown his sorrows with a bottle."

"You got the hots for Ned?" Faye asked, smirking. "Is that why you're asking about Dorrie?"

"Oh, no, nothing like that," Gina replied, adjusting the roses on her tray.

"You got a man already?"

"Nah, not looking for one, either," Gina replied, moving away to tend to a customer.

Before long, the Third Door was hopping, and Gina found herself sidestepping through another lively Saturday night crowd.

"Did you hear?" Lulu asked, sounding a bit breathless as

she twirled by, balancing a tray full of colorful drinks. "Benny Goodman might be stopping by later. He's home from New York, you know."

That *was* news. Even though Benny was just in his early twenties, he was one of their neighborhood's most famous sons. He'd grown up over on Maxwell Street, just a few blocks away, his family living alongside the many other Jewish immigrants who had fled from Russia before the revolution there. Though he was the bee's knees in New York, it seemed he hadn't forgotten his Chicago roots.

As Gina made her rounds, she kept her eye out for Marty, hoping this time he'd give her some answers. There was something funny going on, she could just feel it.

Yet Marty didn't arrive until nearly nine, just before the headliners were scheduled to perform. Glimpsing him across the room, she was about to approach him until she caught sight of Gooch staring in her direction.

Time to give Gooch something else to look at, she thought. At that moment, a rather sloshed woman moved unsteadily in front of her.

Here's my chance, she thought, taking a deep breath. Pretending to trip, Gina pushed against the woman's hip, causing her to topple directly into the lap of a man sitting with his date, who steadied her with a wide grin on his face.

"Say, whatcha doing with my fiancé?" the man's companion growled. "And what are you smiling at, Georgie?"

"Pardon me," Gina said pertly, stepping around the ensuing skirmish. As she'd hoped, Gooch had to intervene—the two women were already nearly at blows—so he was no longer keeping tabs on Gina.

Gina slid over to Marty as he was taking a picture of

a couple clinking their martini glasses together. The woman, whose shock of red curly hair was clearly from a bottle, was wearing a blue boa made of tightly woven ostrich feathers, which she had playfully thrown over the man's shoulder. For his part, the man's tailored tweed suit marked him as a man of means.

"This'll be a real nice memento of our time together, sweetie," the woman said, clutching the man's arm.

"I can remember just fine without a picture," Gina heard the man reply. As the woman began to pout, he quickly gave in. "How much?" he asked Marty, pulling out his wallet.

"A buck," Marty replied, positioning his camera. "Steady, steady. Big smile. Eyes open," she heard him say. "Come by Tuesday night. I'll have it ready for you by then." He pulled out a small notepad. "Name?"

"Mimi," the woman simpered. "This here's Jacky. I mean Jack," she added when the man glared at her.

"Whatdaya need our names for?" Jack asked Marty.

Marty pushed back his spectacles and gave them a bland smile. "I don't. I just need something to write down, to keep my prints straight when I develop them. How's about I just write 'Gorgeous Boa and Friend.'"

The woman giggled, and Jack gave a curt nod. "That'll work."

"Just catch me at my break on Tuesday." He pocketed the folded-up bill the man gave him, placing it deep inside his double-breasted suit coat, along with the small notepad. "I'll develop it tomorrow in my darkroom."

Marty was about to move away when Gina seized his elbow. "Hey," she said. "Can I speak to you?"

"Later," he said through clenched teeth. "We can't talk here."

Over the next hour, Gina was too busy to find a time to talk
to Marty, but around ten o'clock she saw him slip out of the
main area of the speakeasy, into the salon.

Well, I'm due for a break anyway, she thought, moving to follow him. When she reached the salon, though, she didn't see
him. *I guess he went through the tunnel. I can still catch up with him.*

Her plan was derailed when Jade flounced into the salon.
"Can you believe I have to switch my set?" Jade asked, strip-
ping off her stockings and shoes and leaving them in a heap
by the stuffed purple sofa.

For the next few minutes, Gina listened to Jade complain
about the other musicians, all the while feeling annoyed that
the starlet was keeping her from pursuing Marty. Finally Jade
went into the women's dressing area to touch up her rouge and
change her costume.

Seizing the opportunity, Gina slipped through the door
and found herself in a fairly dark tunnel, lit only by a few
flickering electronic lights along the passageway. The tunnel
smelled strongly of mold and yeast, and she could see a long
row of barrels lining one long, damp wall. At the end of the
tunnel there was another door, and a ladder on the wall beside it. Marty was nowhere to be seen.

When she reached the large wooden door, she tugged on
it cautiously. It seemed to be locked. If Marty had gone
through that door, there was certainly no way to follow him.
She looked up at the long ladder that led to a window far above
her, which had to open to the gangway that ran between the
alley and the street.

Gina put her hands on the metal ladder and shook it. It
seemed attached to the wall, at least. Taking a deep breath, she

began to ascend the rungs, trying to refrain from stepping on her dress as she climbed. When she reached the top, she could see that the window, slightly ajar, opened upward. An exhilarated feeling of victory and conquest swept over her as she shimmied carefully though the window, trying to keep her precious dress from getting dirty.

Immediately the chilly Chicago air engulfed her, and she almost regretted she'd lacked the foresight to bring a coat. Except the joint had been so hot, the cold air was actually refreshing.

She decided to wait in the gangway itself, right near the window, in case she had to beat a hasty retreat. Hauling herself atop a conveniently positioned barrel to await Marty's return, Gina popped another piece of chewing gum in her mouth. *Don't care if I look like a cow,* she thought, resentfully recalling what the Signora had told her the other day.

The quiet was broken by a murmured conversation from a couple on Harrison Street. She could hear a woman's high melodic laugh, punctuated by the man's deeper chuckle, as the pair passed by the gangway entrance. Gina idly wondered if the couple might be heading to the hotel down the street, or perhaps somewhere more respectable.

The conversation faded as the couple walked away. Soon after, she heard a funny sound at the other end of the gangway, this time in the alley. It sounded like a few people whispering harshly to each other.

Then she saw what looked like a man being pressed against the edge of the wall at the end of the corridor between the two buildings.

"Oof!" The man made a sickening sound, as if he had been punched in the gut. She saw his figure slump to the ground and then heard footsteps moving quickly down the alley, toward the street.

Gina put her hand to her heart. Should she go back inside? Then she heard the man groan and saw him shift slightly. *He's probably all right,* she thought. *Just down for the count. No need to get involved.*

Still, she couldn't quite bring herself leave without checking on the slumped-over figure. Keeping her back close to the brick wall of the building, she tiptoed carefully toward the man, who was now moaning softly. That must have been some wallop. A cold sense of trepidation washed over her.

"Hey, mister," she whispered. "You doing all right?" His hands were gripping his stomach, and his fedora was covering his face.

Thinking he could breathe more easily if she removed it, she pulled the hat off.

Then she gasped, recognizing him. "Marty! Oh my God! Did those men punch you?"

He opened his eyes and turned slightly toward her. He seemed to be trying to focus as he gasped for breath.

"Marty, it's me. Gina. Who did this?"

As he opened his mouth to speak, a trickle of blood ran out from between his lips. With fearful recognition, she moved his hand from his stomach and was sickened to feel a sticky warmth spreading across his coat. Without thinking, she unbuttoned it. There was blood everywhere. "Oh, Marty! Let me get help!"

When she started to stand up, he grabbed at her arm. He mouthed something, but she couldn't make it out.

"What? What did you say?" she cried. "You need help! A doctor!"

"No." His hand dropped to his side, and his eyes fluttered.

Without thinking, she slapped at his cheeks. "Marty, Marty! Wake up! Please, tell me who did this!"

He opened his eyes again. "Camera," he said, scrabbling at his coat, seemingly with all the energy he could muster.

She felt his pocket and pulled out his black leather camera case, which was a little longer and wider than her mother's old Bible The weight suggested that the camera was neatly tucked into its collapsed state within. "Here it is, Marty. Should I give it to someone?"

"No! Hide. It."

"H-hide it? Why?"

His breath was growing shallower and more pained. His lips were still moving, but sounds were no longer coming out. His eyes were imploring, frantic, and she took his hand again to calm him.

"Okay, I'll do it, Marty, I promise." She looked wildly about. Where could she hide it? Not in the alley or behind the barrel, that was for sure. Someone would likely find it there.

At the sound of an odd croaking noise, her eyes flew back to his face. "I'm sorry this happened to you, Marty," she whispered, watching the muscles of his face unclench as death stole over him.

She stared down at him, unable to comprehend what had just happened. His body seemed miles away, and she could feel herself starting to shake.

A sound at the end of the alley caused her to look up, her heart beating. Was someone there? Was someone in the shadows?

Though she couldn't see anyone, the sound brought her to her senses, and she could feel something surge through her body, jolting her into movement. *Hide the camera, Gina. You promised him.*

She stumbled down the alley, trying not to vomit. *Where to go? What should she do?* She could feel the tears starting to slip down her cheeks.

Everything seemed far away and strange. Should she go home? Then the Signora would wonder where she was. The Signora. She should tell her, shouldn't she?

Gina started to move back to the Third Door. Then she stopped. Could she trust the Signora? Or Big Mike? How about Lulu? No, she'd get screwy. Ned? No, she didn't know Ned that well.

Alert the police. That's what she should do. Then she remembered what Ned had said about the cops being in Big Mike's pocket. Was that true?

"Get a grip, Gina," she whispered to herself. She forced herself to think. Should she bang on the main door and call for Gooch? Or should she climb down the way she had come?

"Quit shaking," she ordered herself. "Don't let on that you know what happened, Gina." Then she pinched herself. "That means you have to stop talking to yourself."

No, she couldn't talk to Gooch. Or anyone. At least not until she could figure out who she could trust. She had to go back the way she had come, pretend that she hadn't seen what she'd just seen. Pretend she didn't have his camera.

What to do with the camera? She couldn't exactly hold it in her hands, and her dress was too revealing too hide anything.

With a deep breath, she crept back inside the cellar entrance and carefully climbed one-handed back down the ladder. Mindlessly she stepped, one rung after another, scarcely knowing what she was doing.

When she reached the bottom of the ladder, she looked around for a place to hide the camera. The five musty barrels lined up against the wall offered the obvious choice. Judging by the cobwebs across the top, they hadn't been moved in a while. Crouching down, she quickly tucked the camera behind the middle barrel before trotting unsteadily back toward the salon.

"Get a grip," she told herself. She forced herself to jump back and forth in her heels as a boxer would. Left foot, right foot. Left foot, right foot. She gave a few quick jabs in the air for good measure. The motion helped her regain her focus, and after stopping, she listened closely for sounds inside the salon. All she could hear was the low and steady murmur of voices and muffled songs from the speakeasy. Hopefully the other girls were still out on the floor.

Cautiously she pushed open the door and stepped back inside the salon. When she looked down, though, she noted in horror that her hands were bloodstained, from when she had placed them over Marty's wound.

She hurried to scrub her hands at the sink, using the scented soap, trying not to feel nauseous at the smell of lavender and blood. The blood came off quickly, although she could still see some beneath her fingernails. As she watched the reddish water flow down the sink, she grew dizzy.

Looking straight ahead, though, proved to be a mistake, as she caught a glimpse in the mirror of frantic eyes in a face reddened from crying. To her alarm, she could also see a touch of blood on her cheek, which she swiftly wiped with a wet tissue. Her hands were just back to their customary pink when the Signora came in.

"Long break, Gina," the Signora said to her, a reprimand evident in her tone. "I don't think I've seen you on the floor for almost twenty minutes."

Gina put her hand on her stomach. "I'm sorry, I was having a touch of cramps." The twisting knot in her stomach made cramps a viable excuse.

The Signora looked her up and down. "Your headband is a bit askew," she said.

Gina quickly straightened the offending piece in the mirror. "Thank you, Signora."

The next hour passed in a blur. Gina couldn't remember who she had talked to, what they said to her, or what she might have uttered in return. She only managed to calm her nerves when she took a few sips of whiskey from different patrons' glasses when no one was looking. At one point, she remembered, Roark spoke to her, but she only mustered a smile and handed him another pack of cigarettes, hoping that was what he had asked for.

Every time any of the speakeasy patrons mounted the stairs, Gina expected a great clamor to be heard once they reached the alley, screams and shouts that a man had been found murdered near the opening of the gangway. Yet there were no such cries.

Marty's body must be fairly well hidden in the dark shadows of the gangway, she figured. Had his absence even been noted?

She couldn't stop thinking about it. Finally, between sets,

she sidled up to Ned. "Where's Marty?" she asked as innocently as she could, bracing herself for questions. "I haven't seen him for a while." Feeling her headdress slip, she reached up and took it off and pushed it back on.

"Dunno," he said, staring at her face longer than necessary. "You all right, doll?"

"I'm fine," she said, turning away from him. Did she look flushed? Disheveled? As soon as she had a chance, she rushed back to the powder room to splash more water on her face.

Staring in the bathroom mirror, she pinched her cheeks to make them less pallid and fixed her headdress again. It was then that she noticed the swipe of blood near her hairline. Had Ned seen it? No, he couldn't have. She scrubbed it away.

As she smoothed down her green dress, she saw some blood on the hem, from when she had knelt beside Marty's body. Hiking up her skirt, she quickly rinsed it under the running water, hoping that it might have just looked like a drink had been splashed on the fabric.

She faced the door, wanting more than anything to just go home. But the Signora had already warned her about staying off the floor for too long. Taking a deep breath, she put her hand on the knob and pulled the door open. *Everything will be all right,* she thought fiercely. But how could it be?

When it neared one o'clock, the Signora let them know they would be able to leave. Though still numb from what had happened, to keep her mind from drifting to the image of Marty's bleeding body in the gangway, she'd forced herself to focus on how to smuggle the camera out of the speakeasy without bringing it to anyone's attention. *It's too big for my purse. Too big for my coat pocket. How? How? How?*

Gina left the floor quickly, still trying to figure out how to retrieve the camera. As she changed into her regular clothes, her eyes fell on the stockings that Jade had discarded earlier. They gave her an idea.

A quick glance around confirmed that the salon was empty. Grabbing Jade's stockings, she slipped out of the dressing room and back down the dark tunnel to where the camera was hidden behind the barrels. In the dark, she hiked up her dress and tucked the camera into her garter so that it rested along her inner thigh. She then wrapped one of Jade's stockings around her leg and tied it into place. Pulling her dress back down, she took a practice step. Not only did the camera press sharply into her thigh, but it had already begun to slip. Two steps later, it slid out completely.

"That's not going to work," she muttered to herself, feeling her heart beginning to race again. She *could* just leave the camera there, but once Marty's body was discovered and a hue and cry raised, it could be found before she could hide it again. No, she had to figure it out now. "Think, Gina. Think!"

As she stared at the stockings and garter, a new idea occurred to her. She pushed the camera halfway into Jade's stocking, then tied it tightly to the inside of her upper thigh. Next she wrapped Jade's other stocking around the first so that the camera was securely in place. Finally she pulled her own crumpled stockings up, securing them with her garter, and placed her feet back inside her black pumps.

Gina took another careful step. Good. This time the camera stayed put between her legs. If she walked slightly bow-legged, it would work. Hopefully she'd be able to get home without the whole thing coming loose on the street. The last thing she needed was Lulu asking questions.

She slipped back into the dressing room with no one the wiser and quickly pulled on her coat and hat. With the camera out of view, she already felt better.

"Lulu," she called. "You almost ready?"

Her reply was interrupted by an enraged screech. "Who stole them?" Jade snarled. "Who took my stockings? I left them there!" She pointed to the corner.

Like the other women, Gina rolled her eyes and feigned an impatience she did not feel. She tried not to think about Jade's stockings wrapped around her thigh, weighting her spirits as well as her gait.

She was glad when the Signora arrived to disperse the women. "Enough," she said, eying Jade in disapproval. "It's time for Gina and Lulu to leave."

"I know one of you stole them," Jade hissed at them, seeming to blame all of them at once.

Faye just shrugged. "Not me." Did her eyes linger on Gina?

Gina tugged on Lulu's arm. "Let's go. I'm tired."

After Gooch opened the green door, the women stepped into the alley, Lulu complaining about Jade under her breath. Gina could only concentrate on putting one foot in front of the other, her eyes fixed on the spot by the gangway entrance where Marty's murder had occurred.

I'm just going to pretend to find his body, she thought to herself. *I'll scream when I see it.*

As they passed the entrance to the gangway, Gina peered down the dark narrow corridor, preparing to spot Marty's dead body in the shadows. Then she squinted more directly.

The entrance of the gangway was clear. Marty's body was gone.

Where has the body gone? Gina wondered, in a daze, as she and
Lulu continued to walk home. That was all she could think
about. She could barely keep track of her friend's prattle. Lulu
seemed to be talking faster than usual, or maybe it was just
harder to make sense of her jabbering after what Gina had
witnessed earlier.

Had it even happened? She would doubt everything, except
she could feel the camera tied to her thigh with Jade's stockings. *Could Marty still be alive?* Maybe he had just passed out earlier and had somehow managed to crawl away. Or maybe
someone else had found him and taken him to a doctor or
even a hospital. Maybe he was recovering right now over in
Rush Medical College. Maybe tomorrow he'd be asking for
his camera back, as if nothing had ever happened.

Then she remembered the blood. Blood from Marty's
mouth. Blood seeping through his jacket. How could he be
alive? No, surely he was dead. So had someone moved him?
Who would do that? Maybe it was the person who had killed
him. Why had he been killed? Try as she might, she could not
keep the questions from bouncing wildly through her mind.

A shadowy Cadillac passed by them, causing the two
women to instinctively pull together more closely. Was someone watching them? Gina tightened her grip on Lulu's arm,
seeking some comfort and warmth.

Don't be ridiculous, Gina, she scolded herself. *No one is watching you.*

Yet had someone seen her, bending over Marty's body?
Perhaps they'd seen her take the camera. What was on Marty's camera? Why was it so important that she hide it? Why
had he insisted that she tell no one?

Lulu, it seemed, had some questions of her own. "What do you think of Jade accusing us like that?" Lulu asked, still indignant. "That hussy thought we'd stolen her stockings!"

"She's nuts," Gina agreed, feeling chained by the purloined silks tied around her legs.

Maybe she'd be able to slip them back into Jade's belongings when no one was looking. Right now, she had far bigger things to worry about than a pair of stolen stockings.

A few minutes later, the women reached Lulu's two-flat brownstone and parted ways. When she reached her own home, Gina slipped inside. Her father's bedroom door was closed.

Should I tell Papa? she wondered, raising her hand to knock on the door. She felt a strong urge to shake him awake, cry on his shoulder, and tell the whole terrible story. Papa would know what to do. Papa would know what to do with the camera.

Then she dropped her hand back to her side without knocking. What if he *didn't* know what to do? What if she was in danger? What if telling him put him in danger, too? No, it was best to lay low for a while. Keep it all to herself.

Creeping inside her tiny bedroom, Gina took off her stockings and untied the camera from around her thigh. Sitting cross-legged on the floor beside the bed, the camera in her lap, she ran her hands along the loose floorboard her mother had shown her long ago. She remembered how her mother had giggled like a little girl herself. *You never know when you might need a special hiding place,* she had said. *I had one myself, in my bedroom growing up.* Over the years, Gina would hide little treasures she had found on the street. An old jump rope. A little doll.

Some shiny glass. Now, it seemed only fitting that it would hide Marty's camera.

Pulling off her dress, she climbed into her bed and huddled under her heavy covers, shaking until she finally succumbed to terribly disturbed dreams.

CHAPTER 8

After a few hours of fitful, restless sleep, Gina awoke with a start, the image of Marty's dead body still a shock to her senses. From the slight crack in her curtains, she could see that dawn was just breaking.

Gina listened for sounds that her father might have already woken up, but it was silent. Satisfied, she rolled out of bed and opened the curtains to bring in the early morning light. She pulled out the camera from under the floorboard and stared down at the flecks of blood on the leather case, trying to set aside the memory of Marty slumped in the alley.

Fighting the rise of bile, she took a Kleenex and carefully scrubbed off the blood. When she opened the case, she discovered that the interior was divided into three pockets. The large pocket held Marty's camera, while each of the two smaller pockets positioned below held a small canister of film. She took one of the canisters out of its pocket and shook it, hearing the roll of film inside. She knew enough about film to know she shouldn't open the canister, for fear that the light would ruin the film. The other canister was empty, the film no doubt still inside the camera.

Carefully, she started to slide the camera out of its pocket. As she did so, she discovered that Marty had tucked a small black leather notebook and pen into the same pocket, so that they had nestled behind the camera. She recognized it immediately as the one Marty would write in when he was out on the speakeasy floor.

Setting the camera and case aside, Gina pulled out the notebook and traced the cover with one finger before she could bring herself to look inside. There was nothing particularly distinctive about the notebook, with several rings holding its pages and a simple leather strap keeping it shut. Five-and-dime stores might stock a hundred like it.

As she'd suspected, the notebook appeared to be Marty's record of the photos he'd taken of the Third Door patrons for the last few weeks. Although Marty's script was tight and difficult to read, each entry contained a nickname, a number, and the date the photo had been taken. Some of the names were crossed out. A few had what appeared to be a sum listed beside them, and quite a few were marked "paid."

When she flipped to the last of his notes, she found that the final entry read "Gorgeous Boa and Friend," with the date January 12 and the number 11 beside it. With a pang she remembered the moment. That silly woman and the surly gent were the last people Marty had ever photographed.

She looked closely at the entries that preceded Gorgeous Boa. According to the scrawled dates, Marty had taken five other photographs last night, identified respectively as "Lulu," "Lillian Gish," "Joes and Bettys," "Our Great Soldiers," and "Darrow." Then there was a line break, and the next group of photographs was from January 9. Like the others, these had nicknames: "Benny," "Cat's Meow," "Tootsie," and so on.

Flipping through the book she recognized some familiar names: Faye, Gooch, Jade, Billy Bottles, and others. She didn't see her own name, but when she turned to the evening when she started working, January 6, she saw one called "New Ciggie Girl?" So he *had* taken a picture of her that evening, as she had suspected.

She set the notebook beside the two canisters of film and gingerly picked up the camera.

"Oh, Marty," Gina muttered. "What did you want me to do with this darn thing? What is so important that I couldn't tell anyone?"

Her anger suddenly flaring up, she snatched up the camera case with the intention of stuffing everything back inside. To her surprise, her abrupt movement caused something shiny to fly out of the camera case and land in the soft folds of her skirt.

A key.

She picked it up and examined it. A house key, perhaps? It seemed too small. It looked more like the kind of key that would be used to unlock a drawer or perhaps a small case.

It had to be for something important, however, or why would he keep it with him?

Thoughtfully, she returned everything to the camera case as she had found it and then returned the case to its hiding place beneath the floorboard. Climbing back onto her bed, she stared at a long black crack in her ceiling until it was finally time to get up.

I need to see a newspaper, Gina realized as she stood at the sink, washing the dishes from breakfast. She'd been in a discon-

certing fog for hours now, as the memory of Marty's death
kept washing over her, again and again, in indestructible waves.
She was beginning to question herself, her memory. It couldn't
have been a dream. That's why she needed the newspaper. To
confirm once and for all that Marty had been killed. To find
out who had done him in.

"Hey, Papa," she called out. "How about we go for a walk?
Get some fresh air?"

"Sure thing," he replied, coming to stand in the doorway
of the kitchen. "So long as you aren't walking me to the church.
The next time I go to church, it'll be to have my Last Rites
administered. Even then, I'm not so sure."

"Not to worry," she said, trying not to shiver at his ma-
cabre joke. They hadn't gone to church regularly in quite some
time, and attending service was the last thing she felt she could
do. "I thought I'd get the newspaper. Give us something to
read."

"Oh yeah?" her father said, his tone more hopeful. He
missed getting the newspaper every day, but that was one of
the first things Gina had cut when she had taken over the
family budget six months ago.

After she helped her father pull on his winter layers, they
set out into the cold. Without even discussing it, they walked
toward their usual drugstore, which was several blocks past
the one owned by Big Mike and the Signora. For the first
time, she wondered about that.

"Hey, Papa, you ever been to Mr. Rosenstein's pharmacy?" she asked. "Over on Harrison."

Her father frowned slightly. "No."

She would have asked more, but their attention was caught

by a woman still dressed in full evening garb, complete with ostrich-feather headband, teetering down the street. Her wrap was hardly warm enough for the weather, and when it parted, they could clearly see she was with child.

"Not so hot to trot, is she?" her father said.

Hearing her father's words, a flush of shame flooded her own cheeks. There had been a time once, a few years ago, when she'd thought she was pregnant. Hearing the news, her guy had dutifully proposed, but he had been scarce after that, living up his "final days" as a bachelor in style. She could still remember how, when she'd discovered her mistake a few weeks later, he had crowed over their "near miss" and promptly broken off their engagement. There had been other men since David, but she'd found ways to protect her body and heart from ever being so vulnerable again. Love and marriage were for chumps; she knew that to be true.

Uneasily, she watched the woman. Probably coming home from an all-night bender or a tryst. There were lots of men who wouldn't care that she was already knocked up. Surely this weather wouldn't be good for the baby.

To her surprise, another woman, clad head to toe in black, approached the pregnant woman then, and after a brief exchange, the two walked away together. Gina was fairly certain that the woman had been one of the temperance workers who had been shouting outside the tea room the day before.

"She's from Hull House, I bet you anything," her father commented, referring to the woman in black. "Miss Addams will help that girl get a real job, take care of that baby."

Gina nodded. Her father was referring to the settlement house that had been established a few blocks away by Jane Addams four decades before. The women who worked there were all bent on social reform, trying to improve the lot of the people around them. "Make us lofty," some of her neighbors had sniffed over the music and art programs. "Do-gooders," others said. Gina just knew that though Addams had fought staunchly for women's suffrage, she was also a strong proponent of the temperance movement and Prohibition.

Her father had firsthand knowledge of the place, having been one of the first boys to take classes there as an orphan, after his mother had died of pneumonia, when the house opened in the 1890s. He didn't speak of that time much, but she knew it was there he had learned to spar, alongside the Greeks in the gymnasium. No wonder he had wanted to box and work for Big Mike's father when he got older.

When they reached the drugstore, Gina quickly paid for the newspaper. She had to resist tearing through it, seeking news of Marty's death, but she could tell that a storm was on its way. In her haste to leave, she had forgotten an umbrella.

Sure enough, it soon began to rain—large, heavy drops that pelted her face. Gina felt a violent chill overcome her, and she could see that her father had begun to shiver. Fortunately, they both wore hats, but the last thing she needed was for either of them to get sick. "Let's hurry, Papa," she urged him.

Sticking the newspaper inside her coat, she urged her father to walk a little more quickly, which wasn't easy. Hearing her father's deep sigh made her feel guilty. These walks were probably a bit too hard on him.

When they finally returned home, she settled her father into his favorite cushioned chair in the living room, a cup of tea beside him on a lace-covered table. She sat in a matching chair on the other side of the small table, rushing as quickly as she could through the newspaper. Page after page she turned, from the front to the last, and there was nothing there.

Gina went through the newspaper again, this time more slowly, looking closely at all the sections, running her fingers down each obituary in turn, in case she had overlooked his name. But no mention of a Doyle. There were also no John Does or any stabbing victims listed at all.

For Chicago, it looked to have been a remarkably violence-free evening. Except for the missing body.

Monday morning, Gina decided to check the newspaper again. There *had* to be news by now.

"Just the paper, please," Gina said, laying down the coins at the same drugstore she had visited with her papa the day before. This time, she could not wait to walk back to her flat to read through the pages and sat down on a freezing metal park bench.

"Waste of money," she said out loud, disgruntled. There was still nothing about Marty's death on the front page or even buried within.

She did see another headline, though, that was somewhat shocking. BEERING HEIRESS FOUND DEAD. Underneath was a gorgeous picture of Genevieve Beering, looking vibrant and full of life on the front page of the *Tribune*. Apparently she had missed several social engagements; questions were raised over her absence, and in due time her death was discovered by her companion. No cause of death was listed.

The heiress's death was very much on the tips of everyone's tongues when Gina arrived at the Third Door the following Tuesday evening. "Bet you anything it was suicide," Faye said.

"Why would you think she did that?" Lulu kept asking. "She had *everything*. Money, looks, connections. I don't get it!"

"Maybe that just wasn't enough," Ned pointed out. "Some people need more out of life." His voice was edgy, and once again Gina noted how haggard he had become.

"Well, that's suicide for you," Faye said, with a disdainful twitch of her nose. "No thought to anyone but herself."

"Did she leave a note?" Gina asked. "An explanation?"

"Doesn't seem to have," Jade said. "That's the way of it, I suppose."

"Or there was more to it," Ned replied before turning back to his music.

"Or nothing to it all," Lulu said. "Could have been an accident. Or she took sick. Influenza, maybe. We all know that's been going around again."

"But why not just say so?" Faye asked.

Lulu shrugged. "Didn't want to start a panic?" It was true; they could all remember when the Spanish flu had struck without mercy ten years ago. Since then there had been cases, but nothing with the virulence that Chicago had seen during the Great War.

Gina had just put her cigarette tray on when she heard a sharp whistle from Billy. The Signora was standing there.

"Ladies and gentlemen," she said, her voice calm and authoritative, "I have just received a call that the police will be paying us a visit in short order."

The few customers who were already there looked up in alarm.

"No need to worry," the Signora said soothingly. "Lulu here will take you upstairs to the drugstore, where your *lemonade* and *Cokes* will be refreshed. Others of you"—here she looked meaningfully at the only man who looked openly drunk—"may wish to leave. Faye will show you out."

Quickly, Gina found herself whisking away all the remnants of the cocktails, while Billy poured out lemonade and iced tea. Several customers, after their initial confusion, followed Lulu up the stairs to the drugstore and the tea room, so that they could exit onto Harrison. Others were shepherded by Faye up the stairs to the alley, where they were expected to quietly disperse either to Halsted or Morgan. No one would want to be caught in the alley by the entrance to the speakeasy. Little Johnny led a few of the men to the tunnel. None of the women went that direction, though, Gina vaguely noted. A moment later she learned why.

"Too dirty!" one of the women hissed to her male companion. "I'll take my chances in the tea room, thank you very much."

Within a matter of moments, all of the customers had departed the premises. Billy and Gooch then performed one of the most amazing feats that Gina had ever seen—they pushed the bar directly against the mirrored back wall and then swung the entire wall around, so that the bar, with all its bottles, disappeared from view. They then locked the rotated wall into place.

"Follow me," Billy called to Gina, disappearing through another door to the room on the other side of the dance floor, where the bar was now hiding. Jade and Gooch were both moving the liquor to a small storeroom. "Get a move on, toots," Billy said. "Gotta lock this door before the Drys come."

"Will they come down here?" Gina asked.

"They might," he said. "Just in case they have a warrant to search the whole premises."

Picking up a bottle in each hand, Gina walked quickly to the storeroom. "Where do I put them? Anywhere?"

"Anywhere."

"Be careful," Jade warned. "The last thing we need is to break a bottle."

With all of them working together, they quickly finished hiding the bottles and returned to the main area. Gooch and Big Mike had hidden all the tables and chairs somewhere as well. Ned was still sitting at the piano, singing along loudly as he played one of the great choruses of the Temperance brigade, "Onward, Christian Soldiers."

When the Signora glared at him, he stopped and sheepishly stood up. "Thought it might convey the proper mood," he muttered.

Gina hid a smile.

"Everyone upstairs. Some to the tea room, others to the drugstore," Big Mike called out. He had several brown envelopes in one hand. "They'll be here any minute."

They went up the stairs, and Little Johnny flipped the lights off behind him. As she'd been told, Gina pulled on a blue sweater and tied a white apron about her waist. To her chagrin, when she entered the drugstore, she realized she'd forgotten to put her own patent leather shoes back on and was still wearing the pumps. Hopefully no one would say anything about her mismatched apparel. She went behind the counter, where Benny handed her a white towel with a wink. He went off to stack some cans on a shelf.

Gina edged over to Ned, who had seated himself on a tall stool at the long counter by the soda fountains. "What happens now?" she murmured, setting a cup of lukewarm coffee in front of him.

He opened a *Tribune* to the middle section. "We just need to sit tight. No big deal. Big Mike's got an inside man at the police station. Sometimes, the coppers come back later for a drink—after they've filed an official report with Prohibition agents, that is, dutifully stating that no bootleg alcohol has been discovered here." He pointed to the sign above the fountain that read: IN COMPLIANCE WITH THE 18TH AMENDMENT, NO INTOXICATING LIQUOR ALLOWED ON THE PREMISES.

Although most of the customers had fled, with promises to come back later "if they don't go and dump out your booze," a few had remained. Whether out of loyalty or curiosity, Gina couldn't say. She was annoyed to see that Roark was one of the customers who had taken a seat at the soda counter.

"Can I get you something, *sir*?" she asked.

He looked up at her. "Do you even know how to operate any of the equipment here? Or are you planning to figure it out as you go?"

"As a matter of fact, I do know." Without waiting for him to answer, she banged a saucer and a cup of coffee down in front of him. "This should suffice, I think." Lulu slipped in, wearing a regular day dress. How she'd gotten enough time to change, Gina had no idea. She picked up one of the little baskets and began to place a few cans and supplies inside it, posing as a regular employee of the store.

A few seconds later, two Chicago cops dressed in sharp blue uniforms entered the drugstore, glancing up at the bell above the door as it announced their presence. They looked around skeptically at the customers seated on stools, browsing the shelves, standing in line. One of the cops, a middle-

aged man with graying hair showing under his blue hat, was
holding a manila folder in his right hand. His name, O'Neill,
could be read over his left breast pocket. He looked around,
seeming to be taking everything in. His eyes fell on Roark,
Gina noticed, but he didn't say anything.

"Crowded tonight," the younger one, whose badge named
him as Dawson, commented.

O'Neill nodded but did not reply.

"Good evening, Officers," the Signora greeted them, practically purring. She had slipped on a dark jacket over her evening gown, looking more like the proprietress of a high-end
boutique than a two-bit drugstore. "Captain O'Neill, may I
offer you a phosphate?" She gestured to two stools at the end
of the counter. A brown envelope lay on each one. "How about
an egg cream or piece of pie?"

"All right, cut the malarkey," O'Neill said. "We're not
here on a booze check. We'll leave that for the Drys."

"You're not?" The Signora blinked. "Then why are you
here, Captain O'Neill?"

The captain opened up the folder and held out a photograph. "This man. He worked at this *establishment*, didn't he? I
have it on good authority that he did."

Big Mike pulled out his glasses and, along with the Signora, viewed the photograph. The others shuffled their
feet. Clearly this was not what anyone expected.

Gina felt a qualm as she realized what was coming. Feeling
her face flush, she began wiping down the counter vigorously,
hoping to hide her rising distress.

To her surprise, Ned grabbed her hand. "Relax," he said
through clenched teeth. "You'll give it all away."

Jerking away her hand, Gina stared at him. Did he know? Then she realized he meant the larger show.

She watched the Signora take the photo and then blanch to a deathly pallor. "Oh, no!" she cried. "That's not . . . Marty, is it?" Her question was faint as she clutched her husband's arm for support.

"Marty?! Marty?!" everyone around them began to murmur.

Gina felt Roark stiffen in his chair, clearly listening. She glanced at him, and to her surprise, he was staring at her full on.

She looked away.

"Yes, I'm afraid it is." Big Mike looked down at the photograph with distaste. "What's wrong with him?"

"He's dead," Captain O'Neill said. "Stabbed. At least two, three days ago." Then, taking in their stunned faces, he added, "I'm sorry."

Lulu shrieked and staggered back against a display of soaps, knocking them over and falling full-length on the floor. Taking advantage of the distraction, Gina began to edge from behind the counter.

Roark glanced at her again before looking away, his fingers tapping the rim of his cup. His eyes were unreadable, but he seemed to be taking in everyone's movements and reactions. A few more customers took the opportunity to leave the drugstore, and Gina could see that he had noted that as well.

Captain O'Neill looked around at those who remained, mostly Third Door employees now. "When was the last time any of you saw Mr. Doyle?"

At first, they were all silent, looking to the Signora for guidance. Her face was pale, though, and she seemed genuinely disturbed. Seeing this, her husband helped her to a chair. For her part, Gina was frantically thinking about when exactly she had seen Marty alive inside the walls of the Third Door, in case anyone thought to ask her. A growing sense of unease was overcoming her, and she felt like she might faint.

"Saturday night," the Signora said finally. "He was working. Taking pictures. It was Saturday night. Isn't that right?" She looked to the others for confirmation.

Gina found herself nodding along with the others.

The Signora's look was guarded when she turned back to the captain. "Where was he killed?"

"Well, that's an interesting question. His body was found a few blocks from here, but I'm not at liberty to provide more details than that." Pausing, he glanced at Officer Dawson before continuing. "The coroner is fairly certain, however, that the body was moved after death."

There was a general hubbub in the room, and Gina closed her eyes.

She opened them when someone touched her shoulder. It was Ned. "You're looking a little green, Gina," he whispered. "Why don't you get some fresh air?"

Gina looked around. Captain O'Neill had pulled up one of the cushioned chairs to speak with the Signora and Big Mike. Officer Dawson was asking the staff members questions. This seemed to be a good time to slip away. She nodded at Ned.

"Go ahead," Ned murmured. "You look like you're about to pass out." He pressed her arm lightly as he moved past her. "Don't go too far. You don't want the Signora or Big Mike questioning your loyalty. You understand? The coppers may have questions for you, too." The look he gave her then was definitely one of warning. "Take some time to think about your answers."

He knows I know something, she realized. She remembered the splash of blood she'd washed off her forehead that night. The blood on her dress. *Had* he seen it?

When Gina went out the drugstore's only exit onto Harrison Street, she wasn't quite sure where to go. Her heart was pounding hard, like a drummer with a story to tell.

Without thinking, Gina found herself walking down the gangway toward the alley, past the door she'd slipped out on Saturday night and up to the barrel where she'd sat, chewing her Wrigley's gum. Her half-empty pack was still there, exactly where she'd left it.

Her mouth suddenly felt dry, and she picked up the pack and slid a stick of gum out. It felt a little damp from the recent rain, but she didn't care. She popped it in her mouth.

The minty flavor comforted her, and she looked to the end of the alley, where Marty's murder had occurred. It was hard not to think about him, groaning and bleeding out onto the brick walkway of the alley. Who had done it? Who had killed him?

Once again, a devastating sense of loss washed over her, as she thought about how she'd had so little chance to really know him. Angrily, she brushed the tears away from her face. She kicked at the barrel with her heels, making a sharp knocking sound.

A man appeared at the end of the gangway then, from the end of the street, where she had come. His cap was low and his collar was pulled high, and she gasped as he started toward her.

She slid off the barrel and was about to run down the gangway, away from the man and toward the alley, when she saw his severe limp. In relief, she recognized the man as Roark.

She forced herself to stand beside the barrel as he approached. He stood beside her, a speculative look on his face. "So, is this the bearcat's hangout?"

She shrugged but didn't reply.

"You left the drugstore pretty quickly."

She waved her hand. "I just needed a bit of air. No crime in that."

"No, no crime." He eyed the soggy pack of gum on the barrel. "Yours?" he asked.

She stopped chewing and pushed the gum into her cheek. "Nah, not mine." The lie came easily.

"I see. Maybe it's another bearcat's hangout, too. Another bearcat who chews Wrigley's gum."

Not sure what to say to that, Gina remained silent. To her surprise, though, Roark removed his glove and picked up the pack of gum with his bare hand. "It's wet," he noted. He didn't sound surprised.

"I just found it. Don't know how long it's been out here." Her words sounded a bit sharp to her own ear, and maybe a bit suspicious.

He put his hand on the barrel to support himself, the action bringing his face very close to hers. "Is that so?" he asked. Something flickered in his eyes, and he looked away, a scowl on his face. He set the pack aside and pulling out a flashlight, he kept walking down the gangway to the alley entrance, the light directed in front of him.

When he reached the spot where Marty was murdered, he stopped abruptly and awkwardly crouched down, looking at the ground. She watched as he gingerly touched the ground with his gloved hand, then looked at his finger with a grimace. He laid the flashlight on the ground without turning it off, so that it was still illuminating the surface.

To her surprise, he pulled out a Kodak from his coat pocket and, after opening up the case and unfolding the camera, began to carefully snap a few pictures, almost exactly where Marty's body had been. *What is he doing? Why is he taking photographs?*

She was about to slip down the other end of the gangway, back to the street, when he called out to her. "Hey, Gina! Come over here, would ya?"

Reluctantly, Gina walked over to him, stopping just before the place where Marty had fallen four nights before. Despite herself, her eyes flickered downward. From the dim alley light, she could just make out a dark stain on the ground, where the blood had seeped from the photographer's body. Hastily, she averted her eyes.

"What is it?" she asked.

"What do you think this is?" he asked, pointing to the ground.

"I don't know. Someone spilled something, I suppose."

"Spilled something. Right."

She watched as he continued to study the ground. "Why?"

"Did you hear what the officers said in there? Marty wasn't killed where his body was found."

"Oh." Gina swallowed. "Where was Marty found? Did they say?"

"By the Harrison Street Bridge. Along the tracks."

That area, only a few blocks away, was a known dumping

ground for Chicago gangs. "Oh," Gina said again, unsure what
else to say. "I suppose he got mixed up in something he
shouldn't have."

"So it would seem," Roark said, still studying the ground.

Seeing him so close to where Marty had died made her
nervous. "I should head back in."

"Marty was a friend of mine, did you know that?" Roark
said suddenly. "Taught me what I know about photography."

Gina hadn't known that. "I didn't know him very well,"
she replied. *Even though he was my mother's cousin. We had no connection at all. Until he lay there bleeding. And I held his hand until he passed
away.* Gina pushed the thought away, remaining silent.

He straightened up and looked straight into her eyes. "I
saw your face just now. In the drugstore. When the police
came in."

"Oh? W-what do you mean?" Her heart started to beat
faster.

"You knew what the police were going to say. You knew
that they were going to say that Marty had been killed. How
could you have known that, I wonder?"

"I d-didn't know about it, I swear. I j-just felt shocked, like
everyone else," she said. "Besides, *you* didn't seem so surprised,"
she added, going on the offense. "I noticed that myself."

Unexpectedly, he nodded. "You're right," he said. "I received a tip. I thought it would be a good idea to be on hand
when the news was delivered."

"A tip?" she asked. "Why would *you* get a tip?"

"I still have some friends on the force." At her look, he
explained. "I was a cop. Until this." He gestured to his injured
leg. "I don't talk about it much. Now I just do photographs for

them, down at the station when guys get booked, sometimes out on the streets when a call comes in."

"Oh, I thought—"

"That I was injured in the war?"

She nodded.

"Well, I had my share of bullet holes as a soldier, too. Except this injury happened last year." His tone was fierce, and brooked no further questions. He took a step closer. "You know what I think?"

She stayed silent, resisting the urge to back away.

"I think you know something about Marty's death."

"W-what?" she stammered, trying to keep her breathing steady. "Why would you say that? I d-don't."

"When was the last time you saw Marty?"

"Saturday night, I suppose. I'm not sure." She squinted, as if trying to remember. "Just for a few minutes. I don't remember seeing him after that." *Until I saw him right here, dying. Around ten o'clock. On the worst evening of my life.*

"You know what's interesting?" he asked.

"What?" The response was automatic; she really didn't want to know.

"Marty always had his camera on him, anywhere he went."

"So?"

"So they didn't find it on his body."

"Oh." Gina paused. "Well, I suppose that whoever killed Marty took it. Stands to reason."

"That's what the police assume."

Suddenly, despite the chill in the air, she felt flushed. "You don't think so?"

"I don't know." He tapped on his own camera, which was hanging from a strap around his neck. "I just hope that whoever took Marty's camera knows not to expose the film to light. There might be something important on it."

"The murderer will probably sell it."

"I suppose. Unless he was killed for the camera—for the pictures on it."

Marty's dying whisper came to her then. "Do you think that's why he was killed?"

He studied her again. "Can't rule it out."

The cold wind began to whip up in earnest. The flush she had just felt dissipated, and now all she could feel was a deep biting chill in her bones. "I'd better head back in," she said. "The Signora will be expecting me back."

"Of course. Everyone needs their fizzy soft drinks." As she turned to go, he grabbed her arm. "Oh, Gina?"

"What?" Looking up, she was once again caught in the startling intensity of his gaze, and it bothered her.

"Don't tell anyone about anything you may have seen. You understand?"

Her eyes flew over his face, and she saw no mockery there, only concern—and an anger, too. "I don't know what you're talking about. I haven't seen anything."

"Gina, I'm just telling you. There's not a lot of people you can trust around here." He took a step closer, still gripping her arm. "If I can tell that you're hiding something, someone else might figure it out, too."

"I suppose I can trust you?" she asked bitterly. She shook off his hand. "What, on your say-so?"

He stepped back. "Yes, actually. I wish you would. It would be a shame for a girl like you to end up dumped under the Harrison Street Bridge."

She suppressed a shudder. "I can take care of myself."

"I hope so."

As she strode away, it was hard not to hear his words bouncing about her mind. *If I can tell that you're hiding something, someone else might figure it out, too.*

CHAPTER 9

When Gina returned to the drugstore, she found that the cops were just leaving. The brown envelopes that the Signora had left on the stools were nowhere to be seen. As she suspected, no one was above the take.

Although the Signora raised an arched eyebrow when she saw Gina, she didn't say anything. Her face was unusually pale, although when she spoke, her voice was stern and to the point. "All right, time to set up. Back to work, everyone," she said, clapping her hands. "I don't want to hear you discussing this. Gooch, put the signal back on."

Gina followed Lulu and the others down the narrow steps back into the speakeasy. Following the others' lead, she began to help reassemble the club, to ready the place once again for guests. There was a numbness to all their movements, and she saw even Gooch brush a tear away. She could see, too, the speculation on everyone's faces, but no one dared discuss Marty's death, at least not when the Signora was in earshot.

When Roark passed by her, their eyes met, but the look he gave her was inscrutable. She watched him say something to Clarence Darrow, who turned and gave her a thoughtful glance. Suddenly uncomfortable, she busied herself with her tray, awaiting the return of the other patrons. Roark disappeared into the back room, presumably to start a new game of poker with his fellow soldiers.

Within the hour, the patrons began to drift back inside, with the less sophisticated among them whispering excitedly about the "raid."

Overhearing them, Jade sneered. "They'd be in the crapper if that had been a real raid."

As Gina walked over to a corner table, a man seated at another table suddenly thrust out his arm as she passed, effectively keeping her from moving. "Hey, toots," he said. "Where's that Harp?"

"Who?" Gina asked, finding her cheeks hurt when she moved her jaw. It was then she realized she'd been clenching her teeth since she'd spoken to Roark in the gangway.

"The photographer? Marty?"

"What's it to you?" Gina said, stepping neatly away from the man's wandering hands before he could land one on her hip. The man looked slightly familiar.

"He took a photograph of me last Saturday. Told me to come by today and he'd have it ready for me." He looked around. "So where is he? I want it."

Comprehension dawning, Gina remembered the man from Saturday night. This was Jack, of Jack and Mimi fame. "Gorgeous Boa," Marty had named the man's friend.

Unsure what to tell him, Gina edged away from the man. "Uh, I'll find out for you," she said.

She knocked on the door of the Signora's salon. The proprietress opened the door a few inches, clearly indicating that she did not wish Gina to enter the room. "What is it?" she asked, her tone sharp.

"There's a patron asking for Marty. Said he took a photograph on Saturday," Gina whispered. "Marty told him to come back today, told him that he'd have it ready for him."

The Signora took a deep sip from the martini glass in her hand. Since she had started at the Third Door, this was the first time that Gina had seen the Signora take a drink. "The camera," the Signora said. "I'd forgotten about that." Her voice was uncharacteristically soft, as if she were talking to herself. "His photographs. I don't know if he developed them before . . . before . . ." Her voice trailed off, and she looked somewhere far away.

Gina silently finished the unspoken thought. *Before he was murdered.*

It was hard not to picture the camera and canister of film under the floorboard. She was certain Marty had not had time to develop the last roll of film before he was killed. Of course, she could not say that to the Signora.

"Oh." Gina waited. "What do I tell him, then?"

The Signora waved her hand. "Tell him we don't have it. Offer the man a drink. On the house. That should suffice."

Gina nodded and turned away. Before the door completely shut, she heard the Signora speak to someone who was in the room. "The camera! What do we do about that?"

The door shut then. Gina craned her neck, trying to hear more through the wooden door. Why was the Signora so concerned about Marty's missing camera? Unless, perhaps, there was something on the film that she did not wish anyone to see.

Her head was still pressed against the door when Ned rounded the corner. He stopped short when he saw her, and she stepped back hastily. He gave her a peculiar look. "I had to speak to the Signora," she said quickly, trying to make it appear that she was just stepping out of the woman's salon, instead of eavesdropping. "Going back to work now," she added.

Ned gave her a funny little bow. "Carry on," he said, his eyes still narrowed.

Slipping past him, Gina returned to Jack, who was just finishing up what looked to be a Rum Runner at the bar. She waved to the bartender. "Another of the same, Billy. Signora's orders."

The bartender nodded.

"On the house," she said, placing the drink in front of Jack. Roark, who was sitting at the bar, raised an eyebrow.

"Well, what do you know, toots?" Jack said, patting the empty stool beside him. "Why don't you take a break and sit with Jack a little while."

Gina rolled her eyes. Clearly, he had gotten the wrong idea about her intentions. "I don't think so."

"Well, when's he coming back?" Jack persisted. "What did you find out?"

Luckily, Billy Bottles intervened. "Marty's dead, fellow."

"Dead?" the man repeated, looking startled. "Where's his camera? How do I get my photograph?"

"Dunno," Gina replied.

As she started to move away, the guy took hold of her wrist. "Look here, sweetheart," he said. "I need that film. The negative, you get me? If you bring it to me, you'll get a nice reward." He slipped a bill onto her tray, under a pack of cigarettes. "Here's a little something to get you motivated."

"Why? What do you need the negative for?" Gina asked. She kept her tone low, hoping that the din of the speakeasy would keep Roark and Billy from overhearing their exchange. "Gonna develop the picture yourself?"

The man grabbed her wrist again. "That money means you don't ask questions, doll, and you keep your mouth shut. You get me?"

She pulled her hand away. "Yeah, I get you, *Jack.*" *I also get that I'm never turning that film over to you,* she thought. It just had seemed more dangerous to tell him no. Besides, maybe she could string him along, find out why it mattered so much to him. "It's not like I knew the guy that well."

He grinned. "Just be sure to keep those pretty eyes peeled. Ask around. I bet you can find it." Downing his drink, he set the glass on the counter. "I'll be back in a few days."

As he walked away, Roark spoke right into her ear. "What are you up to, Gina?" he asked.

When she turned to face him, she could see he looked furious. He continued before she could reply. "That's a real wrongheaded way to make money. Why would you help a guy like that anyway?"

"Mind your own beeswax, why don't you?" she replied, walking away. She was getting mighty sick of men telling her what to do.

A few hours later, just after Lulu's second set, an impossibly bleached blond woman stopped by the bar, coming to stand beside Gina where she was waiting for Billy to finish making some gin rickeys. Gina recognized her at once. It was Mimi, the woman who had accompanied Jack on the night Marty was murdered. Once again, she had a long boa tossed over her shoulder, although this time the feathers were a deep red.

Gina sidled up to her with the cigarette tray. As before, the woman ordered a pack of Marlboros, this time fishing through her own clutch for the necessary coins.

"Hey, sweets," she said, accepting the smokes from Gina, "You seen that photographer around? I want to pay for that photograph he took last Saturday night. You know, the one with me and my *friend*." She pulled out a small compact and pursed her lips.

Gina tried to affect a nonchalance she didn't feel. "No, Marty's dead." She figured since Billy had spilled the beans to Jack earlier, she could do the same.

Still looking in the tiny compact mirror, Mimi formed her lips into a perfect O. "How awful," she said, pulling out her lipstick and applying the same heavy red that her lips were already drenched in. "What happened?"

"He was killed. Murdered."

This time Mimi did look up at Gina. "You don't say. Who did it, do you know?"

"Don't know. His body was found under the Harrison Street Bridge."

"Oh," Mimi said, looking back into the mirror. "You know what *that* means," she said. "Better to not know more."

"I suppose," Gina replied, and started to move away.

"Listen, doll, I really need that photograph. Can you get it for me?"

"I don't know," Gina said, backing away. Something about the woman's furtive smile suddenly bothered her.

"You need some money? I get it." As Jack had done earlier, she slipped a few bills onto Gina's tray. "You gotta understand.

I need that photograph. Just for a little payment I got coming. A bit of insurance, if you know what I mean."

"Insurance?" Gina asked, slipping a box of Marlboros over the bills. Why not? It would buy her papa a little more medicine. She glanced over at Gooch, who was frowning in her general direction. A chill coursed over her. Had he seen the exchange?

"That rat Jack's gone and left me," Mimi sputtered, her baby face suddenly looking ugly and wrinkled. "The fink's gone back to his wife. Said it's over between us. Two nights we had together. Two goddamn wonderful nights," she added, before her blue eyes narrowed. "Then he dumps me! Dumps me! Can you believe that? What a bunch of hooey!"

Gina could believe it easily but cast about for more agreeable words. "What a bum!"

Mistaking Gina's ironic tone for sympathy, Mimi continued. "So you can see I *need* that picture. One gal to another." Her tone turned wheedling. "You'll help me out, won'tcha?"

"Sure, sure," Gina said, edging away.

Later, as Gina waited for Billy to fix a tray of drinks while the girls were dancing on the floor, Mr. Darrow said something to her that she didn't quite catch.

"What did you say?" she asked, trying to be heard over the trumpets and piano.

"I just commented on the fact that it is so very strange not to see Marty around."

"I suppose," she said, wishing she could slip her shoes off without anyone seeing her. Her feet were killing her.

"A camera is an amazing instrument," he said. "Do you agree, Miss Ricci?"

"Aw, please, Mr. Darrow, call me Gina," she replied. "Yeah, I suppose so. I've never looked inside one, though. No one has brought one by for my papa to fix, I don't think." She turned back to Billy, noting the three drinks on the tray. "One more gin and tonic."

"You said three for table four," the bartender replied, sounding more surly than usual.

"No, I said four for table three," she said, glancing over at the table in question. Sure enough, there were two couples waiting on their drinks, just as she noted. "See, four people."

"Sure, sure," he said, reaching for the gin. Before he poured the liquid into the cocktail glass, he first poured out a full shot, which he proceeded to down in one gulp.

"A strange instrument," Mr. Darrow said again, clearly in a musing mood. "Catches so much more than those being photographed may realize. Expressions of hope, worry, anger, despair, happiness—all caught in an instant, for all eternity. Unlike a seated portrait, of course, which captures more of how the artist sees the subject."

"Yes, that's true." Gina thought about Jack and Mimi, both slipping money onto her tray. One wanted to keep the photograph hidden, if not destroy it. The other wanted it brought to light, used for some bitter gains of her own.

Billy placed the last drink on her tray. "Get a move on, toots," he said.

"I'm going, I'm going," Gina said, adding some napkins to her tray.

CHAPTER 10

Gina rolled out of bed with a sigh. Marty's funeral was that afternoon, and she was dreading it already. In her mind, she knew she needed to attend, out of respect for both Marty and her mother, but she wasn't quite sure she could bring herself to go.

To kill time, Gina had decided to head over to the drugstore to get some medicine for her papa. His palsy had been awful bad of late. Last night, when she had arrived home around one in the morning, he'd been awake and in pain. She thought she'd get him some nice bath salts as well, which she hoped would ease the fatigue in his joints and muscles. Might as well see if there were any perfumes to be had, too, since she had already used up her only bottle of scent. Even after the cost of Madame Laupin's frocks had been deducted from her pay, she was pleased to have a little more spending money than she could ever remember having.

As she waited for Mr. Rosenstein to fill her papa's prescription, Gina walked up and down the aisles, sucking on a butterscotch. The sight of cameras on display stopped her, her heart giving a lurch as she thought about Marty and his camera, tucked away under the floorboard.

A thought struck her then, and she stood stock-still in the middle of the aisle. Perhaps she could just take Marty's camera somewhere and get the film developed. She could find out what he'd been hiding, and then—

Here, her imagination stopped short. What in heaven's name would she do when she saw the images that Marty had begged her to hide? She had no clue. That was not something to worry about now, she decided.

Benny came over then. "You thinking about getting a camera?" he asked. "We've got the latest Kodaks for ladies. Stylish, like yourself."

"Stylish, that's me," she said, pretending to spritz herself dramatically with the perfume she'd selected.

He pulled out a bright pink camera case and opened it up to disclose a bright pink padded interior. "See, the camera goes here, and there's where you keep your extra roll of film. It's called a Vanity."

She took it from him, turning it about in real admiration. She pointed to a little pink compartment that had been snapped shut. "What's in there?"

Benny grinned. "Open it and see."

Curious, she unsnapped the top to find a space for a small tube of lipstick and a compact. "How darling!" she exclaimed, imagining what it would be like to own such a clever thing.

Then, remembering why she was looking at the cameras in the first place, she asked as casually as she could, "How would I get the photographs developed?"

"That's easy," Benny replied. "Take the roll to the Kodak store, over on Polk. They'll make the photographs for you.

Drop if off and they'll have them ready for you a few days later."

Gina found herself sweating at the thought of a stranger developing Marty's last roll of film. Who knew what was on that roll? Benny's next words made her even more nervous.

"They do a real nice job," he assured her. "When you go in the store, you can see all the photographs hanging out to dry."

"Oh, for everyone to see?" she asked. *Golly, that will never do,* she thought.

"Sure enough," he replied. "Sometimes I've taken my little sister Jasmine in to look at them. Once we were laughing so hard, the manager told us we had to leave. Which we did, but we came back later and soaped his windows." He chuckled a little at the memory.

"What if there's a picture of something, you know, private? Something you might not want strangers to see?" she asked.

Though he cocked his head and gave her a funny look, he still answered her question. "Then you'd better develop them yourself," he said. "Mind you, that's not cheap. Requires lots of equipment. Chemicals, too. We don't carry that stuff. We just sell the cameras and the film, not the kits. And the kits don't always work right, I've heard."

"I see," Gina said, glancing back at the cameras, a new thought forming in her mind. Could she find a way to develop the film herself? How could she start with Marty's film, though? She'd have to take a few rolls herself and practice developing them. It wouldn't matter if she messed up her own rolls. She just couldn't mess up the one Marty had shot. She pointed to the pink Vanity Kodak he'd just been showing her. "How much is that one?"

"Thirty dollars," Benny replied, regret in his voice. "We do have a few used ones, for a quarter of the price. I just don't know how well they work, to be honest."

After examining the three used cameras, Gina selected the one that appeared to be in the best condition. "I'll take this one, Benny, with a box of film, please," she said. On a whim, she put the perfume she'd been considering on the counter as well. Why not?

Although she did feel a twinge as she handed over some folded-up bills. *Papa won't remember that we only had meat twice this week,* she silently reasoned.

Before she left, she had Benny show her how to load the camera and unwind the film when it was done. The process was simple enough, but she left the store still feeling vaguely uneasy. Could she really learn to develop photographs? What if she messed up? What if she never learned what Marty had hoped to keep hidden?

Gina stood in front of the mirror, and carefully fixed her black cloche hat. After she returned home and made her father a midmorning snack, Gina wanted nothing more than to try out the camera, but it was time to ready herself for Marty's funeral.

She felt strange about attending the funeral alone. Yet her Papa had made it quite clear that he wouldn't have gone even if he hadn't been in so much pain, and he didn't understand why she was going either. Nor did it seem likely that any of the girls from the Third Door were going. She'd overheard Lulu and the other girls talking about how much they all hated going to funerals. Even Ned seemed to want nothing to do with it.

Deep inside, she just knew that her mother would expect her to pay her respects to her cousin. It was clear that Marty had been fond of her mother. Perhaps Marty had been a favorite, too. With a pang she realized she'd never know. "I'm leaving now, Papa," she called.

He glanced at her and did a double take when he took in her long black dress. It must have reminded him, as it did her, of Aidan's funeral so long ago. He scowled now, perhaps at that memory. "Do as you please," he said, before turning back to his newspaper.

About forty minutes later, Gina hopped off the bus on State Street and began to walk slowly north toward Holy Name Cathedral. The church itself loomed above her, its shadow reflecting the dark shadows she felt deep inside herself. She hadn't attended Mass in years. She could almost hear the taunting voices of the nuns from her elementary school whispering that she was lapsed.

As she watched a pair of older women dressed entirely in black walk into the church, she wondered if the Signora or Big Mike would be there.

Gina sighed. It was too late to worry about that now.

Before she walked in, Gina stopped to look at the cornerstone, which still showed the bullet holes from where the gangster Hymie Weiss had been gunned down in front of the Cathedral by Capone's men a few years before. Everyone had heard about the hit, and she'd heard many mothers had taken their sons there as a bit of a cautionary tale. Although what the tale was, she wasn't quite sure, other than don't futz around with Al Capone.

Suppressing a shiver, Gina mounted the flat stone steps,

walked through the arched entrance, and entered the dark interior of the cathedral. Before passing into the nave, Gina picked up a Mass card from a small tray beside several lit candles.

After sliding into a back pew, she looked at the card. On the front was a portrait of a sorrowful Madonna holding an earnest baby Jesus, his finger crooked in blessing. On the back was a Bible verse from Jeremiah 31:3. "The Lord hath appeared of old unto me, saying, Yea, I have loved thee with an everlasting love: therefore with lovingkindness have I drawn thee."

Below the verse was his name. Martin Liam Doyle. Born Monday, November 2, 1885, Chicago, Illinois. Died Sunday, January 13, 1929. Chicago, Illinois.

Tears welled up in her eyes as she took in the incorrect date of Marty's death. No one knew that he had actually been killed the night before what was printed on the card. *Marty staring up at her.* Then that whisper. *Take my camera. Hide it.* What had he wanted her to do with it?

Gina sighed, pushing back into the uncomfortably hard wooden pew.

What if she had told people what had happened? What if she had told them about Marty's death? *You could have been a target, too, Gina,* the dark little voice deep inside her intoned. *So could Papa. Best to keep it all to yourself. Figure it out for yourself.*

Being among all the mourners made her feel like she was losing her mother and Aidan all over again, and the darkness that had been twisting her insides threatened to overwhelm her. To keep herself from breaking into unstoppable sobs— which she feared would happen—she tried to focus on the people who were slowly filling the pews toward the front of the nave. The church was about one-third full, and she started to listen to the jumble of conversations going on around her. A few snippets floated toward her.

"Hadn't come home in years, I heard," one older woman said with a sniff.

"Practically killed his mother," the woman next to her agreed. "He never did marry, you know." That last statement was issued in an equally damning tone.

"Oh, that Marty," the first woman said. "He always was a bit of a scamp."

"Tragic end, of course."

"Of course," the first woman concurred. "Still, he likely had it coming, seeing who he ran about with all those years. Scofflaws!"

"Did you know, he worked in . . . one of *those* places!" The women's voices dropped. They could have been speaking about someone working at a brothel, but perhaps to these women's minds a speakeasy was equally sordid. Gina tossed her head. Probably a bunch of temperance do-gooders. Although most of the ones that lived in her neighborhood were Methodists. Maybe it was different on the North Side.

That reminded her of the thought that had been plaguing her since she had first decided to attend the funeral. Were any of her mother's family members here? They had to be.

Just then, the great wooden doors opened again and a priest entered, dressed in white robes and carrying a cross. The congregation all stood at once in tribute. Behind him were other members of the clergy, all carrying lighted candles. The priest preceded the casket, which was borne on the shoulders of six pallbearers. Behind the casket were three mourners dressed heavily in black. One was an old woman who moved very slowly, supported by a man on either side, one older and one younger.

Gina regarded them carefully. Given their status behind the casket, they must be immediate members of Marty's family. Perhaps hers as well.

She watched the men carefully lay their great gleaming burden in front of the altar. She gulped, thinking about Marty stretched out inside the coffin.

She was so lost in thought that she did not realize that everyone had been seated in the pews and she was the only one still standing, giving her an unrestricted view of the entire congregation. She saw Gooch sitting next to a woman whose face was heavily veiled under a fashionable hat. From the elegant slope of the woman's form, she suspected it was the Signora. Since everyone was still watching the pallbearers setting the coffin in place, she was able to steal a few more glances around. She did not recognize anyone else.

One of the pallbearers turned back toward the congregation, unexpectedly meeting her gaze. She could see a startled look cross his face, even across all the pews, and she sat down hastily, trying too late to hide from the public scrutiny.

A man seated toward the back turned around as well, presumably following the direction of the pallbearer's surprised gaze. She took a sharp intake of breath when she recognized Roark. What was he doing there?

The funeral Mass passed slowly, but Gina found herself remembering the rhythms of the church service. The Latin phrases came back to her, as did the call and response. Stand up, give the response, sit back down, kneel, pray, listen, pray, shake hands. Every time they were asked to stand, she tried to see if there was anyone else there that she knew, but the block of people was too great.

When the priest administered Communion, Gina stayed in her pew, somewhat self-consciously. Not wanting to meet any curious eyes, she focused on the priest as he offered the vessel full of wine for everyone to drink. Churches were one of the only places where wine could be publicly consumed, since they were not selling it to their parishioners. Of course, she had also heard that sales of church wine had risen sharply in recent years, and it was easy to imagine that at least some of the barrels were ending up in less godly hands.

After the Mass was complete, the priest spoke in English. "The family has invited you to a luncheon at the residence of the decedent's mother, Mrs. John Doyle, at one o'clock to complete our celebration of the late Martin Doyle's life." He gave the address of a well-to-do area on Oak. "This now concludes this morning's Mass." He gestured for the pallbearers to position themselves by the coffin again.

The priest led them out, swinging the censer to spread the burning incense's fragrant smoke through the congregation. As they passed, the same pallbearer again swiveled his gaze toward Gina, a puzzled look on his face.

While many of the congregation started to walk toward Oak Street, Gina stood on the steps, in the shadows, watching Marty's casket be loaded into the waiting funeral coach that would take him to the cemetery for his eternal rest.

Gooch and the Signora walked quickly past her toward a black car waiting on the southern corner of Superior and State. Neither of them seemed to have spoken or interacted with any of the other mourners.

"I just need to pick up some corned beef," she heard an older woman say to her husband. "I'll meet you over there."

Gina moved back inside the church, thinking to light a candle for Marty and one for Aidan as well. A heavy feeling of loss washed over her, and she looked toward the glass windows to keep her tears from falling.

When someone jostled her arm, she glanced over. It was Roark.

"Why are you here?" he asked.

She continued to light the candles, silently saying a small prayer. "Same as you, I guess. To pay my respects." Her words sounded hollow, false even to her own ears. She didn't blame him for the suspicious frown he gave her. "Of course," he said, walking away from her.

Sudden tears stinging in her eyes, Gina walked quickly out of the great wooden doors of the church. She was about to flee down the stone steps when one of the pallbearers hailed her.

"Young lady," he called, carefully helping an old woman in black down the stairs. Gina recognized her as the woman who had walked behind Marty's casket before the Mass. "Please, wait."

Reluctantly, Gina descended the stairs and moved toward them, trying to think what to say. Luckily the man, who was probably in his early fifties, spoke again. "May I ask how you knew my brother, Marty Doyle? You look familiar."

Gina gulped. This was Marty's brother, which meant, of course, that this was another of her mother's cousins. For a moment she gaped at him, unsure what to say and feeling completely addled.

The old woman surveyed her keenly, then swatted the man

lightly on the arm. "Of course she looks familiar, you numbskull. Sometimes my son Eddie's a bit of a dunce, aren't you, Eddie?" She continued to eye Gina's features. "I recognize that wayward chin, that defiant look. You have the same look in your eyes that my niece Molly had, just before she ran off with that Italian fellow and wrote herself right out of the family."

Gina stiffened. "That 'Italian fellow' was my father, Frank Ricci. I am sorry, Mrs. Doyle, for your loss. I was here to pay my respects, and I was just leaving."

"Turning your back on the family?"

"No more than they turned on us."

"Your mother made her choice to go with your father. She chose a life without us."

Her son was still trying to work it out. "You're Molly's daughter. That makes Mother your—"

"Great-aunt," Gina and Mrs. Doyle said at the same time.

They didn't have very long to ponder the significance, as the driver of the funeral coach called out that he was ready to start the processional to the graveyard.

Mrs. Doyle straightened her shoulders. "This is not the place or time to go into this. You will join us at my home. Eddie, give the girl our address. I'll not have it any other way." She spoke firmly, and Gina found herself accepting a business card from Mr. Doyle with the address scrawled on the back. "We'll be there directly after the burial. Do join us. There is much we need to discuss."

Trying to maintain a sense of calm, Gina walked up to the Doyles' home right at one o'clock, just as nearby church bells tolled the hour. She'd spent the last hour, wandering aimlessly around outside the church, trying to overcome a growing sense of panic and fear over the upcoming meeting. In the back of her mind, she'd known she might meet some of Marty's relatives—*her* relatives—but now that this was actually happening, she was feeling nervous and tongue-tied.

She consulted Mr. Doyle's card, to make sure she was at the correct address, even though it was obvious from all the people dressed in black and carrying covered dishes. She kept her fingers crossed that Roark would not be there.

Quickly straightening her coat and hat, Gina hoped she would look presentable when she entered the house. It was then that she noticed some men in dark suits standing by the door.

Their movements reminded her of how Gooch and Little Jimmy moved and acted at the Third Door. Were they guards? For a moment, she wondered if she was supposed to know a password. What would happen if she didn't?

"Get a grip, Gina," she muttered to herself. Approaching the men, she asked, "Is this Mrs. John Doyle's home?" She felt stupid and nervous. Should she show them the card from Eddie Doyle?

She needn't have worried. One of the men gave her a terse nod and cocked his head. "Inside."

Inside, she walked into the grandest home she'd ever seen, with a gleaming wooden staircase rising gracefully to the second floor, a parlor to the right, and a closed-off room to her left. Everywhere mourners clumped together in murmured conversations and muffled laughter. As she walked into the parlor, she passed a huge table full of heaping trays of food. Ham, Irish soda bread, corned beef sandwiches, tiny cookies. On another table by a floor-to-ceiling window, there was a great glass tureen full of soup, and another full of a pink

frothy liquid that looked like punch. In another corner, there
was still another tureen with a number of glasses near it. Men
were gathered beside it, pouring themselves a familiar-looking
brown liquid. Whiskey.

With her stomach growling, she took a china plate from
one end of the table and began to stuff it full of meats, cheeses,
and salads, not caring if she was transgressing convention or
propriety. She went to a corner table to eat, while still watching
everything around her.

Could any of these people be her relatives? Should she try
speaking to anyone? Right now, she just wanted to stuff her
mouth full of food.

She was in midbite when a white-haired man approached
her. "Miss Ricci?" he asked.

Trying to swallow the huge chunk of brown soda bread,
she just nodded.

"Allow me to introduce myself. I am Hiram Dern, a friend
of the family and their attorney. The Doyles asked me to have
you join them in their study when you arrived. Follow me, if
you would. I don't like to keep them waiting."

Reluctantly, Gina abandoned her plate of food, hoping she
could retrieve it later.

She followed Mr. Dern down a long corridor to a back
room. It opened into a large study full of gold-embossed books
and gleaming dark wood. Mrs. Doyle and Eddie Doyle were
seated on fancy chairs around a low table, along with another
much older gentleman with thick white hair, bright blue eyes,
and red cheeks. A dour-looking woman dressed in a somber
gray dress was seated beside Mrs. Doyle. Her hair, pulled back
in a severe bun, showed she was not a flapper or a New Woman.
Nor was she a woman born with prewar gentility. This was

a woman with presence, a woman who brooked no nonsense. She was probably in her thirties or early forties and had the air of someone who would rather be outside than in a room seated on a sofa sipping tea.

Eddie stood up when she entered, and Mrs. Doyle gave her a terse nod. "Prompt, at least," she commented. A cookie and a cup of tea were untouched in front of her.

He extended his hand toward her. "Gina," he said. "How good of you to join us. I'd like to introduce you to my father, your great-uncle John Doyle."

"Forgive me, my dear," the white-haired man said. "I cannot get up and about like I used to, particularly after the funeral. I will ask you to sit beside me, so that I can see you more clearly."

With a start, she recognized her brother in her great-uncle's features.

"What is it?" he asked, seeing her expression.

"It's just that you remind me of my brother, Aidan, who passed in the Great War."

Instinctively, everyone in the room made the sign of the cross.

The woman in the dark uniform coughed. The sound caused everyone to turn to her.

Mrs. Doyle turned to her. "Let us not forget to introduce you to your mother's cousin, Marty's sister, Nancy. She's a spinster."

Nancy Doyle grimaced. "Thank you for that, Mother. Also, let us not forget, a police woman. On the force for twelve years." Although she seemed to have announced her employment with a bit of a jab toward her parents, there was also pride underlying her words.

Surely there were very few women on the police force, Gina thought as she regarded the woman. She must have joined during the war, when the young men around her were conscripted to fight overseas. That she had been allowed to remain on the force later was likely a testament to her fortitude. But it was hard to make sense of that right now. Her head spinning from meeting all these new relatives at once, Gina could only smile wanly at Nancy.

Nancy did not return her smile. "How long have you known Marty?" she asked, her eyes narrowing. "We understand that you work at the Third Door, too."

There was no pretense that she worked at the pharmacy or any other such hooey, Gina noticed. "How did you know that I work there?" she countered. "Did Marty tell you about me?"

Nancy's look of pain looked real. "None of us have spoken to Marty for a very long time."

Mr. Dern exchanged a look with Mrs. Doyle. "How long did you know Marty? Was he friendly with your father? Is that how you came to work at the Third Door?"

Gina noticed that no one had answered her question. Maybe Gooch had told them. Still, she answered the attorney's question. "I only met Marty a couple of weeks ago, when I first started to work at the Third Door. Shortly after, he told me he was my mother's cousin. I wish I *had* known him better. I am . . ." She hesitated, not wishing to divulge too much. "I'm interested in learning more about photography. I would have liked to learn from him."

Another speculative glance followed, this time between Nancy and her grandmother.

The attorney nodded. "How *did* you come to work there?

Perhaps Marty mentioned it to your father? They don't exactly put adverts in the paper, do they?"

"No," she said slowly, remembering Marty's indignation with the Signora. "My friend told me that they needed another girl there."

"A fortuitous coincidence, then," Mr. Doyle said, clapping his hands together.

Gina smiled at her great-uncle. He, at least, seemed genuinely pleased to meet her. "I suppose," she replied. "Marty told me that he didn't want me working there." She bit her lip then and looked away. She didn't know why she had said that.

The attorney nodded. "Protective," he said, looking around at the others, as if this confirmed something for him.

The others exchanged another glance. Clearly, a hidden conversation was occurring, one to which she was not privy. She waited for someone to elaborate, but no one did.

She turned back to her great-aunt, who was still looking at her with curiosity and something else. "Please, Mrs. Doyle," she said. "Why did you ask me to see you?"

Her great-aunt nodded at her lawyer. "I'll let Mr. Dern explain."

The lawyer cleared his throat. "Martin Liam Doyle, having died without issue, has designated you his primary beneficiary and heir."

"What?!" Gina searched their faces. Was this a joke? An odd joke, to be sure. Indeed, they all looked solemn. Nancy seemed put out but not surprised.

Mr. Dern continued. "His will left everything to your mother, Molly O'Brien, who, it seems, was his favorite cousin. Turns out, he never updated his will, even after her death,

I was going to inform you tomorrow, and then you showed up at the funeral today."

Nancy and Eddie both gave a little grunt at the attorney's words, the sullen sounds lingering in the air.

"Marty did tell me that my mother had been his favorite," Gina agreed, looking at Marty's brother and sister. "I'm afraid I don't understand what this means."

A snort again, this time from Nancy.

Ignoring the sudden tension, the attorney continued. "Since your mother has passed, her inheritance will pass to her issue, which means you and your brother, Aidan. Since your brother passed in the Great War, *you* are Martin Doyle's primary beneficiary."

Behind them, Nancy muttered something under her breath that Gina couldn't quite catch.

This time the lawyer wagged a warning figure at Nancy before continuing. "Thus, this means that Mr. Doyle's possessions will pass to you, as you are above the age of majority," the lawyer continued. "This will, of course, be after the funeral and interment costs and all other debts are paid. There may be very little after that," he warned her. "Assuming that we can confirm your identity."

"Of course. I didn't know, I didn't expect—" Feeling helpless, Gina let her voice drop off. Marty's family, *her* family, continued to size her up, regarding her as one might view a strange animal.

Mr. Dern continued in his dry way, as if she had not spoken. "Mr. Doyle leased two flats in one of the buildings above the Third Door, as you may know. One of them was his personal apartment, and the other he used as his photography studio. His rent has been paid through June, as he had a specific relationship with his landlords," the lawyer continued. "You will of course inherit all of his furniture and other effects, whatever those may be." After scrutinizing her face, he turned to Eddie. "I think Miss Ricci could do with a drink."

"Of course," Eddie replied, as he hastily poured some whiskey into a glass and placed it in her hand. "This must be a shock."

The others watched as she took a deep gulp of the liquid, which burned her tongue and throat unmercifully.

"*Is* it a shock for you?" Nancy asked. "Are you quite sure that you knew nothing of this bequest?"

Gina took another deep gulp, and the hot, bitter taste of whiskey washed uncomfortably down her throat. "I knew nothing about it."

"You have to admit," Nancy interrupted, "that the timing of Marty's death is fortunate. For you."

"Fortunate?" Gina asked. "Whatever do you mean?"

"Your father is no longer able to fix things like he used to, is he?"

"Why, no," Gina began, surprised that Nancy knew about this, but her uncle Eddie cut her off.

"You and your father, you are in deep financial trouble, are you not?" he asked, regarding her closely.

"Yes, well," Gina stammered, "no. I'd just gotten the job. We're doing well enough." Gina stood up then, anger coursing over her. "I didn't even know about Marty, let alone about this inheritance. To say it was good timing, well, that is terrible. I have no other family, and I would have liked to know him! I would like to have found a connection to my mother again."

Tears as hot as the whiskey burned in her eyes. "I don't

know what you might be accusing me of, but I certainly did not ask or expect anything from Marty, who I only just met. To say I was here for anything else at all, well, that impugns me, him, and worst of all my mother." Gina set down the glass down hard on the edge of the desk. "If you'll excuse me."

Her great-uncle stood up then, a smile on his lips. "Gina, you're quite wrong."

Gina glared at him. "Wrong how?"

"That he was the only connection to your family, to your mother. We're so very sorry to have said good-bye to Marty, but we're very glad that you've come back into our lives. Your parents did you wrong by keeping you away all these years."

Gina stiffened. "My mother said her family cast her out. That *you* cast her out. Even Marty told me that you would be unlikely to welcome me."

There was a shuffling among her relatives, and her great-uncle laid a hand on his wife's arm. "Let's move past that. We are in a different era now, are we not?" With considerable effort, he held out his elbow for Gina to take. When she hesitated, he leaned over and drew her hand onto the crook of his arm.

Nodding to the lawyer to open the heavy oak door, her great-uncle pulled her through the ornate doorway. "Come, my dear. I should very much like to introduce my great-niece to the world."

CHAPTER 11

When Gina returned home from the luncheon, she was exhausted. So many new cousins and aunts she couldn't even make sense of it all, some smiling, some looking at her in suspicion, some giving her little hugs, others turning away from her. She'd stayed at the Doyles' home for another hour before she grew too overwhelmed and left, only to discover it had begun to snow. After waiting to no avail for the bus, she ended up walking along the bus route, catching it with just two miles to go. At least she'd managed to save her shoes from getting ruined.

"Papa?" she called out, dropping her bag and keys on the table. She wanted to talk things over with her father right away. She knocked on her father's bedroom door and went in. To her surprise, the room was empty. That was odd. Her father didn't usually venture out on his own these days.

Gina went to the flat above hers and knocked on her neighbor's door. "Mrs. Hayford," she called. "It's me, Gina."

The door opened slightly and a middle-aged woman looked out. "Hello, dear, what is it?"

"Have you seen my papa?"

"Oh, yes, dear. I believe he went out," Mrs. Hayford replied, pulling her shawl closer around her as the chilly wind swept through the open door.

"Where did he go?"

"Down to the barbershop, I heard him say." She shook her head. "Guess he wanted a shave and a trim."

"More likely he just misses his pals," Gina replied. Although on the one hand she was glad that her papa felt up to seeing his friends, on the other, she felt a bit miffed that he'd ventured out into the growing storm without her.

Slipping on boots, Gina set out for the barbershop over on Carpenter. Although her father's palsy was manageable, it was hard not to worry that he might take a treacherous spin on the ice and break a bone—or worse. Within a block, she regretted that she had not changed out of the thin black dress that she had worn to the funeral. The snow had starting coming down harder and the wind had begun to pick up, so that the chill burrowed right into her bones.

When she arrived at the barbershop and opened the door, a little bell jangled above her head. The shop was full of thick masculine aromas—men's facial soap, cologne, sweat. She was immediately an object of the men's interest when she walked in, blowing on her hands and stamping the snow from her boots.

"Hey, Gina," the barber called, stopping in midshave. As always, her dad's longtime friend Al was dressed in his crisp white jacket and black bow tie. He jerked his thumb toward the back of the room. "Your pop's over there."

She found her father sitting on a black leather chair in the back corner of the shop, clouds of wispy gray-and-black hair blowing about him on the floor. She did like seeing his face neatly shaved, without any of the cuts he often inflicted on himself. The banter that had stopped when she entered the room soon resumed. The shop looked darker than usual. "I think Al needs to screw a few lightbulbs in," she joked to her dad.

Following her glance toward the burned-out electric lights in the ceiling, he gave her a meaningful look. "Shhh," he said, putting his fingers to his lips. "Turns out that Al made a deal that wasn't on the up-and-up."

"What do you mean?" she asked, plopping down in a red chair next to her father. Commonwealth Edison wasn't a business particularly known for making deals with its customers. You paid or you didn't. For sure if you didn't, your electricity was cut. That was it. No deals to be had.

"Light fixing," her dad whispered. "He had a guy turning back the dials on the meter. Only problem is, the electric company caught on and changed the whole gizmo. I even looked at it. Nothing can be done now. Told Al that he's gotta pay the whole bill, unless he wants to cut hair in the dark. Rotten shame."

"Wasn't hurting anyone," Al grumbled, overhearing their conversation. "Just trying to save a few bucks."

The other men were all shaking their heads in solidarity. That the scheme was illegal didn't seem to bother anyone.

She smoothed the folds of her long black dress. The gesture appeared to remind her father where she had been earlier. "How was the funeral?" he asked, his manner gruff.

"Fine, I suppose. It was a funeral." She didn't want to say anything about the conversation she had had with Marty's family, since others sitting around the small barbershop were already listening in.

"Whose funeral?" Al asked, wiping the soft lather from his blade.

"Marty Doyle's," her father replied, before she could say anything.

Al glanced over at them, moving the blade away from the man's throat. "You don't say? Marty Doyle's funeral?"

One of the other men spoke up. "Doyle? I heard about that. He was killed, down by the Harrison Street Bridge, wasn't it?"

"That's right," Gina replied, turning back to her father, hoping he'd take the hint. She didn't want to discuss the topic anymore, even though the men still did.

"Heard it was one of Capone's men," Al said, meeting Gina's eyes in the mirror. His voice then dropped, as everyone's did when they mentioned the Chicago gang leader. "Whacked him real good."

He began to add a soapy lather to the man's face, still watching Gina in the mirror in a way that made her uncomfortable. "Why'd you go to his funeral?" There was curiosity, but some suspicion, too.

Catching her father's eye, Gina could tell he'd grown more wary. Although his head was shaking a bit from the palsy, he had clearly caught on that there was something she needed to discuss with him in private. "Just paying my respects," she said, trying to sound casual. "I worked with him a while." She turned back to her father. "Papa, are you ready to go? Let's head home."

Their walk home was hard going, particularly since they had to push against the blowing wind and snow. Her father clung to her, and as they walked, she told him all about the service and meeting members of the family at the Doyle home. He grunted when she mentioned that Nancy Doyle was a police-woman. "I remember her," he said. "Tough as tacks."

Then, with some trepidation, she told him about the will. "I don't want you taking anything from them."

"It's an *inheritance*, Papa! Marty left it to me," she said. "Well, he left everything to Mama before he went to war. When she passed, Aidan and me became the beneficiaries. I guess he never got around to changing his will." *Or he just didn't have anyone else*, she thought with a pang.

When they reached the front door, her father stopped short. "You left the front door open? In a storm?!"

"No, I'm sure I locked it," she said. "Maybe the wind—?"

"Shhh," he interrupted her. "Stay here."

He began to move toward the stairs, trying to grip the railing. Ignoring his command, Gina mounted the steps directly behind him and was right at his elbow as he pushed the door open.

Staring inside, they both gasped. "What in the world?" she heard her father say. Gina just held her hand to her mouth in disbelief.

The whole front room was in disarray. Sofa pillows had been slashed, their stuffing spilling everywhere. Books and other items from the old oak bookcase that her father had made for her mother before Gina was born littered the floor.

Ignoring her strong instinct to flee, Gina opened the door wider, and they stepped inside.

"H-hello?" she called out, immediately feeling stupid when her father glared at her.

"We're coming in!" her father shouted with a surprisingly

deep voice. "You'd better show yourself or there'll be hell to pay when I find you."

They waited, still met only by a deep stillness. Together they moved toward the kitchen. No one was there. Gina stood silently, her heart beating hard, barely daring to breathe. She was ready to flee should anyone step out of either bedroom or the bathroom.

"Oh, no!" she heard her father call, and she followed him into his bedroom. Her mama's jewelry box had been upended on the bed. Jewelry was spilled everywhere, as were the photographs they had been looking at the other day.

Trying to stay calm, she touched her father's shoulder. "I'm going to call the police."

While they were waiting for the coppers, Gina discovered that her father's radio had been stolen, but thankfully the thief had not discovered the tiny cache of dollars she'd kept hidden in a tomato soup jar in the back of the kitchen cupboard. The camera, too, was still tucked away underneath the floorboard, just where she'd left it, along with the notebook and key. All was intact.

Mrs. Hayford started crying when Gina went to check on her. "I never heard anything, dear! My hearing's not so good, and I had my radio on." Her eyes were wide and frightened. "This neighborhood! What's it coming to?"

The police arrived shortly after, their paddy wagon effectively blocking any traffic from passing on the narrow street. When the two cops walked toward them, Gina was surprised to see Officer Dawson, the young cop who had come to the Third Door to ask questions about Marty's death.

The older cop, Officer Jamison, went straight up to her father and began making inquiries. Officer Dawson glanced at her and then did a double take. She could tell he recognized her but couldn't immediately place her, and she didn't feel inclined to enlighten him.

Seeing the question on his lips, Gina hurried past him to help her father answer the other policeman's questions. She pointed out the scattered objects that had been on the shelves, told them about the missing radio, and showed them her mother's overturned jewelry box. Strangely enough, all of the jewelry appeared to still be there.

"Some expensive-looking pieces there," Officer Jamison commented. "Costume?"

Her father scowled. "All real," he said, having prided himself on never having to pawn her jewelry.

"Interesting."

The policemen continued their exploration. Gina watched, a detached daze coming over her. She wanted to take the objects from their curious hands and push the cops right out the door. Already drained by Marty's murder and the funeral, she thought she would just topple over in complete weariness if they didn't leave soon.

She was alert enough, though, to hear Officer Dawson's comment. "Odd time of day for a robbery," he said.

Officer Jamison nodded. "All of it's odd. Broad daylight. Thursday afternoon. At the start of a snowstorm. Unusual."

Officer Dawson turned to her. "Miss Ricci, you said you were attending a funeral and had just returned to your home around three thirty?"

"Yes, that's so."

"Your home had not been disturbed at that point?"

"No, and my father was getting a shave at the barbershop. Mrs. Hayford told me so."

Officer Jamison noted something in his notepad.

Officer Dawson continued. "When you left, did you lock the front door?"

"Of course," she replied, trying not to get angry. "As you can see, someone broke the door in."

The cops walked over and inspected the door. Gina could see where the wood had splintered. "One quick shove and the door just gave way," Officer Jamison said. "Still, the burglar risked bringing attention to himself. We'll canvass the neighbors when we're done here. See if anyone saw anything."

Good luck with that, Gina thought. In this neighborhood, they'd be lucky if anyone would even talk to either of these Irish cops, let alone snitch on someone else.

Officer Dawson glanced back over his notes. "So, whose funeral were you at?" He held his pen ready.

Before Gina could deflect, her father answered the question. "Martin Doyle's. He was related to Gina, on her mother's side. Second cousin or something like that."

Officer Dawson's eyes flicked back to Gina, and she could see the recognition flood across his face. It was obvious that now he remembered her from the drugstore. "Marty Doyle's niece? Interesting."

Officer Jamison wasn't paying attention to his partner. "Did you see anyone suspicious on the street? Someone who might have been watching the house? Or you?"

Gina felt a shiver run over her. "What do you mean?"

"I suspect someone was watching you, waiting for you

both to leave. Might even have known you'd be gone long enough to break in. That takes guts. It also means someone was casing the joint."

"Someone was looking for something specific," Officer Dawson added.

"Like what?" Gina asked, her heart beginning to pound. "The radio?"

"No offense meant, Miss Ricci, but there are other ways to get a radio. You mentioned that yours wasn't so new, right? A few years old, I think you said." Officer Dawson eyed her. "You're sure that nothing else is missing? None of your mother's jewelry? What about yours, miss?"

Gina shook her head, having already found that her few pieces of costume jewelry were still intact. What could the thief have been after? She thought about the camera, still hidden beneath the floorboard.

Hoping her face hadn't betrayed her thoughts, she shrugged. "Nothing else seems to have been taken." She made an elaborate pretense of looking at her watch. "If you're all done here, I'd like to get my home back in order so I can start making some dinner for my father."

"Of course," he said. The officer's eyes were still narrowed. "If you find anything else has been stolen, let us know."

As soon as Gina had shut the door behind the police, and wedged a chair under the knob to keep the door secure she turned back to her father. As usual his hands were shaking a bit, but she couldn't tell if that was his regular palsy or anger. "Whiskey, Papa?" she asked.

Without waiting for him to reply, she pulled a bottle of whiskey from behind the icebox and poured into two glasses, an extra slosh in each. "I could reheat some soup for dinner," she offered, her voice wan. "There's some bread in the bin."

"I'm not hungry," he said, bending down to kiss the top of her head. He picked up his drink in two hands. "This will do me just fine."

Her heart still pounding, Gina took a great gulp of whiskey before going into her own bedroom. She heard her father close his door, and then she shut her own and lay on the bed.

Could the thief have been looking for the camera? Except that no one knew she had it. Or did they?

She remembered again that step in the darkness when she knelt over Marty's body. Had someone been there? Had someone seen her take the camera from his jacket?

With a sigh, she closed her eyes. None of this made any sense. The weariness and emotion she'd been keeping at bay finally overcame her, and she lay on the bed and sobbed.

Lulu nudged her. "You've got a gent asking for you," she said. A day had passed since she had attended Marty's funeral. "Over there, in the corner."

"For me? He wants cigarettes or something?"

"I suppose. I already brought him whiskey. A real flat tire, that one."

Gina walked over to the man in the corner, who was sitting with his back to the wall, looking straight and out of place. Not even tapping his foot to Ned's lively tune.

Putting her brightest smile on her face, she held out her cigarette tray. "Cigar, sir?"

"Sure, Miss Ricci," the man replied.

With a start, Gina recognized him. It was Mr. Dern, the

Doyles' family attorney. She took the cigar and cut the end off, handing it to him when she was done. Instead of lighting it, he slipped it inside the breast pocket of his jacket. He then slid a few dollars onto her tray, more than what the cigar had cost, with a meaningful glance. "Better put that away," he said. "There are thieves about."

When she picked up the money, she saw that he had also left three keys on a metal ring. "To Marty's flat and darkroom. Both are on Polk and Morgan." He pointed upwards, in the direction of Madame Laupine's. "On the third floor. 3A and 3B. The third key, I understand, is to the outer door," he said. "Your grandmother didn't see any reason to delay your inheritance."

"Jeepers!"

"This is, you must understand, against my better judgment." His cough was more an affectation than the result of a scratchy throat. "This sort of business should be done in my office, with signed papers, not in a 'gin joint.'" The last two words were spoken with considerable disdain.

"Oh, yes, of course," Gina said, momentarily distracted by a skirmish going on at a nearby table. One man had grabbed another by his tie, and Gooch was already on it.

"As it turns out, there's more to be paid out to you, you understand."

"Oh yeah?" she asked, her attention fully returned. "I thought you said that you expected there to be very little inheritance."

"You are fortunate in that Mr. Doyle was not in debt. Quite the opposite, in fact," Mr. Dern went on in his dry lawyer's manner. "He paid his rent six months in advance to his landlords—the Castallazzos, as you may have figured out."

Gina twirled one of her corkscrew curls. She had already worked out they might be his landlords, given that all the businesses on the block seemed to be under their thumb.

The attorney continued. "We've settled all of Mr. Doyle's small charges at local businesses. He really didn't seem to run on credit, as so many do, and appeared to have a lean lifestyle overall." He paused.

"Mr. Dern?"

"There could also have been, you understand, *other debts,* which may still surface." Mr. Dern scratched his chin. Gina's face must have betrayed a bit of the inner distress she was feeling, for the lawyer suddenly seemed human. "In the same way that I would advise my own daughter, I invite you to come to me should such *alternative debts* present themselves, and we shall decide together what is to be done. Until then, let us not be concerned about such things."

Something about all this seemed a bit off. "So why just these keys?" she asked, not caring how greedy she sounded. "Why aren't I getting everything at once?"

The lawyer hesitated. "Before the bequest can be finalized, Mrs. Doyle would like to know that she can trust you. Can she trust you, Miss Ricci?"

"Trust me? How?"

"If you know anything—or perhaps learn anything—about Marty's death, she would like to know. There is, shall we say, a great deal of interest from my employer in knowing who killed her son."

"You think I can help find out?" The tingle was becoming full-fledged goosebumps now.

"Mrs. Doyle, I shall say, took a fancy to you. She would like you to have access to his equipment and anything else you might discover. She'd like you to convey any information you have back to her. Do you understand?"

At Gina's small nod, he stood up and downed the glass of whiskey. "I'll be in touch," he said.

"Mr. Dern," Gina called before the attorney had taken more than a few steps. She narrowed the gap between them so that no one would hear her question. "Who knows that Marty bequeathed his belongings to me?"

The lawyer scratched his chin thoughtfully. "Officially, just those of us who were in the parlor at the Doyles' house, after Marty's funeral. However, others might suspect a connection of sorts, given the Doyles' claim to you as their grand-niece." He looked up at her, his brown eyes watchful. "Why do you ask?"

She didn't want to say anything about the break-in that had occurred. "No reason," she replied. "I was just curious how public these sorts of things tended to be."

"Not public at all," he said. "However, given the nature of his untimely death, the fewer people who know about this, the better that will be for you." After he let that sink in, he added, "Remember, Miss Ricci. The Doyles will expect you to demonstrate loyalty to them." He turned then and mounted the stairs with great agility, despite his seemingly advanced years.

"Be their stool pigeon, sounds more like," Gina muttered, feeling the weight of the keys in her pocket. *What secrets might Marty's flat hold?* she wondered, as she moved off to serve another customer.

CHAPTER 12

"I'm going to Marty's flat today," Gina said to her father, handing him a plate of scrambled eggs and some slightly burned toast. "The Doyles' attorney, Mr. Dern, gave me a key. I thought I might poke around, see if there is anything of value."

"Not proper for a girl to go through a bachelor's things."

Her father seemed extra grumpy this morning. They hadn't discussed Marty's will since that moment before the burglary, and she could tell he was still put out. "Do you want to come with me?" she asked, hoping he would decline. Mr. Dern had said Marty's flats were on the third floor, and it was unlikely there was an elevator. Besides, she wanted time to look through everything, on her own.

He rustled the newspaper that Mrs. Hayford had dropped off earlier. "Probably just a bunch of junk. The Doyles probably want you to clear out the flat for them."

She sighed. "You're probably right, Papa," she said. Standing up, she dropped a kiss on his forehead."

Now he did look up. "Be careful, Gina. I mean it."

After asking Mrs. Hayford to check in on her papa, Gina walked quickly over to Morgan and Polk, finding the unobtrusive entrance to the flats between the shops. The smallest key fit the outer door. Around her neck she was wearing the key that she'd found inside Marty's camera case, looped onto a long silver chain that used to belong to her mother.

Taking a deep breath, Gina began to mount the steps to 3A. The stairwell was dimly lit and overly quiet. She began to think it was a bad idea to have come alone.

"Maybe no one else even lives here," she muttered to herself.

However, as she passed by 2A, an old woman glowered out at her through a slightly opened door.

Gina smiled at her by way of greeting, and the woman shut the door without saying a word.

When she reached the third floor, she found a small corridor with one door on either side, facing each other, one marked 3A and the other 3B. Gina pulled out the keys and inserted one of them into the door of 3A. Cautiously, she opened the door, unsure if she would be walking into the darkroom or Marty's flat. Feeling for the light switch, she flicked it on.

It appeared that she'd entered Marty's flat, with a living room space and a kitchen visible just beyond. There were another two doors as well, which she assumed led to a bedroom and a bathroom. All of the windows had been shuttered and the curtains were drawn as well. The place was a complete mess.

"What a dump," she said out loud.

As she looked around, an uneasiness came over her. There

was something about the nature of the disarray that bothered her. It reminded her of how her own home had looked after the break-in. The books on the shelf appeared to have been pushed over, knickknacks were facing in all directions, and some of the framed photographs were askew, as if someone had been looking behind them. There were lamps on end tables on either end of the sofa, but both were close to the edge, as if they had been picked up and moved without being replaced properly.

She waited for a moment, keeping perfectly still. She didn't hear anything in the flat. If there had been an intruder, the person had long since fled. Still, as a precaution, she kept the door of the flat open as she began to explore.

Besides the combined living room and kitchen, there was just a small bedroom and a bathroom. She only glanced into the bedroom, which also looked to have things strewn around it. She shut the door, feeling like she had violated Marty's privacy.

Moving back into the living room, she looked at some of the framed photographs on the shelves. Marty had taken lots of pictures of people in motion, but often when they were still as well. All were compelling, showing emotions and attitudes. Marty had been truly talented.

Leaving 3A unlocked, Gina crossed the corridor to open 3B, Marty's darkroom. The smell of chemicals overcame her in a rush, and for a moment she felt faint. This flat was much darker; The shades had all been drawn, although some afternoon sunlight still streamed through them in places.

She reached to flick on the lights, as she had done in the other flat, but nothing happened. Marty did not seem to have connected lamps as he had done in his living area. There was just enough light to see a single lamp on a small wooden table, which she turned on. She then pushed back the shades and opened the windows so she could breathe more freely. She began to look around.

This living room space was far sparser, but there were clotheslines running across the length of the room, with a few photographs clipped to them. Some newspaper was messily spread underneath, most likely to catch drips.

Gina glanced through some of the piles of photographs, noticing some familiar sights, like the Goodman Theatre, Navy Pier, and Holy Name Cathedral, where Marty's funeral Mass had just been held. There was another of the Harrison Street Bridge. When she saw that one, she shivered. *That's where his body was found,* she thought, feeling momentarily queasy.

Moving along, she opened the door to the kitchen area, finding that Marty had converted this to the darkroom proper. While there was a sink, there was neither an icebox nor an oven. There was also a large metal tub on the floor, beneath several clotheslines. The windows were completely covered with black curtains, and a single red light hung from the ceiling. Gina flicked the light on and off, having never seen a red bulb before. On the counter, there were empty trays. Opening the cabinets, she found more pans, both large and small, a few pieces of odd-looking equipment, and some strange chemicals in containers marked simply A, B, and C.

She sighed. "How can I ever learn this?" she said out loud.

"Why do you need to?"

Gina whirled around. To her surprise, Nancy Doyle was staring at her, hands on her hips. Marty's sister was wearing another gray dress, neat but otherwise not notable. "Just couldn't wait to check out your inheritance, could you?" she asked, spite evident in her voice. "I didn't think the will was considered valid yet."

"Is anyone contesting the will? That's not the impression I got the other day from your mother. Besides, I was given keys." Gina's voice was high-pitched, defensive. "From Mr. Dern. On behalf of the Doyles. You can ask him. I'm not trespassing."

Nancy continued to glower at her, arms crossed over her drab coat. "Hmph."

"In fact, I think *you're* the one who's trespassing," Gina added, her backbone returning.

Nancy ignored her. "Wormed your way into the family quickly enough, didn't you?"

Gina blinked, not sure how to respond. Perhaps Marty should have bequeathed his property to his sister, but for whatever reason, he had not done so. "Well, it's not my fault that Marty cared more for my mother than he did for you."

Nancy didn't even flinch. "That may be so." She opened one of the darkroom cabinets and scowled when she saw only chemicals. "Got anything to drink in this joint?"

Gina sighed. She wasn't sure if she should take Nancy back to Marty's flat, but it seemed worse to push her off. Besides, Nancy was her family, too, even if she didn't seem willing to acknowledge their relationship. More importantly, Gina still had questions that Nancy might be able to answer.

"This way," Gina said, gesturing to Marty's flat. "I was going to check out what food he might have had anyway."

Moving back into Marty's kitchen, Gina opened the icebox and grimaced when the rank odor of spoiled goods reached her nose. She'd take care of that tomorrow. She shut the icebox door again quickly and began to open the kitchen cabinets to see what else might be on hand.

Nancy watched as Gina poked around in the metal containers and sniffed the contents of different jars and bowls. "You're telling me that you didn't know about Marty's will when you started working at the Third Door?" Nancy asked. "Check up there."

Standing on her tiptoes, Gina opened one of the upper cabinets, finding a half-full bottle of whiskey along with several mismatched glasses. "I didn't even know Marty when I started working there."

"So you said."

"Well, it's true."

Nancy sniffed. "You know, I've never been here. Marty and I weren't close. We were . . . estranged."

"There's no ice," Gina said, sitting down. She uncorked the bottle. "It'll have to be neat."

"Neat's fine." Nancy watched Gina pour the amber liquid into the glasses. "Nice to know that even though we'd barely spoken in the last twenty years, we still shared a taste for the same whiskey. To Marty," she said, before taking a deep swallow.

"To Marty," Gina echoed, taking a far smaller sip. Still, the strong liquor made her bold. "Why were you estranged? Did you two have a falling-out?"

Nancy finished her glass. "After your mother left the family fold, it didn't take too much longer for Marty to leave as well." She poured herself another two fingers. "I find it hard to believe that you never met Marty. Before you came here, I mean. Given that your mother was his *favorite*." Her words, while bitter, sounded more forlorn than angry.

"It's true. Neither of my parents ever mentioned him. Not even once that I can remember," Gina replied, before changing the subject. "Did you know my mama?"

Nancy turned back to look at her. "A little bit. She was younger than me, and I'm afraid she seemed silly to me, at the time. I remember the scandal when she ran off. How could I not? Everyone was furious." She rubbed her forehead between her eyes. "The last time I saw your mother was at your grandmother's funeral. My aunt Mary—she'd died of cholera. Your mother came alone. From what I understand, she passed away shortly after."

Gina forced herself to remember that terrible time when her mother had laid in her bed, dying. She'd been so young. The fever had taken her quick, Gina hadn't even understood what was happening until after it was over. Her papa had always been so sad when she asked him about her mother's death, and angry too. She wondered now if her mother had been nursing a deeply grieved and broken heart when she died.

"Marty and I were the only ones from the family to attend your mother's funeral," Nancy said, looking away. "My mother and father simply would not come. They felt she had marred the family's name by marrying your father."

"They seem to have accepted me now." Gina frowned. "Or have they?"

Nancy eyed her. "You seem more perceptive than I remember your mother being. The truth is, I'm as surprised by this sea change as you are. Maybe they've come to regret how they treated Molly." Nancy switched topics. "Do you like working in that gin joint of yours?"

"I like it well enough. It pays the bills."

"You've come into money now. Isn't that enough for you?"

There was something probing under Nancy's questions. She was trying to find something out, and it made Gina uneasy. Now it was her turn to switch topics. "Do you like working for the police? What do you do?"

"Oh, I mostly work with female criminals—alleged and convicted. Mostly prostitution, some petty theft. Sometimes I'm the one to work with female victims, for *other* types of crimes."

"Did you work Dorrie Edwards's case?" Gina asked.

"Dorrie Edwards?" Nancy shook her head. "The name rings a bell. Who was she?"

"She used to work at the Third Door. I replaced her. She was killed on the L, just before Christmas. Stabbed."

Nancy gave a low whistle. "You don't say? Nah, I never get assigned to murders." She pursed her lips. "Edwards was murdered just before you started working at the Third Door? And you took her spot?"

"Oh, for heaven's sake. I didn't murder Dorrie for a chance to work at the Third Door!"

"Didn't say you did."

"What about Marty?" Gina asked. "Have they learned anything more?"

"Like what?"

"Like who killed him?"

Nancy looked annoyed. "Nah. They know he was my brother." Correctly reading Gina's skepticism, she continued. "No, it's true. Even though I'm on the force, they still keep it from me. Being that I'm just a *policewoman*." She began to drum her fingers on the table, looking like she wished she could drum some heads.

"Do you know Mr. Roark?"

"Yeah, I know him. His wife, too. He's been off the force for a while. Mostly just taking crime scene photographs now, from what I understand."

His wife? Gina hadn't known Roark was married. She didn't know why that surprised her, but it did. She wondered what his wife was like.

Nancy paused, looking like she was going to say something else. When she did, it was not what Gina was expecting. "You know, I saw him once. Marty. He was taking photographs, out on the street. I watched him for a while."

Seeing that Nancy seemed to have a specific purpose in bringing this up, Gina waited for her to continue. "He'd take a picture, and then he'd scribble something into a little book." She paused again. "You know, his camera hasn't been found."

"No?"

"It's odd. There were some things still in his pockets. Money. His keys." She nodded at the ring of three keys in Gina's hand. "Those."

Gina set them down on the counter in distaste. "I . . . I didn't realize."

Nancy went on. "His wallet and identification weren't on him, either. Neither was his notebook. Have you seen it?"

Gina pictured the notebook in the camera case, hidden under the floorboard in her bedroom. She shook her head. "I haven't had a chance to look through his things. I suppose it might be here." She looked around. "Although I have the feeling that someone has already searched the place."

Nancy nodded. "The police probably did. I can see if I can look in the file. See what they might have found."

Might have been the police, Gina thought. *Or perhaps it was someone else. Maybe even the same person who broke into our flat.*

Nancy stood up then and stretched her shoulders. She began to study the faces in the photographs on the shelves.

"Anybody you know?" Gina asked.

"Marty was a mystery to me." Like Gina, she seemed amazed by her brother's work, but also a bit sad. "I knew he was talented, but this is incredible." She poured herself some more whiskey without asking and took a long sip.

Gina wasn't sure if she should say anything. Nancy definitely did not seem like the kind of woman who would take kindly to a hug or even a friendly pat on the shoulder.

Her sympathy dissipated, though, when Nancy began pulling out cabinet drawers, inspecting Marty's belongings in a willy-nilly way that bugged Gina. A sister should show more respect.

"Hey, do you mind?" she asked.

"Funny that you ask. I do mind, actually." Nancy slammed a drawer shut. "I mind that my brother thought more of you—or at least your dead mother—than he did of me."

Her anger gave Gina pause. How would she have felt if Aidan had left his belongings to a stranger? Not very good, that was certain. "I'm sorry," she said.

In her remorse, she almost offered to let Nancy come back and help her look through Marty's effects. Then she recalled the image of him dying, trying to protect something or someone. She had to honor his final wishes.

"I need to get to my shift," she said, pointedly opening the door. She gestured for Nancy to leave.

Frowning, Nancy set her emptied glass down on the table. As she walked out, she leaned down, so close that Gina almost gagged from the smell of whiskey on her breath. "I'll go, but I'm not done here—or with you."

With that, she stalked out of the flat, her serviceable matron's boots clomping heavily on the stairs. When she reached the second-floor landing, she spoke to someone there. Probably Marty's downstairs neighbor. Slowly, Gina shut the door, an odd feeling washing over her. Perhaps the Signora was not the only one with spies at her beck and call.

"So how did that camera work for you?" Benny asked, watching her wipe down the counter. He had a broom, which he was supposed to be using to sweep the floor, but he'd barely swiped it twice in the last thirty minutes. Nor had he restocked any of the shelves as Mr. Rosenstein had instructed before he had left the pharmacy to deliver some medicine to an elderly neighbor. A chemistry book was open on the counter. "Take any photographs yet?"

"I used up a roll of film, but I haven't had it developed," she replied. "So I'm not sure if the camera works well or not."

"Just take the film over to the Kodak shop I told you about. They'll be ready in a few days."

"I know," Gina replied. "I was thinking of learning to develop the images myself."

Benny looked skeptical. "I'm sure, miss, it would be easier for you to simply bring the photographs in to be developed. Those chemicals aren't cheap."

"Oh, I've got a darkroom," she said, a bit more airily than she intended. She regretted the admission a moment later when Roark came out of nowhere and sat down at the counter. She hoped he hadn't overheard her comment. "What will you have?" she asked him.

"I'll take an orange soda." At her raised eyebrow, he grinned. "What can I say? I've gotta have my fizzy drinks like everybody else."

Unfortunately, Benny continued their earlier line of conversation. "Well," he said, "since you have your own darkroom, you just need someone to teach you."

"Yes, I suppose," she said hurriedly, as she poured Roark's drink. Moving too quickly, she ended up slamming the soft drink in front of Roark, so that a few orange drops spilled on the white counter.

"Careful," Roark said, wiping the drops away with his sleeve. "So, you've got photographs you'd like to develop? And access to your own darkroom? How interesting."

"Well, it's none of your beeswax," she said, hoping that he would drop the subject. "I'd better go help Benny restock the shelves. We just got a new shipment in."

"Gina. I told you before, you can trust me." His voice was low, and unexpectedly he laid his hand over hers where it rested on the countertop.

The sudden warmth from the contact startled them both, and she withdrew her hand quickly. She remembered what Nancy had said earlier about knowing his wife, even though she hadn't noticed a ring. He flushed slightly, and Gina realized that he had used his deformed hand to touch her.

Before she could explain her reaction, he had moved on, his voice harder now. "Just be straight with me. Whose darkroom do you have access to? Marty's, right?"

Suddenly it didn't seem to make much sense to keep the secret any longer. "Yeah."

"How did you get this access?"

"He gave me a key, all right?"

"He did? Why did he do that?" There was an abrupt shift in his tone, to curiosity mixed with disappointment. "I didn't know you two were so *close.*"

She knew exactly what he was getting at, and part of her wanted him to stew in his own juices. Of course, the other part of her wanted to preserve Marty's reputation, and her own. "He and my mother were cousins. They were the ones who were close, at least when they were young," she said, trying to keep her tone even. "I barely knew him."

"I see. That's why you were at his funeral. And you have the key because——?"

"He left me his equipment. I found out after, when I spoke to his family at the reception." She corrected herself. "My family."

He stirred his fizzy drink with his straw, evidently sifting through the information. "You know, that's a real shame."

"What is?"

"That you never got to know him."

"Yeah, well. That's how things go." Gina began to wipe the counter vigorously. "I just wish I had gotten to know him better. I'd have liked to learn more about photography."

She watched Roark grimace after taking his first sip of his fizzy drink. "Not to your liking," she said stiffly. She wasn't sure if she'd mixed the syrup and soda water correctly.

"Just missing something." She half expected him to pull out a flask like most other men did, but instead he leaned over and helped himself to a cherry. He picked up what they'd been discussing earlier. "You know, I could help you. With the photography, I mean. Not the soda making. You're on your own with that."

Gina rolled her eyes. "How long have you been taking photographs?" she asked.

His eyes flicked up at her, and she could tell he was weighing his answer. "When I first got home from the war, I was in bad shape." He looked ruefully down at his hand, but didn't hide it from view. "Ran into Marty, and I guess he took pity on me. Long story short, he taught me the basics. Got me connected at the *Tribune*."

"So you worked for the newspaper."

"For a bit. The work wasn't steady. So I joined the force, like my old man had done before me. When they learned I was a photographer, I became the go-to guy, photographing crime scenes. I was on the job when I got injured again, last year." He gestured to his cane. "Gotta use this while my leg heals. Doc says a few more months."

"Was it hard to learn how to take photographs?"

"Not so hard. The trick was learning the best shots and angles, and of course how to develop the film properly. Film can be easily overexposed, with too much light, or underexposed, with too little light." He glanced at her. "Why do you ask?"

"I was just wondering how hard it would be to learn to develop photographs. When I saw Marty's darkroom, I thought about giving it a shot. I guess it's not so hard."

Roark glanced at her again. "No, it's not hard. Especially not for a girl like you."

"A girl like me?" she asked.

"You know—capable."

"Capable?"

"Don't look so insulted," he said, wiping his mouth. "Do you have some photographs that need to be developed?"

"Well, recently I bought a Kodak for my father," she said, lying easily. "He could use a hobby, you know? I thought since I inherited Marty's equipment, I could develop them for him."

"I see." He seemed to be considering something. "Would you like me to teach you?"

"Why would you do that?" she asked, her eyes narrowing a bit. "I could see if someone over at the Kodak store could teach me."

"Sure, you could do that. Except you might want to be careful about who you share your secrets with."

"I can share them with you?"

His eyes held hers. "Yes. I think Marty would have wanted me to help you."

Marty's dying whisper flitted through her mind then, a warning and a reminder about who could be trusted with the camera.

She was about to reply when Little Johnny entered the drugstore. "You, Gina," he said, pointing at her. "The Signora wants to see you."

"Yeah, sure," she said, trying to sound nonchalant, even though her heart had started to beat quickly. What did the Signora want? "I'll be there as soon as I finish up here."

"Kid, when the Signora says she wants to talk to you, then you don't keep her waiting."

Her eyes darted toward Benny, who had lost his habitual

grin and edged to the far end of the counter. She then glanced at Roark, who shrugged, a slight crease of worry appearing in his forehead.

Little Johnny gestured toward the door. "Let's go."

CHAPTER 13

"Gina," the Signora said, all graciousness and charm. "Please come in."

She'd never been fully inside the Signora's private salon before, and as she stepped in, she was immediately taken by its overall sleek elegance. The walls were covered by turquoise paper, and diamond-shaped mirrors were positioned in all directions. In the center there were two emerald-green sofas facing each other, and two shell-shaped peach chairs on either end. A long and low patterned wood table stood in the middle. A beaded curtain led to an alcove, where the Signora presumably changed her clothes each evening.

"Sit down," the Signora commanded, gesturing toward the sofa closest to the door.

When Gina sat down, she realized that the sofas were each outlined by wooden snakes with entwining heads and tails, then saw that the design on the table was also of intertwined snakes. For some reason, she shivered.

Gooch stepped out of the corner then, taking a stance behind the Signora, who had seated herself on the sofa opposite Gina. He cracked his knuckles before crossing his arms.

Gina sat stiffly, her hands on her knees, as she waited for the Signora to speak. The woman's dark gray eyes were calculating as she regarded Gina, much as an animal might regard its prey. Or as a snake might consider a mouse.

"Gina," she said, finally breaking the silence. "How are you?"

The way she asked made Gina stiffen. Her question did not seem casual. "What do you mean, Signora?"

The Signora studied her, making Gina's heart beat uncomfortably. "You seem nervous."

Gina glanced at Gooch, who just gazed back at her impassively. "I hope I am working to your satisfaction, Signora," Gina said, trying to keep her words from sounding rushed. "I know I have made some mistakes, but I am trying my best, I assure you." She pushed her hair back from her face, trying to wipe away some of the moisture that was suddenly forming on her forehead.

The Signora waved her hand. "Don't be alarmed, Gina. Your progress here has been satisfactory."

"Oh." Gina hesitated. "Thank you."

"I wanted to ask after your family."

"My family? My papa, you mean? He is doing well. Most days, at least." Pride kept her from telling them about the difficulties her father had been experiencing of late.

The Signora's face softened ever so slightly. "I am glad to hear it. Your papa and I were friends—of sorts—a very long time ago." She glanced at Gooch, and now it was the Signora who seemed uncomfortable. Then she seemed to recall herself, switching the conversation. "I understand that your flat was broken into recently."

Gina blinked. "Why, yes. It was." She would have stopped

there, but the Signora seemed to be waiting for more information. "We weren't there when it happened, so I'm glad about
that."

"That's fortunate. I hope that you did not lose too much
of value in the robbery?"

"No, nothing, really. My father's radio, unfortunately. I'm
fixing another one for him, since he does enjoy his music. They
didn't seem interested in my mother's jewelry or anything else."
She hesitated, but then decided to ask a question of her own.
"Signora, how did you know about the break-in? I hadn't told
anyone here."

Gooch shifted his stance slightly behind the Signora, his
arms still crossed. His face was like cut granite, not even a
twitch to suggest what he was thinking.

"Word gets around," the Signora said, running her hand
along the arm of the sofa as if stroking the wooden snake. Her
own body seemed coiled, ready to strike. "Tell me, Gina. How
is the *rest* of your family?"

"Signora?"

"Don't be coy, Gina." She leaned closer. "I know Marty
was a relative of yours."

"Yes. My mother's cousin."

"Did you know Marty well before you started working
here?"

"I didn't know him at all." Gina gulped, an unexpected
lump rising in her throat. "I wish I had, though. Before."

"He left you his property?" the Signora pressed. Gina got
the feeling she already knew the answer to every question she
posed.

"Yes," Gina said warily. "By way of my mother."

The Signora smiled at her. Again, Gina couldn't quite

decide if the smile was friendly or not. "I was his landlord, and of course, with his passing, now yours."

"Oh, yes. I just learned that." They seemed to be arriving at the heart of the conversation. "Do you want me to clear out his belongings?" Her heart sank at the thought. She had no idea where she would store them.

"Oh, no, not at all. Marty has paid a few months ahead, so you need not concern yourself about that. Indeed, I only charge him a pittance for the second flat, seeing as how the darkroom is a business expense. You can spend the time you need, sorting through his belongings. In fact, I am willing to extend the contract for a while, so you need not worry."

"Thank you, Signora," Gina said cautiously. There had to be a catch.

"I must warn you." She paused. "We may need to hire a new photographer in due time who would make use of the darkroom."

"Yes, I understand," Gina replied.

"Even more distastefully, I must warn you that given the way Marty died, you may find something unpleasant among his belongings. Perhaps you would like some assistance? There may be some things in his possession that are not—shall we say—appropriate viewing for a girl such as yourself. Perhaps Mr. Gooch can help you."

"Thank you, Signora," she said, knowing that she would not allow Gooch to go through Marty's belongings. "I'll let you know if I require any assistance from Gooch or anyone else."

The Signora looked slightly taken aback. She was clearly not used to people responding in that fashion, and Gina wondered if perhaps she had gone too far. But she was forceful when she spoke again. "Gina, did Marty tell you something? Let you know who he might have been on the outs with?"

Both she and Gooch leaned slightly forward, anticipating her answer.

Gina closed her eyes, trying to shake away the memory of Marty's last breathless words. "No, Signora," she said. "Like I said, I really didn't know him at all."

After getting dressed for the evening and slipping on her tray, Gina could not stop thinking about getting the film in the camera developed. *I need to speak to Roark. He can show me what to do.*

Her chance finally came when Faye went on break. She slipped into the back room, where the ex-servicemen were playing their customary hands of poker. Upon seeing her, a few of them gave her catcalls. She winked at them in return. "Hello, fellows."

"Hey there, dollface," Donny said, holding up his empty glass. "I'm in the mood for a gin rickey."

Gina made her way around the room, exchanging jokes and taking orders. As she had hoped, Roark was seated near Donny, his eyes intent on his cards. His hand was wrapped around an empty glass.

"Another whiskey?" she asked him, reaching for the glass. "Or did the fizzy drink fill you up?"

"What did the Signora want?" he asked, his voice low.

She shrugged. "A bit of this, a bit of that. Wanted to express her condolences on Marty's passing."

He seemed skeptical. "Nothing else?"

She took the glass from him and placed it on her tray. "I take it that's a yes on the whiskey."

He shrugged. "Why not?"

When she returned a few minutes later with the drinks, she bent over slightly so she could speak softly in his ear. In doing so, she caught a whiff of his aftershave. A pleasant smell, not cloying like some. "I've given it some thought," she whispered. "I'd like to take you up on your offer."

She thought she had kept her voice low, but evidently others had caught the exchange. Some of the veterans around them began to hoot and holler.

"All right, Lieutenant!" one of them said. "Way to get back on the horse!"

"She ain't no horse!" Donny said, smiling up at Gina. She smiled back at him, though she could feel her face flushing.

Roark looked a bit embarrassed as well. Standing up, he took her by the elbow and ushered her out. "Monday morning's fine," he said, sounding a bit irritated. "Leave your Sunday for church. If that's your thing."

She raised her eyebrow. Other than Marty's funeral, she hadn't attended church in years. "It's not. But I do need to catch up on my sleep. How about ten a.m. Monday morning? Will that work?"

"All right." He ran his eyes over her body with unexpected familiarity, and she stepped away, feeling uncertain. He coughed. "Make sure you wear something old. You don't want the chemicals ruining your dress."

"Ha! Except for this dress, old is all I've got." When he didn't return her laugh, she rolled her eyes. "I'll see you then. Ten a.m."

"Hey toots what's your hurry?" Donny called. "The lieu-tenant can't have you all to himself!"

"Duty calls. Gotta get back to the front!" she said, tossing the ex-serviceman a little salute, suddenly feeling lighter than she had in a while.

When she walked out of the back room, Gina encountered Faye, who gave her a suspicious look. "All yours," she said, with a little curtsey. "I was only checking that they were fine. I just did a round, but I think that corner table will want some more highballs. They're in a wild mood tonight."

"Don't get too cozy with them," Faye warned her as she passed.

When she returned to the bar, Mr. Darrow called her over. "That man was looking for you," he said, casually lifting one finger off his glass to point to someone behind her. "I believe you spoke with him the other night."

"Yeah?" Equally casually, she turned to follow the direc-tion of his pointing finger. She was not surprised to see Jack, talking to some other men at a corner table. "Oh, him," she said, turning back around.

"Are you having trouble with that man?" Mr. Darrow asked.

She grinned at his concern. "Why, will you bounce him if I am? Take over Gooch's job?"

"Young lady," Mr. Darrow said, sounding more stern this time, "I suggest that if you *are* having trouble with the gentle-man you allow Gooch and Little Johnny to do their jobs."

"Oh, it's nothing I can't handle," Gina said, hoping that was true. She'd already decided that she'd put Jack off for a while, until after she had developed the film. She looked at

Mr. Darrow curiously. "Do you know him? Have you seen him before?"

Mr. Darrow sipped his gin and tonic. "Hard to say. I don't think I've seen him here, but he does seem familiar somehow." He shook his head. "It will come to me."

She began to straighten her tray. "You know all the regulars, don't you?"

"Most, I daresay," Mr. Darrow replied. "Been one myself, ever since the place opened in '26."

"I suppose Mr. Roark is one, too. Do you know him pretty well?"

"Roark? No, he's only been coming here for a few months. He mostly just plays cards with the other ex-servicemen."

"He seems to be here nearly every night now," Gina said, carefully straightening a row of packs of Wrigley's Spearmint gum.

Mr. Darrow glanced at her. "Maybe someone caught his fancy."

"He's hitched, I heard." She started wiping her tray, feeling foolish. Half the men who came in this joint were probably married, even if they didn't act like it. Even Mr. Darrow appeared to be married, judging by the ring on his finger.

"Could be. If so, he's never mentioned a wife." He took another sip of gin. "Could be his past is catching up with him. He's certainly not the first ex-serviceman to find solace in a bottle, and he certainly won't be the last." He tapped his head. "Some soldiers never really recover from war."

Shell shock. Gina remembered her papa talking about it once, when the neighbor across the street, newly returned from the war, had woken up the whole neighborhood every night with his relentless screams. No one seemed to know how to deal with it. Eventually, his relatives came, and he was escorted away to a sanitorium downstate. Even though she knew that shell shock could happen to anyone who'd been through the Great War, it was hard to imagine such weakness in Roark.

Now she had other things to think about. She sauntered up to Jack, where he was still in conversation with the other men. "Pardon me, gentlemen. Need some ciggies? Or perhaps a drink?"

The men looked pointedly at their nearly full drinks, which Jade or Lulu must have recently refreshed, and waved her off.

Smiling, she turned and headed back toward the bar. She'd only taken a few steps away from the table when Jack caught up with her and blocked her path. He stared down at her with icy blue eyes. "All right, Gina, what do you have for me?"

"Nothing yet," she said, trying to sound pert, despite her sudden fear. Maybe she was a bit out of her depth.

Jack grabbed her wrist, startling her and almost causing her to squeal in pain. "Now, I find that real peculiar."

"What?" Gina said, sneaking a glance around for Gooch or Little Johnny. "What's peculiar?"

"Well, I heard on real good authority that you've been asking about photography. That you have access to a darkroom. Marty's darkroom, in fact."

"Oh yeah? Where'd you hear that line?" Gina asked, bringing down her elbow in a way that effectively rammed into his side. She heard a satisfying gasp of pain, but still he hadn't let go.

"Makes me wonder if you have something to develop."

His hand on her wrist tightened a bit more. "I can make it worth your while, if you give me those pictures."

Gina glanced around again, and this time Gooch had noticed her plight and crossed the crowded room. "Mind getting your hand off the lady?" Gooch asked, his tone menacing.

Jack released her wrist, and Gina rubbed at the red marks his tight grip had left on her skin. "This hellcat's no lady," he said.

"You all right?" Gooch said, glancing at Gina.

"I'm fine," she said. "It's all right."

"You get back to serving, then. Me and him, we're gonna have a little chat."

Jack grinned and put his hand on his hip so that his jacket opened up, revealing a sleek gray handgun tucked neatly in its black leather holster. "You don't want to mess with me," he said to Gooch.

"Gina," Gooch said out of the corner of his mouth, "move it."

Hearing the command in his voice, Gina stepped hastily away, bumping directly into Roark.

They both watched as Gooch wrapped Jack's arm neatly around his back, and propelled him up the stairs. Out of nowhere, Little Johnny materialized and helped usher Jack out.

The few guests who had noticed the confrontation turned back to dancing and sipping their bright-colored drinks. Just another night at the Third Door.

"What was that about?" Roark asked, his mouth close to Gina's ear.

"People think I'm easy pickings. Gotta learn that I'm not."

Gina moved away then, heading back to pick up some drink orders from Billy Bottles. She didn't know if Roark was watching her, but when she looked around again, he was gone.

CHAPTER 14

Trying to keep the chill morning air from entering the house, Gina peeked out onto the porch to see if the milk had been delivered yet. Sure enough, two full bottles of milk were waiting, along with something else that had been covered by an old gray blanket. Pulling on her coat, she stepped out onto the porch in her slippered feet and pulled off the blanket.

"What in the world?" she said, staring down in surprise.

The object turned out to be a radio. But not just any radio—the one that had been stolen from their home a few days earlier. Crouching down beside it, she traced the familiar scratches along its oak surface before turning it this way and that. It appeared to be intact. There was no note or anything to indicate who had taken it—or more oddly, why it had been returned.

Standing on the porch steps, she peered up and down the street, on the off chance the person who had left it for them might still be lurking about. But the street was still in the last sleepy stages of dawn, where only the deliverymen were out and about.

Trying not to feel ungrateful, Gina lugged the radio back

into its customary position in the living room. It seemed perfectly fine when she plugged it in, and after tuning the dials, the sounds of the Monday morning exercise show filled the room. "Breathe in, breathe out," the host said. "Now march in place..."

Hearing the health drills, her father appeared in the living room, wearing his tattered blue robe. "Where'd that come from?" he asked.

"Oh, Papa, can you believe it? Someone gave us our radio back!" She beamed, thinking he would be happy.

"That's all great and good," he said, "but who was the scoundrel who took it in the first place?"

Gina just shook her head. It was all very odd indeed.

Gina mounted the stairs to Marty's flat, holding a small tin of biscuits she'd made earlier. She was still pondering the mystery of the radio as she rounded the second-floor landing. As before, the elderly lady opened the crack of the door and peered out, not saying a word. "Good morning," Gina called, but the woman just shut the door. *Am I going to be getting a visit from Policewoman Doyle now?* She wanted to ask, but didn't.

Roark hadn't gotten there yet, so she let herself into 3A, taking a few minutes to straighten some of the shelves. She spent a little bit of time poking through Marty's drawers, trying to see if there was anything that might shed some insight into his life—or death. Marty appeared to have been a fairly solitary person. Here and there were some odd art deco knickknacks, mostly sad-looking porcelain clowns. After a first cursory glance through every drawer, she began to look more slowly through his clothes, discovering that he kept them folded and carefully maintained. Since Marty and her father were of different sizes, she thought maybe she'd take the clothes to Hull House, to be distributed among the needy.

When Roark arrived a little while later, she felt a bit self-conscious as she led him into Marty's darkroom flat across the corridor. "Here's my camera," she said, handing Roark the Kodak, hoping to skip over any awkward chitchat.

He looked at it, turning it over in his hands. "Had this a while?" he asked, running his finger along the worn surface. He seemed surprised.

"I bought it used," she replied, carefully not adding that she'd acquired it just a few days before. She didn't want to give him any reason to connect her purchase of the camera with Marty's missing one. "I wanted to start my dad on a hobby, and this seemed as good a time as any to do so."

"So you said." He handed it back to her.

Gina gestured to the kitchen area that Marty had converted to the darkroom. "This way."

Roark nodded. "Yes, I know." He opened the door. "Come on, then."

Gina followed him into the darkroom and watched as he looked through the cabinets. "Good, good," he muttered, rubbing his hands together. Like the other time she had been there, the room was cold. "At least Marty kept the place well stocked."

Without saying anything more, he began to move about busily, setting up several long, shallow pans next to one another, pulling down the three large jugs marked A, B, and C. She stepped back to give him space, but they were still very close together. After he filled one of the pans with water, he opened one of the jugs and poured a strong-smelling chemical

into the pan. Gina wrinkled her nose, and her eyes teared up
a bit.

"All right," he said, turning back to her. "Most importantly, you can't let any light touch this film. You understand?"

"Yeah, I get it."

"First, you need to wind up the film like this." He mimicked a winding movement.

"Yeah, Benny showed me that already."

After she wound up the film, he continued. "Before I turn
off the lights, I'll explain the steps. First I'm going to crack
open the case that holds the film, and I'm going to cut off one
end of the film and then the other with these scissors." He
pointed to a shiny pair of shears on the darkroom table. "Then
we'll be able to load the film onto the reel. You need to make
sure you handle the edges as little as possible."

He picked up the reel. "Then we snake the film through
the reel so that we'll be able to wind it up onto the reel. After
that, we'll be able to turn on a little light."

"All that without the lights on?"

"Yes, of course." His tone was matter-of-fact, not conde-
scending.

Gina relaxed. He did seem to know what he was doing,
and she needed to learn everything she could from him. *Eye
on the prize,* she could almost hear her papa saying. She didn't
realize she had clenched her hands into fists until Roark
looked at her.

"What on earth are you doing?" he asked.

"Nothing. Let's get going."

"If you say so," he said, flicking off the lights, plunging
the room into darkness.

Gina sucked in her breath. She'd never been in a room so dark. She couldn't even see her hand in front of her face and could only sense Roark's presence, in a way that made her unexpectedly nervous.

"Are you all right?" He sounded a bit impatient. "Not afraid of the dark, are you?"

"No. So first we crack open the case to remove the film, right?" Her words sounded overly loud. She began to feel around on the table in front of her, nearly knocking it off the table.

"Easy, bearcat," he said. She felt him take her hand and guide it to the opener. "Place it there. Yes, that's right. Now, when I say to, you're going to crack it open—"

Before he was through speaking, Gina had already done it. "Now we cut off the ends of the film with the scissors, right?" She picked up the scissors. "Better step away."

After carefully snipping both edges, she picked up the reel and tried to thread the film as he had described earlier.

"Make sure you only touch the edges," he reminded her. "Otherwise you'll ruin the film before we start."

"I get it," she muttered. Carefully she felt the reel, trying to find a way to thread the end. It was proving more difficult than she expected, and after several tries, she heard him chuckle.

"How about you let me help you?" Again he reached for her hands and very carefully turned the reel. "See, you can feel the threads here," he said. "Now gently tuck the end inside . . . that's right. Now you can wrap the rest of the film around it. Careful, careful."

Holding her breath, she rolled up the film. He was still very close to her, so that her shoulder was very nearly in his chest. "Not bad for your first time," he said. It sounded like he was smiling.

"I'm capable, remember?"

"I remember. Now we put the reel inside this container and add the developer. We have to swish it around for a few minutes—let me set the timer—and then we dump it down the drain. You have to be careful not to do this too hard . . . yes, that's right. You've got it." He took a step back. "You changed your perfume."

Startled, she almost stopped swirling, but then stubbornly didn't reply. There was something intimate—searching, even—in his tone, and she wasn't sure if she liked it.

"It smells like lilacs," he mused. Then, growing more businesslike, he continued, "All right, now we add the stop bath—this keeps the negative from continuing to develop. We swish around some more, for another minute." When that was done, it was time to rinse the film off in water. He flipped the lights back on. "All done." He took the strip of twelve negatives from her. She could see images on it. Carefully he shook the strip free of excess water.

"Good news," he said, holding the strip up. "There are some images on here. You didn't ruin the film."

A thrill of victory soared through her, and she darted closer to look.

"Nope, no peeking," he said, taking a clip from the table. He affixed the strip of negatives to the line. "They need to dry first, and we hang them from the line over the sink like so. Then we can use the enlarger and make some prints."

"How long will it take for them to dry?"

"Oh, a few hours," he replied. "Can I take you somewhere for breakfast?"

She looked doubtfully at her unfashionable old dress, feeling decidedly frumpy. "How about I make some coffee in Marty's flat? I've also got some biscuits."

"All right, then."

They went over to Marty's kitchen in the other flat, and Gina found a plate for the biscuits while the water boiled for the coffee. "I haven't got any cream. Or butter for the biscuits. I think there's sugar in the tin."

"That's all right. I've had worse. Soldier, remember?" Roark wandered around looking at Marty's photographs, only returning when the coffee was ready.

She continued to ask him some questions about film: what it meant to be overexposed and underexposed, how a flash worked exactly, how much light was needed for different kinds of pictures.

Finally, after he had explained some things, he held up his hands with a slight grin. "I'll be right back," he said, picking up the key she had left by the door on his way out. She heard him unlock the door to the other flat. In a moment, he came back with some negatives that Marty had already created, along with a newspaper that had been left behind. "If there's not very much detail and a lot of shadow, then the pictures were underexposed in the development process," he explained. "If the images were overly bright, then they were overexposed." He held the strip of negatives to the light. "Here's a trick. Try holding a newspaper up behind these negatives, like this. If you can read the paper, then that means the negatives were overexposed."

"I see." Then she thought about how Marty had recorded his prints in his notebook by describing their content. "Isn't it possible to write directly on a negative, before the film has been exposed? To record a date or location, or something else you'd want to remember."

"Yeah, Kodak makes a thing they call an autographic camera," he replied. "I don't like it, though. It can mess up the film before it's even out of the camera. Purely for amateurs." He took a bite of the biscuit. She half expected him to grimace as he had after he had the fizzy soda, but instead he ate it, licking his fingers. "Delicious," he said, appearing lost in thought.

An odd contentment stole over her then, as she contemplated his unshaven jaw out of the corner of her eye. It had been a long time since she had sat with a man in such casual intimacy. In the past, her fiancé would stop by their flat for a quick meal, but he tended to converse more with her papa about the Cubs or whatever else was important to him on any given day.

Watching him reach for a second biscuit, she idly wondered if his wife baked.

At the thought, though, she drew herself up with a start. Did his wife even know that Roark was here? Spending time with another woman, alone in her flat? "Let's finish this tomorrow," she said, her sudden feelings of guilt making her tone harsher than she intended.

He looked slightly confused. "I thought you wanted to learn how to make prints. They should be almost dry now."

"Oh, I have other things I need to do," she said, not meeting his eye.

He glanced down at his watch. It was almost ten thirty. "Yes, I suppose so." He stood up and placed his cup and saucer by the sink, a surprising courteous gesture. His tone was cool when he turned back to her. "How about I come back tomorrow? Then we'll create the prints from the negatives. It won't take too long. No more than two hours, before we hang them up to dry. Then you'll have learned everything I can teach you."

Now feeling guilty about her abrupt dismissal, Gina tried to press more biscuits on him. He waved them off, as well as her thanks, and walked quickly out the door, as if he couldn't bear to be there even another minute.

Around four the next day, she returned to Marty's flat to find Roark waiting by the door, impatient to get started on the next stage of the printing process.

"All right," he said, examining the negatives. "First we clean them with a little rubbing alcohol. Then we carefully cut them into three strips of four." He pushed the scissors toward her, and she did as he instructed.

He pointed to a large piece of equipment. "This is called the enlarger. We use this to start the enlarging process. This is where we transfer the negatives to photographic paper, which is how we make the prints."

Laying out three pans, he filled one with developer, one with the stop bath, and the other with water. Each pan had a pair of tongs in front of it. "This time we can work in red light," he said, pulling a chain and turning on the single red light hanging from the ceiling. With some relief, she could see him fairly clearly.

Picking up the first strip of negatives, he placed it in the enlarger. "See, we place a sheet of photographic paper here, look through here, alter the aperture as needed for the right amount of light—let's start with the smallest amount of light, because I can see these were taken outside," he pointed to a dial on the side, "and focus using these buttons to ensure that the image is sharp and clear. Then we set the timer when we're ready and all the image to be projected onto the paper where it will be captured. Usually about thirty seconds. We'll do a test first."

He took the sheet of photographic film and slid it carefully into the first pan of developer. Immediately an image of Gina's upstairs neighbor, which she had taken when she first got the camera, started to emerge. "We agitate it carefully, in a rolling motion, like this—be careful not to splash. Just don't get any of the developer into the other pans or it will mess everything up." He set the timer. "We have to do this for a minute, and then we move it to the stop bath with the tongs."

When the time was up, he slid the developed image into the stop bath. "This will take a few minutes," he said. "You can start enlarging the second image now, as I showed you."

Gina began to look through the enlarger at the second negative, an image of Mrs. Hayford's dog.

"So," Roark said casually, "you got this camera for your papa, did you?"

She thought a touch of honesty would ease the lie. "Yes, he hasn't been well. I thought photography might be an interesting hobby for him."

"Are you planning to set up your own darkroom for him, then? Or are you planning to stay here?"

"I haven't decided. I may not have many options. The Signora says they'll be hiring another photographer at some point. I don't need to move his things out right away."

"Interesting." He moved the first photograph to the bath of water. "Now we'll leave this here for a while." He watched as she carefully put the second photograph into the developer and began to agitate it. "Your father took these recently, I take it?"

"Yes," she said, lying easily.

They continued in silence for a while. Roark had filled a second pan with water, so eventually all of the prints ended up getting rinsed off at once. "Now we hang them on the drying line."

As they hung up the prints on the same line where they had hung the negatives earlier, Gina quietly gloated over the images, delighted by how well a few of them turned out. She'd taken some around her neighborhood, and some down at Navy Pier, focusing on boats on the water, seagulls, and the grand building at the eastern end of the pier.

Standing beside her, he said, "Your father has quite an eye."

Though pleased, she tried to suppress her smile. "Thanks. I'll let him know."

"Just to remind you, it's pretty easy to ruin film without the proper equipment."

"I understand."

"So if you have another roll of film that you want to develop, you need to be really careful."

"I *understand*," she said again.

"Just so you do," he said. He glanced at his watch. "You'd better get ready for your shift. It's almost six o'clock."

After he left, she locked the darkroom door and entered 3A, carrying the bag of clothes she'd brought with her. Even though no one was there, she stepped into Marty's bedroom to change into her customary dress and fix her hair. As she moved around, the key she'd been wearing caught on a tiny neck hair, reminding her of it's presence and that she still hadn't seen anything in Marty's flats that it might unlock.

A glance at the clock on the wall alerted her that it was time to head down to the Third Door. With a sigh, she locked the door of Marty's flat behind her. Maybe tomorrow she'd discover what that key opened.

Gina was leaning over to serve some drinks a few hours later when she heard a commotion over by the stairs, including several outraged female shrieks. Craning her neck, she could just make out Mimi, without her boa this time, holding up an empty cocktail glass in a triumphant way. A satisfied smirk could be seen on her face as the crowd around her yukked it up.

"What in the world—?" Gina asked. She could see now that another woman was completely soaked. Her face was streaming with some liquid, and Gina could see a cherry in her hair. One of her friends was dabbing at her face, and another seemed to be trying to pull her in the direction of the ladies' room.

Faye and Jade were both snickering. "Looks like the mistress and the wife have finally met," Jade said, with one hand half covering her mouth to keep her voice from carrying to the wrong ears.

"Ah," Gina said. "I guess Mimi didn't need that photograph after all."

"Marty's photograph?" Jade asked. "What do you mean? Do *you* know where it is? Jack said he'd pay me a pretty penny if I found it for him."

"Nah, I don't know."

"Really? Did you look around his flat?" Faye asked, her

voice syrupy sweet. "I'd have done that first thing. Being you're his *heir* and all."

Jade took a step closer. "I could help you look. Jack was willing to pay some real scratch. We could go halves."

"Not anymore, I'd bet," Gina said, instinctively taking a step back. She gestured toward where the fracas had just occurred. "Looks like the secret's out."

"Besides," Faye added, "Big Mike wouldn't like you working your own angle with the patrons."

Gina was dabbing on a bit more rouge when she heard the sound of someone heaving behind one of the doors in the ladies' room. A moment later one of the women who'd surrounded Jack's wife earlier came stumbling out. She looked a bit green.

"Can I call you a cab, miss?" Gina asked, watching the woman splash water on her face. "You're not looking so good."

The woman glanced up at her, holding the sink firmly in both hands. "Hey, doll, you're filling in Dorrie's spot?"

Gina nodded. "Yeah, you knew her?

The woman looked a little sad. "Oh, Dorrie. Not real smart, but sweet. Tried to be tougher than she looked, but she wasn't fooling anyone." She began to pinch her cheeks, trying to give her face a better color. "You heard what happened to her, I bet. A real shame."

"Yeah."

"Name's Maxine," the woman said, pursing her lips in the mirror before applying a bright red color. "I used to work in one of these places a few years back. Knew a lot of dumb Doras, just like Dorrie." She giggled. "Our gin joint was over on Wells. The Drys shut it down in '27."

Slipping her tube of lipstick back inside her handbag, she added, "I met my guy there. A real dewdropper, he turned out to be." She shook the expensive charm bracelets on her arm. "These were the best things I got out of that deal."

"Charming," Gina said, laughing along with her. "More charming than him, I bet."

"You said it." Maxine began to fix her waves carefully with a comb. "I guess we all come to the same end, regardless of who does us in. I'm telling you, get yourself a husband before you catch the eye of the wrong guy, like I did. 'Specially if you want a kid or two. Won't get 'em with a guy from a place like this. If you do, he'll drop you real fast."

Gina shrugged. "Better off without a guy like that."

Maxine took another long swig of her cocktail. "Just heard about Marty, though. A real shame."

"Yes," Gina said.

"Shame the Signora got her hooks into him," she said. Only she slurred her words, and it sounded more like *Shame the Sin-yoor-ah gotter hoos in him.*

"What do you mean?" Gina asked.

"Oh, doll, you know how these places work," Maxine said, still struggling to enunciate. Her eyes were shutting. "Or at least you should. She owned the man." She hiccupped then, the action bringing a dazed grin to her face. "I'm *so-o-o* zozzled."

"I had no idea," Gina said with a straight face. Why did women always have to tell everyone how drunk they were? "How about I point you in the direction of your friends."

At that, Maxine began to giggle. "Did you see Norma got that drink poured over her head? She had a cherry in her h-hair!"

"Yeah, I saw."

Maxine rolled her eyes. "It's that two-timing Jack's fault. I don't see the fuss, personally."

As she helped Maxine slosh back toward her friends, Gina thought about what the woman had said. What *had* Marty been doing for the Signora? This was something she had to figure out.

CHAPTER 15

Gina paused as she reached the second-floor landing on her way to Marty's flat, another roll of the film she'd taken at Navy Pier in her embroidered handbag. The door of 2A had creaked open, and the woman stepped out into the hallway. The woman's grayish blue housecoat had seen better days, and her drab yellow scarf covered a gray bun, peasant-style.

Stepped straight out of the Old World, Gina thought. With her hawkish eyes and shoulders that hunched up like a vulture's, the woman looked formidable. A strong and forceful presence not to be ignored.

"Hello," Gina said, standing a bit straighter.

"Who are you?" The woman's accent was thick. Russian.

"Gina." Then, when the woman continued to stare at her with dark and beady eyes, Gina added her surname. "Ricci."

"You were here yesterday. And the day before."

"I have a key," Gina said. Though she bristled at the woman's accusing tone, she thought it would be better to explain. "I am—was—a relative of Marty's. A close one."

"Hmmm." Again the scrutiny. "Police catch his killer?"

"Not yet."

The woman shrugged. "The police in this city!..." She muttered something in Russian.

"What did you say? What did that mean?"

"Just something we say in Russian. *The eye can see it, but the tooth can't bite it.*"

Gina pondered that a moment. "Did you ever see—?" She broke off, trying to figure out what she was asking. *What? What could the woman have seen?* "Anything?" she added a bit lamely.

The woman stayed silent. This conversation was going nowhere fast.

Gina sought to break through the impasse. Behind the woman, she noticed an electric lamp on the table, flicking on and off. "Does your lamp always do that? Maybe I could look at it for you." At the woman's skeptical expression, Gina continued. "My papa, he fixes things. He trained me, too. I could look at it. Maybe set it right?"

Without a word, the woman stepped aside to let her enter the room.

The apartment was dark, its windows covered with heavy curtains that likely provided warmth in the winter but let little light in, creating a cavelike and secretive effect. All around the room there were porcelain and cloisonné knickknacks, and several shelves were adorned with Russian nesting dolls. On one wall was a wedding portrait of a young woman dressed in white and a man in a suit with a tall black hat. Both were ramrod straight, only their sleeves touching, forced smiles on both their faces. There was something a little familiar about both figures.

"How beautiful," Gina said, peering at the features of the woman in the photograph. "Is that you?"

"*Ja,*" the woman replied. "This man, he was my husband, Anton." Her eyes softened as she looked at the stern young man in the portrait. "May he rest in peace."

Gina picked up the lamp and examined it. "I'm just going to unplug it." When she did the room became even darker, and with a sigh the woman pushed open the curtains, allowing the midafternoon light to stream through the dirty glass. "I am Mrs. Lesky."

Taking the lamp shade off, Gina sat down on an over-stuffed chair without asking. Mrs. Lesky watched her.

"Were you and Marty neighbors for a very long time?"

Mrs. Lesky shrugged. "What is a long time? A few years, yes, we were neighbors."

"Are you friends with Marty's sister? Nancy Doyle?"

"Acquaintances, perhaps." There was a slyness to her voice.

Gina looked at the telephone on the table beside the sofa. "Did you call her when I came the other day?"

The woman was still watching her. "I may have made a call, that is so."

"To the Signora, too?"

"Ah, the Signora. No, not her. She's been good enough to me over the last few years, that is true. Still, my rent is high. Thank God, my son pays what I cannot. He works for her."

"Your son works for her, Mrs. Lesky?" Gina glanced back at the photograph, studying the faces again. She remembered Ned's rhyme the day she began at the Third Door. "Oh! Your son is Little Johnny."

"I do not call him by that name. To me, he has not been 'little' for a very long time."

"No, not so little," Gina agreed, peering inside the fixture.

Unscrewing the bulb, she could see that a wire had slipped from its position. Easy enough to fix if she had the proper tools. "Do you own pliers, by any chance?" she asked.

"Pliers?" the woman asked, and then her brow cleared. She opened a drawer in a cabinet and handed Gina a small tool.

With a few twists, Gina was able to rewire the lamp. After screwing the bulb back into its stocket, she carefully replaced the lamp and plugged it back in. The lamp turned on, without a single flicker.

The faintest smile crossed Mrs. Lesky's lips. *"Spasibo,"* she said. "Thank you." Crossing the room, she opened the door. "I have delayed you long enough."

As Gina started to walk out, Mrs. Lesky touched her sleeve. "About Mr. Doyle, he asked me once about life under the tsar. Anton and me, we fled after Tsar Alexander II was assassinated, for there was no place for us. He said he understood that."

"Why?" Gina asked. "What did he mean?"

"Marty was not one to tell the tales, that I know." Her eyes flicked back to her husband's portrait, as if seeking confirmation. "Of course, as my husband discovered, secrets have a way of getting out." With that she closed the door.

Having taken her leave of Mrs. Lesky, Gina let herself into Marty's darkroom. The air in the room was silent and still, and almost felt like it had been waiting for her to return. "Don't go blooey, Gina," she said out loud. "Get ahold of yourself."

Slowly she began to lay out the chemicals, water, scissors, reel, canister, and other equipment, just as Roark had shown her, so she could easily reach everything in the darkness. The

black curtains were closed tightly over the windows. Everything was in place.

She continued to gaze down at the equipment, flexing and
unflexing her fingers. As before, Marty's flat was quite cold,
but she didn't want to ask the Signora to adjust the heat. She
didn't want anyone asking her questions about what she might
be doing in Marty's flat, particularly what she might be doing
in Marty's darkroom. When she had a chance, she'd look over
the furnace and the boiler and see if she might be able to figure
out the problem for herself.

At the moment, though, staring down at the equipment,
she knew she had to quit stalling.

"Just begin already," she told herself.

Taking a deep breath, Gina turned off the lights and
opened the canister of film, hoping that she was doing everything as Roark had explained. As she settled down, she slipped
into her customary focused mode, preparing and mixing and
washing the chemicals over the exposed film as easily as she
could fix a radio.

After a while, images were emerging in the negatives, just
as they had the other day with Roark. It was then she realized she'd been clenching her teeth, and she unlocked her jaw
and rubbed at the joint.

Some of the images, she could tell already, were going to
be difficult to discern. She wondered if she had overexposed
them when she had pointed her camera in the direction of
the sun. "I'll worry about that later," she said, as she washed
off the negatives and hung them over the tub to dry.

Gina came back the next morning to make the prints from
the now-dried negatives. After she cleaned them with alcohol

and cut them into strips, she looked at them in the enlarger. Disappointed, she could see that some were certainly overexposed, and several were overdeveloped. Four of the twelve frames were worth trying to make into photographs, and, after several more tries making prints, she began to figure out how to sharpen their focus. She also experimented a bit with the length of time that the prints were exposed to light, as well as how long she left them in the developer. Most were a mess.

Still, a few had turned out beautifully. She wondered what Roark would think of this first batch of developed photographs. Then a slightly annoyed thought chased the first. Why did it matter what he thought? Feeling impatient with herself, she left Marty's flat to make dinner for her papa before her shift at the Third Door.

As she passed by the bakery, Gina heard a familiar whistle from above. Not surprisingly, she could see Emil grinning down at her from his customary spot on the balcony.

"Hey there!" she called, waving at the boy. "Where's Zosia today?"

"Helping Mama and Papa in the bakery," he replied, his grin growing broader. Clearly he thought that he'd got the better end of the deal.

A customer stepped out of the bakery then, and a wave of sweet cinnamon air wafted over her. "Mmmm," she murmured, and on a whim entered the shop.

Zosia was at the counter fixing a display of delicate cookies, keeping them precariously stacked one on top of the other. Seeing Gina, she smoothed her apron and gave her a bright smile. "Hello, Miss Gina. How may I help you?"

"I thought I might get a nice pastry for my papa." Her eyes ran over the glass case, her mouth watering at the sight of all the enticingly displayed sweets on the doily-covered trays. "Did you arrange all these? You're very good at it."

Zosia shrugged. "I suppose. I'd like to learn how to bake them, but Mama says I'm too young. They don't want me to waste the batter."

Gina nodded. Eggs, milk, and sugar were certainly dear.

"I'm going to show them, though," Zosia said, lowering her tone. "You'll see."

"Show them what?" Gina asked, drawn into the girl's conspiratorial ways.

"I'm taking a cooking class at Hull House," Zosia replied. "They don't mind if I make a mess."

"Keen," Gina said. The mention of Hull House reminded her of the temperance workers, Dorrie's mother, and, of course, Dorrie.

Zosia pushed a porcelain tray of crumbled pastries toward her. "Please, try."

Gina picked a bit of strawberry tart from the tray and popped it into her mouth. "Gee, that's good!"

A look of pride came over Zosia's face. "I told you," she said. "Mama and Papa, they make the best *fraisier.*"

"Indeed. I don't even know why you'd need candy from Dorrie," Gina said conversationally, licking her fingers.

"We like American candy. Milky Ways and Charleston Chews," Zosia said, wiping away some crumbs. "And sometimes, Dorrie gave us money, too."

Gina pointed to the *fraisier.* "I'll take two of those for my papa."

"Ten cents."

Gina opened her change purse and pushed a quarter across the counter. "Keep the change. I just have a quick question."

Zosia eyed the outlandish tip and then searched Gina's face, a look of comprehension crossing her own features. Then, with a resigned sigh, she put the quarter in the till and slipped fifteen cents into her own pocket.

"Can you tell me why Dorrie was giving you money?" Gina asked.

Zosia's shoulders relaxed slightly, as if she'd been bracing herself for a different question. "I suppose it doesn't matter now. She wanted me and Emil to just let her know about things we might see from her balcony."

"Oh yeah? Like what?"

Zosia giggled. "Like people kissing. We saw Dorrie and Ned kiss sometimes, when he'd walk her home. She just laughed when we told her. Said she'd give us extra candy to keep that to ourselves, though, since she wasn't supposed to be stepping out with anyone who worked with her."

"Anything else?"

"Sometimes we saw Faye kissing someone. Under the streetlight. But then one time she slapped him, so we thought maybe they'd called it splits."

"Did you know who the man was?" Gina asked. "Was he a customer here?"

"I think so. At least, I'd seen him before." She gestured for Gina to come closer. "But we saw something else, too, which you might find interesting." She looked expectantly at the change purse in Gina's hand.

Sighing, Gina duly pushed across another quarter, which the girl deftly pocketed. "We saw Big Mike kissing someone, too," she whispered, looking furtively around. "It wasn't the Signora."

"Did the Signora know, do you think?"

"I-I don't know." The little stammer gave her away. Zosia must have wondered if she'd done the right thing. She tied the pastry box with a bit of brown string and pushed it across the counter to Gina, thanking her in Polish.

Gina took the hint and left the bakery. As she walked home, she thought about what Zosia had told her. So Dorrie had been paying the kids for secrets. Questions began to bubble up. Who else might Dorrie have paid for information, and had she known a secret that got her killed?

Gina stood regarding Hull House, a bit put off by the looming exterior of the Italianate mansion. The brown-brick settlement house was enormous and stretched the entire length of the block. Since her conversation with Zosia the day before, she'd been thinking she'd like to learn more about Dorrie, and talking to her mother might be a good place to start. Maybe Mrs. Edwards would be there with the other reformers, or she might be able to sniff out an address for her home.

The plan had seemed so reasonable when she woke up that morning. Now she was having second thoughts and began to turn away.

Just then someone called out to her from the porch. "Miss! Wait!" An older woman dressed in an old-style white dress hurried down the walkway. "Is there something we can help you with?" She glanced at Gina's stomach in a knowing way. "A place we can send you?"

"Oh, no, ma'am. Not that," Gina said, speaking quickly.

"I mean, yes, you can help me. I was wondering if Mrs. Edwards might be here. I know that she volunteers here."

"Oh, Mrs. Edwards? I believe she's in the back, sorting old clothes for the poor. Why don't you come into the parlor and I'll fetch her?"

The woman ushered Gina inside the house, and she found herself alone in a very grand parlor filled with overstuffed Victorian-era sofas. She didn't feel comfortable sitting down, so instead she positioned herself by the window, looking out onto the street.

A few minutes later, Mrs. Edwards came into the room. She stopped short when she saw Gina, but then extended her hand in greeting. She did not have the same wild look in her eyes as when Gina had first seen her in the tea shop, but there was great sorrow and despair etched into her cheeks. "You," she said. "I know you. From the *tea shop*." There was a tinge of sarcasm to her voice. "Who sent you? The Signora?"

"No, Mrs. Edwards. No one sent me," she said. Deciding to be straightforward she added, "I do work at the Third Door, though."

The woman gestured to the sofa. "Pray, sit." When Gina had settled herself uncomfortably next to her, Mrs. Edwards asked, "Did you know Dorrie?" Her hopeful look was hard to bear.

Gina fiddled her hands in her lap. "No, I didn't. I just started, after New Year's Eve."

"You replaced her."

"Yes." There didn't seem any point in denying that fact.

"Oh. She was my only daughter. Did you know that?"

Gina shook her head.

Mrs. Edwards brushed a tear away. "Tell me. Why are you

here? I don't know you. And you didn't know my daughter. Why did you ask to see me?" Though she struggled to remain composed, Gina detected a note of agitation in her voice.

"Mrs. Edwards," Gina said, trying to keep her tone soothing, "what do you think happened to your daughter? To Dorrie?"

She saw the muscles in the woman's cheek tighten. "It was the alcohol and working in *that place* that ruined her, you know. I never wanted her to work there. Those owners lack souls, and they don't care who they are corrupting."

"Oh," Gina said, not sure what else to say. The woman had looked calm, but now she was taking on that crazed look she'd had the day she'd lambasted the Signora at the tea room. *Mad*, Ned had said.

"Her daddy came home drunk every night of the week, did you know that? Especially on Saturdays. Thought it was his right to drink up all my hard-earned washing money. Said it was a man's right to enjoy the fruits of his labor. What about my labor? He did whatever he wanted when he came home." She gave Gina a fierce look. "I mean anything." She grimaced. "I thought Dorrie understood the dangers of drink. Thought I raised her better than that. Then she turned around and betrayed me to the quick when she ran off to work at that *den of iniquity*." She spat out the last three words.

Gathering her nerve, Gina posed the question she'd been rehearsing in her mind. "Mrs. Edwards, that day at the tea shop, you said something to the Signora. You said you knew she had asked Dorrie to do *something* that ended up with her being killed. What did you mean by that?"

The woman brushed a tear from her cheek. "The police tried to tell me that she was just in the wrong place at the wrong time. Pshaw. I know she was being asked to deliver messages."

"Messages? What sort of messages?"

"She never told me exactly. I know she spent a lot of time with gents, too. I didn't like that. She wasn't raised that way."

"Gents? Was there someone in particular?"

Pulling out a handkerchief, she blew her nose heartily into the bleached white square. "Well, there was that piano man, of course. *Ned.* Not a *serious* man at all." Her disapproval was complete. "Only after a *good time* with my daughter."

Gina swallowed. "Do you think Ned might have—"

"Killed Dorrie?" Grimacing, Mrs. Edwards finished the thought. "Nah. He doesn't have it in him. I'm telling you—it has something to do with those messages she was running for those Castallazzos. Someone killed the messenger. My darling girl." Her eyes flooded with tears.

Gina looked around the parlor, searching for something to say. "I heard she had a beautiful voice."

"Dorrie used to sing the sweetest little songs here, before the devil found her," she said, pointing at the piano. "Guess that's how she got connected with that 'Neddy' in the first place. Him a crooner, her with tunes and kicks. Lord knows I loved my daughter, but there wasn't any calming her down. Hot to trot she was, and the Castallazzos knew that. Took advantage of her, they did." She stared down at Gina. "That place is the devil's lounge—best you remember that, girl, or you'll follow the same sad path of my daughter."

Gina edged toward the door. "I'll be going now."

The woman's eyes had taken on that unfocused look they'd had when Gina first saw her. "The Castallazzos will get theirs, though, I promise you that."

A chill went down Gina's spine. "What do you mean?" she asked, backing up another step.

"Well, I'm not going to take a pineapple to the place. I'll leave the bombings to others." Her laugh was bitter. "There will be a reckoning for their sins, mark my words. In the hereafter, I have no doubt, but here on this temporal plane, too. They will cross the wrong person and it will all come crashing down."

On her way out the door, Gina nearly ran into two women entering Hull House. One was an elderly but spry-looking woman, perhaps in her early eighties, and the other was a smartly dressed, athletic young woman.

"Slowly, child, slowly," the older woman admonished her. Gina recognized Jane Addams, the founder of Hull House, having seen her around the neighborhood her entire life. "We are busy, but not so much that we should run into each other."

The other, more stylishly dressed woman smiled down at Gina. With a sense of shock, Gina recognized her as well. This was none other than Amelia Earhart, the famed aviator. "Pray, tell us. Are you here for one of Miss Addams's fine programs? I should like to hear all about it. We're looking to do more at our sister settlement house in New York City."

Gina didn't know what to say, her tongue having escaped her.

Miss Addams sounded stern. "Speak up, girl. I was just telling Miss Earhart about the progress so many of the young women have been making. Do not make a liar of me."

"Now, now, Jane," Miss Earhart soothed her. "You've scared the girl out of her wits."

"She works at one of those moonshine parlors," Mrs. Edwards said from behind them. "Same one that killed my daughter."

Miss Addams and Miss Earhart looked her over. Gina braced herself for an angry harangue, but none came. Instead, Miss Addams touched her arm. "There's always time, child," she said. "We do not seek to condemn."

"Just to educate," Miss Earhart added, her blue eyes appraising. "Those places do kill."

"Indeed they do," Mrs. Edwards said pointedly. "Pray heed what I told you."

"I'd best be off," Gina said, before turning and practically running down the path, away from Hull House.

CHAPTER 16

As luck would have it, Gina had to wait almost a full day before she was able to return to Marty's flat with a third roll of film, full of pictures she'd taken on her way. Though the weather had been a balmy forty-three degrees the day before, winds blowing in from Canada off Lake Michigan had plunged Chicago into another freezing cold spell. Everywhere the streets were frozen, even iced over in patches, making it perilous to get around.

When she arrived at Marty's flat, she began to develop the new roll of practice film in the darkroom. This time, everything proceeded at a much quicker pace, and she soon was pleased to see more details emerge in the negatives as they developed in the bath. Feeling more confident that this time she had exposed and developed the film properly, she mentally applauded herself.

While the negatives hung to dry, she went back into Marty's flat and put on a kettle for tea. As she waited for the water to boil, she idly looked through some of the stacks of photographs again, this time examining their composition and form with a more critical eye. She looked at the images of

people as well, many taken out on the street. He'd taken a few
of Mrs. Lesky, too, one catching a poignant expression on the
woman's face as she gazed at a framed picture of her husband.
A wonderful image, to be sure, and Gina thought she might
give it to Mrs. Lesky.

After a while, she began to notice something surprising
about the photographs. Not a single one had been taken at
the Third Door. They'd been taken, for the most part, outside in the open, far away from the place.

Why was that? After all, she'd seen Marty taking photographs in the speakeasy on numerous occasions, and she was
sure that those photographs were the main source of his
employment—not to mention income. So where were all the
images from the speakeasy?

He had obviously put them somewhere or given them to
someone, as they were nowhere to be found. Or had someone
stolen them? She remembered how the apartment had looked
like it had been rifled through. Or was it possible that he had
kept them hidden?

She added a dollop of whiskey to her tea. "Oh, Marty,"
she said, taking a deep gulp of the fire-burning stuff. "What
a mystery you were."

Setting down her cup, she went into his bedroom and lay
on the floor next to his bed so that she could see if anything
was underneath. Unfortunately, there was nothing under the
bed except for great amounts of dust that wafted up and tickled her nose, causing her to have a fit of violent sneezing.

After she recovered, she lay on the floor again, tracing the
patterns on the floorboards beneath her. Her mind flashed to
the spot under the floorboard at her own home where she had
hidden the camera. Her mother was the one who had shown

her that spot, long ago. What if this was a family trait? Perhaps Marty, like his cousin, used similar spaces to hide his
secrets.

As she began to tap around on the floor, she found a loose
board that made a rather hollow sound when knocked. "Ap-
plesauce!" she exclaimed, growing even more excited when she
saw that several nails had already been removed. That had to be
on purpose.

Sure enough, it was pretty easy to lift up two floorboards,
exposing a small chest about two feet long by one foot wide.
Her heart began to beat faster when she saw that the chest
had a small lock. Just the right size for a small key to open.

Pulling out the key around her neck, she inserted it into
the lock. Carefully she turned the key and opened the lid of the
chest, scarcely daring to breathe. Inside were clear sleeves containing film negatives, and a small stack of photographs
bound together with a leather string.

There was also an album covered in fancy but yellowed
lace—a family album, she quickly discovered. Her family. As
she paged through, she came to a picture of her mother, and
her eyes started to fill with tears.

Gina set the album aside, resolving to examine it in greater
detail later. Instead, she focused on looking through the loose
photographs, hoping that the secrets Marty was hiding beneath the floorboard would not be too much for her to bear.

Glancing through them, she could see that most of these
images had been taken at the Third Door. Movie stars, baseball players, famous boxers. Babe Ruth. Benny Goodman.
Lulu hadn't been lying about their visits. Such images might
fetch a pretty penny from *Variety* or some other entertainment
rag. There were others of hot-to-trot women, hanging on the

arms of men dressed in immaculate pinstripe suits. Gang members with their molls, if she had to guess.

Thankfully, none were indecent. They were mostly of couples kissing, holding hands, dancing closely, clinking cocktail glasses, or in other intimate moments. In a few, the couples appeared dismayed or angry, and Gina assumed that they were unaware that Marty was taking their picture.

A few she lingered over and set aside. The first was a picture of four women with Ned. Faye, Jade, and Lulu were all smiling, while a fourth woman, wearing a black dress and headpiece, wore a pouting look. She thought it might be Dorrie, especially after she found another picture of the same girl, this time carrying a cigarette tray and looking slyly up at Roark. Gina found herself staring at that one before setting it aside.

She also discovered that Marty had taken a picture of her, that first night she worked at the Third Door, just as she had suspected at the time. Feeling a bit vain, Gina glanced at the photograph more closely. The camera had caught her wide smile, as well as the gap between her front teeth. It had also caught the quirk of her eyebrows, which she knew was the expression she adopted when someone was handing her a line.

Flipping the photographs over, she realized that all of them had numbers penned on the back, and they appeared to be numbered sequentially. Intrigued, she pulled out Marty's small notebook, which she had removed from the camera case that morning, to see if she could make sense now of how Marty kept track of his images.

Slowly, she systematically compared the numbers on the photographs with the notations in Marty's notebook, working to decipher his code. The number seemed to be the date, the roll number, and the position of the image on the roll. Then he would include a code name, followed by something that appeared to note payment. A few of the entries were starred or underlined. The photos with Dorrie had been taken on December 15, 1928, just a week before the cigarette girl had been murdered.

After pouring herself some more whiskey, Gina seated herself on Marty's green sofa and picked up her family's photograph album, handling the crumbling black leather cover and yellowed pages with care. Inside there were pictures of her father as a boxer, and some of her mother and her parents and her Doyle grandparents. She recognized Eddie, as well as Marty and Nancy.

She sighed, once again wishing she had known more about this side of the family. Her mother's familiar handwriting had labeled most of these images at the bottom. She must have still been in contact with Marty until just before she died, even though Gina was sure she had never met him as a child. On the last few pages, a new, unfamiliar handwriting appeared.

Dear Molly's wedding, it said, underneath a picture of her parents standing under a bough of flowers. Then another picture, clearly taken at a distance, of her brother, Aidan, maybe around six, holding on to her hand, when she was about one. The caption read *Darling Molly's children.*

A lump formed in her throat as she thought about her brother, laughing and joking around, so full of life before the Great War took away everything that mattered. She continued to turn pages carefully. She stopped when she came across another picture of her parents, when they were still quite young, alongside a second man. The three were standing in front of a Ferris wheel. The writing underneath read *Lincoln Park. 1898.*

Studying the photograph more closely, she realized that the other man was none other than Big Mike, owner of the Third Door. Judging by their close stance, the three had once been friends. Her mother and father were turned toward the photographer, with stiff smiles on their faces, while Big Mike's face was turned so that he was smiling at her mother. There was a fondness in his expression that caught her attention. Could Big Mike have had feelings for her mother, all those years ago? That might explain the occasional animus she felt from the Signora. But on the other hand, maybe it didn't.

A clattering at the window caused her to start, pulling her out of her reverie. Seeing the window rattling, she went and got the little tool kit she had found among Marty's things and began to examine the window frame. She could see that there was a loose chain, so she tightened it. It was always good to have something to fix when the world around her seemed like it was falling apart.

"Papa," she said to her father the next morning, softly so that she would not startle him. He was trying unsuccessfully to fix a clock that a neighbor had brought by the other day. From behind the doorframe, she watched him struggle to even open the base of the clock, where the gears and springs could be found. When he looked up at her, she continued. "I was wondering if I could show you something." She held up the lace-covered photograph album that she had retrieved from underneath the floorboards in Marty's flat.

He winced when he saw the album, as if he knew it would

hold painful memories of their family's past. When he didn't take it from her, she opened it to the photograph of her and Aidan.

"My dear boy," he said, tracing his finger over his late son's face.

Not wishing to deepen her father's melancholy, Gina quickly flipped several pages. "Do you remember any of these people?" she asked, pointing to her mother with Marty and some individuals who looked like younger versions of the people she'd met at the funeral.

"Gina, sweetheart, I don't really remember your mother's family." He looked deeply sad and ashamed. "I should have asked her more about them, but she was just so intent on getting away from her home. Then Aidan was born, and I suppose the questions never seemed to really matter. Your mother was so deeply happy, and so was I."

She bent her head; for the moment, her questions were stilled.

CHAPTER 17

Gina removed Marty's camera from her purse and laid it on the darkroom table. "Today is the day," she informed it, running her fingers along the scratched brown case. "Today is the day that I learn what secrets you are hiding."

She finally felt ready to develop Marty's last roll of film, which was still safely encased within his camera. That didn't mean she wasn't nervous, though. She could feel herself sweating through her dress as she began to set out the equipment, despite the chill in the apartment.

Carefully she wound the film unto the roll so that it was ready to remove from the camera. Then she turned out the light. "Don't ruin the film, Gina," she said to herself through gritted teeth.

The room now dark, she cracked open the film case, holding her breath until she felt the edge of the film, and cut off the end with her small scissors. Slowly she rolled the film onto the reel, and only when there was nothing left to roll did she take her next breath. Then she began the process of developing the negatives.

As soon as she'd rinsed off the last of the chemicals and

hung the negatives to dry, Gina began to study the images that had emerged, taking care not to touch them. Since she had not yet enlarged them, the details were difficult to decipher. She could make out images of people on a street. Others looked like they might have been taken at the Third Door.

Gina left the darkroom then and paced around Marty's flat, trying to think of ways to busy herself while the negatives dried. Since there were no more rattling windows to fix, she contented herself with flipping through a stack of magazines and pulp comics that Marty had seemed to enjoy reading. He seemed particularly fond of *Under Fire* magazine, especially—judging by the bent corners—those "War and Wing" stories featuring the Great War's flying aces. She wondered what Marty would have thought of her chance encounter with Amelia Earhart at Hull House the other day. He might have had high praise for the woman who had flown halfway around the world.

When she returned to the darkroom, she checked that the negatives were dry and took them over to the enlarger. Barely breathing, she placed the photographic paper carefully and then slipped the film carrier with the first strip of negatives into position. Her heart was beating rapidly, and she had to keep wiping her hands on her dress because her palms were sweating so much. What images would emerge? What was it that Marty hadn't wanted anyone to see?

The first few images seemed nondescript. Taken outside the Drake Hotel on the Gold Coast, they were shots of pedestrians strolling about, some entering or exiting the hotel. Not surprisingly, most looked well-to-do, in their fur coats and matching hats, their servants following them, their arms laden with wrapped packages. In each, she could see a young man

with a cap drawn over his face. In one he was leaning against
a streetlight, reading the day's newspaper; in the second he
was lighting a cigarette. In the third he was speaking to a
woman with a long fur coat, which almost reached her shoes,
and a matching cloche hat. In the fourth, he appeared to be
lighting the woman's cigarette, although her face could not
be clearly seen. All rather mundane. Nothing particularly interesting.

Now that she understood Marty's notation, she opened
the notebook to see what he had written about these images.
She realized that he had not provided descriptions for the first
five photographs. Maybe when he took pictures on his own
time, for his own purposes, he didn't capture the information
in his notebook. Perhaps he only noted the photographs that
people might pay for.

Gina then inserted the second set of negatives into the enlarger, looking at the four images in turn. The fifth exposure
on the roll showed the same man, this time staring straight at
Marty. His features were hard to make out. The next three
images had been taken at the Third Door, the night Marty
had died.

She sighed. None of them seemed particularly note-
worthy. The sixth one featured a woman whom Marty's book
referred to as "Clara Bow," likely because the patron had struck
an "It Girl" pose. The seventh was of two young couples mug-
ging for the camera. In the background, Gina could see herself sitting at the piano beside Ned. She vaguely remembered
their conversation. Had this been when they were discussing
Dorrie? The eighth image was of the veterans in the back
room, but again, they were all grinning and raising their
glasses, cards facedown in front of them or still gripped in

their hands. Even Roark had a grin on his face, she noticed. She studied it a bit more, taking in his relaxed demeanor.

Finally it was time to examine the last strip of negatives. Her hands were shaking a bit as she placed them in the enlarger. There were only three exposures because Marty hadn't had the chance to use the last one on the roll. Like the others, they had been taken at the Third Door. The ninth was of Clarence Darrow. In the background, she could see the Signora and Gooch watching two men seated at a corner table. The tenth was of Lulu. Behind Lulu, she could see Mimi sitting on Jack's lap, her hand on Jack's face, perhaps about to pull him close for a kiss. Jack was turned slightly away, as if he'd been conversing with a man standing near the table. The last was the one Gina had seen Marty take, the one of Mimi and Jack, now seated more decorously in two different chairs, Mimi's boa wrapped provocatively around her man. Jack's brow was furrowed, and his lips were tight. His eyes were looking away from Mimi, as if he were trying to distance himself from the woman at his side. Clearly not a married couple, and not even one in love.

Stepping away from the enlarger, Gina felt a great sense of disappointment sweeping over her. She didn't know what she had expected the film to reveal, but none of these images seemed to have much to say. The ones from the Third Door had captured everyday shenanigans, and if there was a story behind the ones taken out on the street, it didn't look particularly interesting.

A glance at her watch showed her that she was going to be late for work. Since the negatives were dry, she carried them over to Marty's flat, where she added them to the locked chest under the floorboards.

On her way out of the flat, she thoughtfully selected two photographs from those Marty had hidden away and placed them in her handbag, after wrapping them in paper. They were the two she thought included Dorrie: the photograph of Ned and the four cocktail waitresses, and the one of the young woman holding a cigarette tray, standing near Roark with a coy smile on her face. On a whim, she grabbed two others from the same stack as well: one of Billy Bottles, with Clarence Darrow and other men seated at the bar in the background, and the other of Lulu posing with two College Joes.

When Gina started her shift a short while later, she spotted Lulu lighting a man's cigarette on the other side of the room, gazing into his eyes. Looked like a pose she'd picked up from the talkies.

"Say, Lulu," she said, when her friend passed by her. "Can I talk to you about something? In private."

Lulu raised her eyebrows. "Sure thing, doll," she said. A few minutes later, she followed Gina into the salon. "What's up, hon? Something the matter?"

Silently, Gina pulled the photograph with Lulu and the other three women from her bodice, where she'd stashed them when she changed. She pointed to the fourth woman in the picture. "Is this——?"

Lulu froze as she looked at the photograph. "Dorrie," she murmured. Then, more sharply, "Why are you showing this to me?"

Before Lulu could ask more questions, Gina held out the image of Dorrie and Roark. Behind them, Faye could be seen serving a soldier a drink, and Ned was staring at Dorrie, a dark look on his face. "Look at this one," Gina said softly. "What do you make of this?"

After a quick curious glance, Lulu scowled. "I don't make anything of it. If you know what's good for you, you'll keep your nose out of things that don't concern you." Before Gina could stop her, she crumpled up the photograph and threw it to the ground. Jade and Faye walked in just then, watching with appraising eyes as Lulu stalked past them in a huff.

Jade lifted her eyebrow. "What was *that* about?" she asked.

Faye, meanwhile, had picked up the photograph and was looking at it. "Where did you get this?" she asked. "Find it in Marty's place?"

Jade came to peek over her shoulder. "What were you doing with it?"

"I found it, and I guess I was just curious," Gina replied.

"You're curious about Dorrie?" Jade curled her lip up in disdain.

Gina thought quickly. "No, about Ned, actually." Better to let them think she had a crush on the local sheik than an interest in the deceased waitress.

Faye smirked, but her eyes looked hard. "Girl, I warned you away from him."

"I know, you're right." Gina slipped the photographs back inside her bodice and returned to the speakeasy floor before the women could say anything more. Out of the corner of her eye she saw that Lulu and Ned were having a heated conversation by the piano.

Seeing that Billy Bottles was at the other end of the bar, Gina moved next to Mr. Darrow, who was seated alone. On a whim, she decided to show him the photographs as well. "Mr. Darrow, if you have a moment," she said, "I wanted to show you a picture that Marty took of you. Before Christmas, I'd guess."

She pulled them from her bodice and showed him the one of Billy. "It's not of you, but you're in the background, just behind Billy."

His eyebrows raised slightly, and he took the photograph. "I don't recall Marty taking this." He straightened his glasses and looked more closely. "Very interesting," he said, tapping the other men at the bar in the background.

"What is it?"

"Those fellows are O'Banion's men. I recognize them from one of my trials. I defended one a while back. Successfully, I must immodestly add." He pulled on his suspenders. "They weren't there because of me, I hasten to add. I haven't seen these men for years." He continued to examine the photograph. "I must say, this is all very interesting."

"What is?"

"I'm no photographer, of course, but I've perused many photos from crime scenes and courtrooms over the last few years, and these are different."

"What do you mean?" Gina asked.

"It's fairly evident. Mr. Doyle was focusing on the background. That is, what was going on *behind* his subjects, who are in the foreground."

"How can you tell?"

"The foregrounded people are slightly out of focus, but in comparison the people in the background are much sharper. I contend that they may have been the actual subjects of his shots."

"Why would he do that?" Gina asked.

He swirled his gin in his glass, causing the ice to clink together. "Why indeed?"

She turned to the other photographs, this time looking more closely at the one with Lulu and the College Joes. She could see now that there were other men behind these three subjects as well. "What about this one?" she asked quietly, sliding it over.

He picked it up and grunted. "Same," he said. "More of O'Banion's men. Could the Castallazzos be getting in with the North Side Irish? Perhaps Marty was keeping tabs on them." He handed the photographs back to her.

She tucked them back inside her dress and moved away thoughtfully.

Ned walked up to her then. "Take a break," he said. "I want to talk to you."

After delivering two drinks to waiting patrons, she followed the piano player out into the salon, which was empty. He took a swig from his ever-present silver flask. "Why are you asking about Dorrie? Lulu told me about the photographs."

"I'm sorry. I was curious."

"She's curious," he muttered, and walked into the long corridor that led to the tunnel away from the speakeasy. "I would give anything to know what happened to Dorrie. Anything, you hear me?"

Gina scrambled after him. "Where was she going that night? You really don't know?"

"I guess she had another guy on the side. Not the first girl to stray, won't be the last." His tone was bitter. "What's this to you? I asked you before. Now I want an answer." He stepped toward her, causing her to take a step back. "You can't just stick your nose where it doesn't belong."

"Say, Ned. Do you think that Marty's death was—"

"What? Marty's death was what? Sad? Disturbing? Uncalled for?"

"—was connected to Dorrie's death?"

Unexpectedly, Ned laughed, sounding genuinely amused. "Been reading that mystery writer, Agatha Christie, have you?"

"No, it's just that—"

He looked down at her and put his face so close that she could practically taste the alcohol on his breath. "You looking to replace Dorrie? You wear her dress, her hairpiece—"

"Only the first night! I didn't know. These are my clothes now."

Ned wasn't done. "Serve her drinks, flirt with her men. How else do you want to replace her?" He ran his hand along her hip. When she flinched, he drew back with a harsh laugh—there was nothing of his earlier amusement to be heard.

"Look, Gina," he said, running his hand through his blond hair. "I don't know where she was going that night."

"Her mother thought she was supposed to deliver a message."

He looked annoyed. "That may be so. If you haven't figured it out by now, people who ask too many questions don't last long enough to hear the answers."

"Is that what happened to Marty? Did he ask too many questions?"

"You just don't get it, do you?"

"Get what?"

A cough behind them caused him to step away.

It was Roark. "Am I interrupting something?" he asked, looking from one to the other. Gina's face flushed as she wondered how much of the interplay between her and Ned he had witnessed. She wondered why she cared.

"Not at all," Ned said, pushing past them. "I have another set to play."

"Like them pretty and drunk, do you?" Roark asked her, watching the pianist slip back into the speakeasy.

Gina rolled her eyes. "Did you know that Ned and Dorrie were an item?"

"An item?" Roark seemed to consider. "Yeah, I suppose I could see that. From what I could see there might have been something between them. Why?"

"I found a picture. He looked plenty jealous." She handed him the picture that Lulu had crumpled earlier.

"Ah, Dorrie." He seemed to be focusing on her smiling face. Then he studied the photograph more closely. "I see what you mean about Ned."

Gina swallowed. She remembered what Zosia had told her about seeing Dorrie kissing Ned out on the street. "Was there a reason for him to be jealous? Was his girl two-timing him?"

"If Dorrie was two-timing him, it wasn't with me." He paused. "She wasn't my type.

The bigger question is—how mad *was* Ned, if he found out that Dorrie was canoodling with another man?"

Gina shivered. There was an answer to his question that she couldn't bring herself to face.

"Gina, I'd like to see you in my salon." The Signora's whisper in her ear was like her dress, velvet and dangerous. Gina had just reentered the main floor. "Now."

"Yes, Signora," she replied, preparing herself for trouble as she followed the Signora back to her private room.

"I'd like to see the photographs that you just showed our patron Mr. Darrow." The Signora extended her hand, making it clear that this was not a request.

Gina felt goosebumps raise across her arms. "The photographs, ma'am?"

"Yes, Gina. The ones that are currently inside your bodice. Please don't make me have Gooch retrieve them."

"No, ma'am, I'll give them to you." Gina pulled the photographs out and handed them to her, trying to keep her hands from shaking.

The Signora studied them in silence. When she finally spoke, her voice chilled Gina to the bone. "I assume that you found these among Marty's belongings."

There seemed no point in lying. "Yes, Signora."

"Did you find others like these? Taken in my establishment?"

Suddenly Marty's dying warning came into Gina's mind. *Hide it,* he had told her. Then she thought about how Marty had hidden these images under the floorboards. Why? The Signora knew that Marty took pictures of patrons there. She'd hired him to do so. "No, I didn't see any," she lied. "Did he usually give them to you?"

The Signora's brow cleared. "Yes, he did. That way, in case anyone wanted to pick up a photograph—a memento of their visit—they could." Although her words were plausible, Gina sensed a lie. "So if you see any more, please give them to me. We wouldn't want these photographs to get into the wrong hands, now would we?"

Gina took a step back. "No, ma'am," she replied.

"Then you may return to your duties now. I don't want my customers kept waiting."

As the servers were changing for their next set, Gina noticed a woman sitting at the end of the bar. She'd placed her purple sequined handbag on the stool beside her, probably to keep unwanted companions at bay. She was sipping a gin and tonic.

Billy Bottles was watching the woman uneasily. Catching Gina's eye, he nodded for her to come over.

"Take care of that, will you?" he muttered, flicking a finger toward the woman. "The Signora don't like that kind of thing. And Gooch is too busy right now to handle it."

Gina looked over. She could see now that the woman was crying, black marks from her mascara streaking down her cheeks. Then she recognized who it was. Greta Van der Veer. Glancing around, she saw Gooch standing over two obviously intoxicated college boys in a menacing way. The phonograph was playing a record while Ned was taking his break.

"Oh, of course," she said. After handing Billy the empty glasses on her tray, she slid over to the woman. "Miss Van der Veer," she said, "may I help you, please?'"

She glanced up at Gina and scowled. "You can't help me," she said, her words slurring together. She swayed a little on the seat and took another gulp before slamming her glass back down on the counter.

"Miss," Gina said, gripping her elbow, "I think you might like to visit the powder room."

Greta shrugged off Gina's hand before taking a huge

slurp of her drink. Out of the corner of her eye, Gina saw that Gooch and Little Johnny busy rounding up two rowdy College Joes. Looked like she'd have to handle this herself. "Don't wanna," she slurred.

Unexpectedly, Ned appeared at Gina's side. "What's going on here?"

"She's zozzled."

"You don't say." He put his hand on the woman's shoulder. "Come on, doll, let's flip this joint. Get you some fresh air."

Reaching up, Greta patted the piano player's cheek, giving him an amused smile. "Think I'll go anywhere with you? Like your dumb little Dorrie did? How'd she get killed anyway?" She smiled darkly at Gina. "Did anyone ever catch Dorrie's murderer?"

Gina's thoughts flashed to the accusation that Dorrie's mother had hurled at the Signora up in the tea room. "No," she said, glancing at Ned. "No, I don't think so."

Ned scowled. "I've had enough of this. Hope Gooch hustles her out good and hard." He walked away.

"They never catch the murderers, have you noticed that?" Miss Van der Veer said, her words in a long, slurred drawl. "Everyone knows, and no one says a thing."

"What do they know? What don't they say?" Gina asked, startled by the woman's words.

Miss Van der Veer squinted up at her. "Say, do I know you?" she asked.

"I saw you here the other night. When you were with—"

"Genevieve Beering. My darling Genevieve. She was murdered. In her prime! Oh God!" The woman began to cry again, loud ugly hiccupping sounds.

"What? Murdered? I thought—"

"Let's get her out of here," Roark said, coming up behind Gina. He leaned down to whisper in her ear. "This is not a conversation we want to have in the open." To Miss Van der Veer he said, more politely than Gina had ever heard him, "Please allow us to escort you somewhere we can talk more privately."

The woman looked defiant but then slumped over in apparent resignation. "All right," she agreed, allowing Gina to put her arm around her waist, resting her head heavily on Gina's shoulder. Gina grabbed a towel from Billy as she passed. Roark limped behind, carrying the woman's drink, as they propelled her into the dark passageway that led outward.

"You're pretty," she said, looking up at Gina. "Don't you think she's pretty?" she asked Roark.

Roark coughed. "Sure."

The woman ran her fingers up Gina's bare arm. "Are you interested in a friend, honey?" Then her eyes welled up. "Genevieve was my friend. My darling Genevieve. You said your name is Gina, right? Genny, Gina, one and the same." Then tears began to slip down her face in earnest and she slumped to the ground, suddenly exhausted. "I miss her! My dear sweet beautiful Genny. No one will ever replace her!" She reached her hand out to retrieve her cocktail from Roark. When he handed it to her, she took another deep sip.

Here was her chance. "Miss Van der Veer," Gina said, sitting down beside the distraught woman, "I am so sorry. Miss Beering must have been such a dear friend." Handing the soft towel to the woman, she helped her dab her eyes, waiting for her weeping to subside. "Tell us, though, why do you say she was murdered? I assumed her death was an accident. The papers never said."

"She just accidentally bludgeoned the back of her own head?!" Miss Van der Veer replied, angrily scrubbing at her eyes, worsening the streaks of black. "I'll never forget how I found her, lying in the middle of the floor in her suite at the Drake Hotel, in a pool of her own blood."

Gina shuddered, remembering how she had found Marty in the alley. Bracing herself, she continued. "Could she have slipped and fallen? Landed too hard on the floor?"

Miss Van der Veer shook her head. "Not likely that she slipped. The floor was carpeted."

Gina kept trying to imagine the scene. "Perhaps she fainted and hit her head on a piece of furniture?"

"That's probably what her killer hoped we'd believe," Miss Van der Veer seethed. "I'm telling you, she was murdered. I'm sure of it. She was on her stomach when I found her."

"Did you alert the police to your suspicions?" Roark asked. "Did they look into them?"

Miss Van der Veer's deep sniff of contempt made it clear what she thought of that idea.

"Well, the coroner would know," he said. "I can speak to him."

Miss Van der Veer clutched his arm. "Pray, be discreet. The idea that Genevieve would be associated with something so sordid—Oh! I can't believe it!" She buried her head in the towel, half sobbing, half snorting.

Gina and Roark exchanged a glance. "Who do you think killed Miss Beering?" Gina asked.

The woman peered up out through the fingers spread across her face. "I shouldn't say."

"You were saying plenty out at the bar," Roark said. "You weren't so concerned with being *discreet* out there when you were tossing back gin rickeys."

Unexpectedly, the woman began weeping even more forcefully into her hands, and Gina shot Roark an annoyed glance. "Allow me, Miss Van der Veer," she said, gently taking back the towel. She wiped the tears and snot from the woman's face as she would from a child's. Then she dipped the edge of the towel in the glass of gin and did her best to remove the black mascara streaks. "There, that's much better. Miss Van der Veer . . . earlier, you mentioned something about Dorrie . . . Did you know what happened to her?"

"Oh, Dorrie," Miss Van der Veer said dismissively. "She was just a messenger for Big Mike. Someone didn't like her message. Obviously."

"What do you know about it?"

Her eyes half closed, she grimaced. "She threatened Genevieve once, warning her about something. The floozy came to the hotel one morning in December, unannounced. I was in the other room, and I distinctly heard her say, 'I'm gonna tell, and you'll be ruined.'"

"Yeah?" Gina replied, remembering what Zosia had said. "What was she referring to? Tell what?"

"I dunno. About her gambling, I think. Genevieve liked the cards. She had to start paying back the Castallazzos—" The woman's eyes rolled back in her head as the gin overtook her. She hiccupped. "But I think she'd already been paying Big Mike back. You know, the *other* way. I think Dorrie was threatening to tell the Signora."

Gina gave her a little shake. "Well, what about Miss Beering? What did she say? Was she angry at Dorrie?"

The woman lolled against Gina, a bit of spittle dripping out of her mouth.

"Wake up! Tell me!" Gina cried, shaking the woman harder.

"I think I'm piffled," Miss Van der Veer mumbled. Roark muffled a snort.

"I think you are," Gina said, giving Roark a warning look. "If you can just tell me—"

Roark suddenly put his hands over Gina's mouth, lightly, just touching her lips. "Shhh," he said. "Someone's coming."

"What's going on here?" the Signora asked, staring down at the three of them. Gooch and Little Johnny appeared behind her like silent statues.

Gina stood up. "Miss Van der Veer, Signora," she said, gesturing to the unconscious woman. "She was in a bad state. Billy Bottles asked me to move her from the bar, thinking you wouldn't like her bothering the other guests. Mr. Roark was kind enough to help me, since Gooch and Little Johnny were otherwise occupied with those college buffoons."

As if on cue, Miss Van der Veer suddenly rolled over and retched. Gina grabbed her head just inches before she would have planted her face in her own vomit.

The Signora's regal gaze was dark and penetrating. "Take her out the back way," she commanded Gooch and Little Johnny, who instantly obeyed. To Roark, she added, "Please accept a drink on the house for your trouble."

"Thank you, Signora," he said, and stepped away without another comment.

Her eyes swept over Gina. "I think you can go home now."

"Already?" Gina blurted out. "It's only eleven!"

"The sets are over. The other girls can handle the rest of the shift."

"Yes, Signora," Gina replied, immediately chastised.

"Remember when I told you earlier that I don't need any gossip among the staff? Just keep your nose to yourself."

CHAPTER 18

Gina had only taken a few steps along Halsted before getting the distinct feeling that someone was behind her. It didn't help that the street was very foggy, so she began to walk quickly, cursing the click of her heels with every step. When she turned around once or twice, the footsteps behind her stopped, too.

Pressing against the stone wall of the building, Gina cast an uneasy glance up and down the street. Behind her, she noticed a large shadowy figure lighting a cigarette. She could tell it was a man, with his fedora pulled down so as to obscure his face.

Had the Signora sent someone after her? She began to walk quickly down the street. Though not fast enough. A man grabbed her arm from behind. "Hey, miss," he hissed. "How's about you hand over that purse!"

Gina froze, feeling unable to move. *This can't be happening.*

"I think you've got something I want," the man said in her ear. Was his voice familiar? "Just hand over your purse. Don't make this any harder than it has to be." His tone was quiet, menacing.

He's going to kill me, Gina thought frantically. *I'm going to die right here on the street.*

Even as she thought that, instinct and fury kicked in. "No!" she shouted, whirling around, planting a fist into his belly, the way her brother had taught her so long ago.

Not expecting the blow, the man bent over in pain, giving her the opportunity to deliver a sharp uppercut to his jaw. As he staggered back, she pressed her advantage, striking and swinging with abandon, disregarding the oofs and gasps coming from the man. She didn't even know what she was thinking; everything was just coming out of her—all the anger, sadness, frustration she'd been feeling since Marty was killed, welling up from a place from deep inside.

Distantly she heard someone screaming, and she looked up, allowing her attacker to stumble away. On the balcony above, she could see Zosia in a white nightgown, her eyes wide and frightened, her yellow hair floating about her in a gossamer way. She looked like an angel.

"You okay, Gina?" she called down, her voice trembling. Then, with admiration, she added, "You sure showed him what's what."

"I'm all right," Gina replied, covering her ferociously beating heart with one hand. She laid her other hand on the brick wall, trying to support herself as her body began to shake.

The door to the dress shop opened and Madame Laupin stepped out, clutching a robe about her. "What is going on here?" she exclaimed. Then she spied Gina huddled against the wall, trying to keep herself from tumbling to the ground. *"Mon Dieu! Mademoiselle!"* she cried. "What happened?"

"S-someone came after me. A man," Gina said, trying to

catch her breath as the enormity of her attack started to over-take her. Tears flew to her eyes. "I need to sit down," she said, trembling now in earnest.

Madame Laupin threw a comforting arm around her, but Gina saw her look anxiously up and down the street. Zosia had disappeared from the balcony. "Come inside, *cherie*. Allow me to give you some brandy. Indeed, I quite insist."

"Thank you, Madame." Gina followed the woman in, past the dress forms and sewing machines, and up the stairs to the small flat above the shop where Madame Laupin lived.

She sat huddled in a kitchen chair, with a blanket pulled over her legs, watching Madame Laupin move purposefully, unscrewing the cap from a bottle.

"Here you are," she said, pressing the cup into Gina's hands. She watched as Gina took a good warming sip. After that, the questions came. "Who was that man, *cherie*? Did you know him? Was he a patron? You know not to involve your-self with men you meet there . . ."

"I don't know," Gina said, rubbing her arm where the man had gripped it. "Maybe. He wanted my purse." *And more likely, my photographs.* She took another deep sip. "He may have fol-lowed me out. His voice sounded familiar."

"That is not good. You must inform the Signora. She pro-tects her girls."

"Yes, of course," Gina replied, even as other thoughts pushed their way into her mind. Had the Signora sent this man to attack her? She didn't think it wise to share her concerns. Instead, noticing a man's jacket by Madame's sewing table, she changed the subject. "Do you create men's clothes, too?"

Madame Laupin laughed. "I'm just reweaving this one. Bullet made a big hole in it, and the owner needs it back."

"Jeepers! A bullet hole?"

Madame put her finger to her lips. *"Fermez la bouche.* Keep your mouth closed, *cherie."*

Gina watched Madame fold the jacket and set it aside, then pick up her own glass of brandy. *"Santé."*

"Cheers," Gina replied. As she clinked her teacup against Madame's glass, a drop of hot brandy landed on her knuckles, which were raw and bleeding from the scrap. "Ouch!"

Madame Laupin set down her glass. "Your hands!" Getting up, she poured some hot water onto a cloth and handed it to her. "Press this to your knuckles. They will feel better soon."

Gratefully, Gina applied the warm compress to her hands. "How long have you worked for the Signora?" she asked.

"Oh, many years," the dressmaker replied. "She saved me from a life of destitution. I began making dresses for her a long time ago, and she has been very generous to me. Very generous. There are many, including yourself, who have benefited from her kindness. Why do you ask?"

"I think that the Signora may have sent that man after me."

Unexpectedly, the dressmaker laughed. "The Signora? No, I should say not." She lowered her voice. "Brute violence is not the Signora's style. Big Mike's perhaps. Do not get on his bad side, I implore you."

"Except, what if I did?" Gina whispered.

"Then I suggest you do whatever is necessary to make amends." She stood up. "Have you recovered sufficiently for your walk home?"

"Yes, Madame, thank you."

When she stepped back outside, Gina looked up and down to make sure that the man was not still waiting for her.

The street was empty. Zosia, she was glad to see, had not returned to her perch on the balcony. Holding up her coat, Gina
ran the rest of the way home without stopping.

Despite her aching knuckles, the next day Gina found herself
filled with a new resolve. She'd woken up throughout the night,
sleeping in fits and starts, recalling the feel of the man's grip
on her arm, and her own unexpected response. The fury she'd
felt! The power, too. What would the man have done? Just
steal her purse? Or would he have killed her? And for what?

On and off throughout the day she thought more about
the man. *It just couldn't have been a coincidence,* she thought. *That
man wanted something from me. Surely not my six dollars in tips.* More
importantly, she couldn't shake the feeling that she had met
him before. She had no doubt that the Signora had sent him
after her, no matter what Madame Laupin thought.

Another flash of anger flowed through her then. "The
Signora may think she controls everyone, but she doesn't control me," Gina grumbled out loud as she buttoned her coat.
She looked at the photograph of Marty with her mother that
she'd she'd removed from Marty's album and placed in a small
frame on her dresser.

"Mama," she said to the picture, "I just have to know more
about what Marty's last pictures may mean." Looking into the
mirror, she fixed her hat and pinched her cheeks to make them
less pale. Then she "I know you'd tell me not to do it, Mama.
That it isn't safe. I know it isn't. But I *owe* it to Marty, and to
you, too."

Her plan was to ask just Mr. Darrow about the subjects of
Marty's photographs taken the night he had died. Before going

to the Third Door, she stopped by Marty's flat to remove the photographs of Jack and Mimi, the one with "Clara Bow," and the one of the two couples snuggling where she could be seen in the background talking to Ned, as well as the one of Mr. Darrow himself. As before, she wrapped them in paper and put them in her purse. She figured she'd approach Mr. Darrow and slip them to him so he could look at them in the privacy of the men's room.

What if you can't trust Mr. Darrow either? Even as the little thought dangled before her, she squashed it. Honestly, if you couldn't trust the country's foremost criminal attorney, even in an age of rampant corruption, who could you really trust?

As it turned out, the point was moot. By seven o'clock, Mr. Darrow had still not shown up, which, experience suggested, meant he had decided not to venture out for the evening.

Surprisingly, Jade had also failed to show up, even an hour into her shift.

"I can't imagine where Jade may be. This means that Lulu and I have to move up our set," Faye said, seeming put out. "You'll have to take my backroom orders."

Though she was disappointed about not being able to talk to Mr. Darrow, being among the ex-servicemen quickly lifted her slightly dampened spirits. They seemed to be in a good mood. Everyone but Roark, that is, who gave her an odd glance when she walked in.

"Say, doll," Donny called to her, nudging his buddy. "How about a new concoction tonight? The lieutenant here is a bit grumpy. We need something to get him peppy again."

"Isn't he always grumpy?" she asked, flashing Roark a smile. To her surprise, he didn't smile, and his eyes looked cold. Startled by his response, she took a step back before turning her attention back to Donny.

"Nothing will help *him*, I think." She smiled down at Donny, putting her hand on her hip. "What would you like? Southsider?"

The men all groaned. The Chicago drink was already a regularly imbibed concoction, it would seem.

"Gin rickey? Sidecar?"

Each suggestion elicited similar groans. She laughed and said, "How about I just surprise you?"

"You do that, doll," Donny grinned back, showing the full plate in his jaw. "We'll get the lieutenant back in good spirits right quick."

She left the room and walked up to the bar. "Yoo-hoo, Billy," she called. "The boys in back want something new."

"They do, do they? I've just the thing," he said, pulling some glassware off the shelf behind him. Looking around, he added, "Jade's still not here? That's not like her."

Gina watched as the bartender mixed up a concoction of absinthe, gin, and vermouth. The result was a bright green drink, which he poured into four glasses. He poured the excess into a shot glass and slid it over to her. "Try it," he ordered, a gleam in his eye. "Good and hard."

After a quick glance around to make sure no one was paying her any mind, Gina tossed it back. The lash of gin coursed down her throat, almost causing her to cough.

"That's a good girl," he said with an approving nod. "Just stay steady on your feet."

He wasn't kidding. She had to put her hand on the counter to maintain her balance. "What'd you call that one?"

He winked. "An Obituary."

Carefully Gina walked back to the cardplayers' table and began serving the drinks to the men. They all laughed when she told them the bartender's name for the drink.

Noticing her hand when she set his cocktail in front of him, Donny asked, "What happened to you?" He pointed at her knuckles, which were still sore and raw. "Punch someone's lights out?"

"Yeah, that's it," she said, fluffing her hair. "A customer told me he didn't like the way I laid down his drink. Took him around back and gave him what's what." She struck her boxing pose, and most of the men whooped and whistled. Roark, she noticed, did not laugh.

She delivered the rest of the drinks and started back to the main room, but before she got to the door Roark caught up to her and said in a low voice, "Gina, what really happened to you?"

"Oh, now you're talking to me?"

"Gina, I—"

"It's nothing," she said, cutting him off.

"Tell me."

He's not going to leave me be until I answer him. She shrugged. "Last night, someone jumped me after I left the Third Door."

"What? Who?"

"I didn't get a good look at him, but his voice was familiar," she said, trying to remember. Did she know him? She went on. "He told me to give him my purse, but I . . . I didn't want to do that. So I hit him."

"You could have been killed! Did he hurt you?" His eyes ran over her, assessing her for other injuries.

"I'm fine."

His face cracked into a grin. "It looks like you got a few hits in, at least."

"Yeah." She started to push past him, even as he stepped aside to allow her to pass. "I told you I can take care of myself."

"I'm starting to see that."

The girls were just finishing their set when Gooch came up to her. "You're wanted in the ladies' dressing room," he said. "All of you. Signora's orders."

When she entered the dressing area, along with Faye, Lulu, and Jade, who had just arrived, she was startled to see Nancy standing there, alongside Officer Dawson, the Signora, and Big Mike.

Was it a raid? What was going on?

She and Lulu exchanged a wondering glance. The police must have been brought in through one of the secret back entrances, because she would have noticed them descending the main stairs from the alley. Everyone would have seen and assumed it was a raid. Gooch came in behind them and leaned against the door, thereby ensuring that no one would be able to enter or exit without his say-so.

"This *policewoman*," the Signora said with scarcely masked disdain, waving at Nancy, "would like to search your belongings."

"What?" Jade and Lulu exclaimed in unison, with Jade adding, "You can't do that!"

"I'm sure we have nothing to hide," Faye said, raising one of her delicately arched eyebrows.

Gina, for her part, had frozen. The photographs from Marty's last roll of film were still in her purse, which was hanging alongside the other girls' bags. Now everyone would see them. She glanced at the Signora. Surely she'd get in trouble for having them. Unless, of course, she claimed that she had planned to give them to the Signora all along. She hadn't shown them to anyone, so that could seem plausible. She could just hand them over now.

Except—she remembered Marty's dying words, asking her to promise to keep them hidden, to keep them safe. Her heart started beating faster.

Despite the women's protests, Nancy dumped Lulu's handbag out on the counter, a hodgepodge of items falling about. Tubes of lipstick, small compacts, some coins, a few dollars. Jade's was much the same.

Officer Dawson followed closely behind her, watching his subordinate's movements with an eagle eye. From Jade's bag, he smoothed out an advertisement. *"Singers wanted!"* he said, reading the headline out loud. *"Auditions at The Sunset Café!* Oh, what do you know, that was tonight."

"That's why you were late? Looking for a new job?" Lulu whispered loudly to Jade, who just frowned at her in return. "Isn't that one of *Capone's* joints?"

Oh, Gina realized, watching the interplay. The Signora certainly did not look pleased.

Jade shrugged. "I could sing with Louis Armstrong, Earl Hines." She looked pointedly at the Signora but didn't say anything more.

Uncomfortably, Gina turned her attention back to Nancy, who had reached her own purse. As she'd done with the others, Nancy removed Gina's change purse and makeup. Then she pulled out the tissue paper containing the photographs. She glanced at them but set them aside without a word. The Signora gave Gina a sharp look, though she didn't say anything.

"What's this all about?" Jade asked. "You've looked in all our purses."

Nancy grimaced. "We received an anonymous tip that one of the girls at this establishment was seen with Genevieve Beering's jewelry in her possession." As she spoke, she picked up Gina's embroidered bag again. With a frown, she used her fingers to probe the material. She glanced at Gina. "Something in here?" she asked.

"No, why?" Gina replied.

Nancy continued to push and pull the material apart, fingering the green thread out along the seam. The others all watched in breathless fascination as if they were catching a burlesque act at the Star and Garter.

There was a slight tearing sound, and triumphantly Nancy withdrew a pearl choker necklace, inlaid with a distinctive set of rubies, surrounded by diamonds, which they all beheld in fascination.

Gina felt the room begin to sway. She recognized the piece immediately. "How did that get there?" she asked faintly. Everyone darted glances at her, confused by what was going on.

Nancy held up a photograph of Genevieve Beering, which looked to have been clipped from a society page. "Take a gander at the necklace that Miss Beering is wearing in this photograph." She held the necklace up to the picture in comparison. "Looks the same, don't you think?" she said. "Miss Van der Veer reported the necklace as missing."

The room was spinning now, and Gina leaned against the makeup counter. How had the deceased heiress's necklace ended up in her purse? Everyone, even Lulu, was staring at her with an expression of shock and suspicion.

"I don't know anything about it," Gina whispered, sitting down hard.

Nancy held the pearls out to the Signora, whose face had paled. "Madam?"

Wordlessly, the Signora took the necklace from the policewoman and held it to the light with the manner of a professional jeweler. Then, with a quick shudder of distaste, she ran the pearls across her own teeth. "Fake," she said, confirming Nancy's mute question. "I have no doubt that it is a very expensive necklace, worth a great deal of money, but the jewels are themselves fake."

"Well, it's a copy, then," Lulu said. "Not Miss Beering's necklace at all."

Nancy shook her head. "According to Miss Van der Veer, Miss Beering had been wearing this copy for months. The original is locked up in a vault somewhere." She paused. "Miss Beering was last seen wearing it the day she was killed."

"So Genevieve Beering was murdered?" Faye exclaimed. "How awful!"

"We heard her death was an accident!" Jade said.

Nancy shrugged. "The coroner confirmed that she'd been killed, by someone hitting her over the back of the head. The Beerings did not wish to be associated with something so sordid."

"So they paid off the coroner," the Signora said knowingly. "Kept the information from the press."

"Except Miss Van der Veer has been talking," Nancy replied.

Remembering the pickled state of the heiress's companion the previous night, Gina could see how that was likely true. Right now she had other things to worry about.

Big Mike picked up on her concern. "How exactly did this necklace end up in my employee's purse?" His face turned menacing as he regarded Gina. "You stole it from her?"

"No! I didn't!" Gina cried, looking around at everyone. "I only ever saw the necklace when she wore it here. Like everyone else! Someone planted it in my purse!"

"Why would anyone do that?" Faye asked. "More likely you took it yourself."

"What? When?"

"I remember when she admired it when Miss Beering was here." Jade said sweetly. "Stands to reason that her killer took her necklace."

Gina's mouth fell open in shock. This couldn't be happening.

"Even a fake one?" Lulu said doubtfully. "I mean, it's pretty and all, but—"

"The killer probably didn't realize it was fake," Faye said, with a snide look at Gina. "She probably hoped to pawn it for a few bucks."

The situation was getting out of hand. Gina turned to the Signora, who was looking at her with her customary hauteur. "Please, Signora! I would never steal. Please, you know my father—!"

"Gina Ricci," Officer Dawson interrupted, full authority in his voice. "You are being brought in for questioning for the theft of this property, and the murder of Genevieve Beering. Officer Doyle, if you would."

A dull rushing filled Gina's ears as she looked around, her shock reflected on the faces of the others. Nancy stepped over to Gina and pulled both of her arms behind her back. There were great gasps all around.

"Is this absolutely necessary?" the Signora asked. "I have my establishment to think of. We cooperated with you."

Nancy and Officer Dawson looked at each other. "We'll take her out the back way, same way we came in." She plucked Gina's coat from the coatrack and put it around her shoulders. "Let's go."

Blinking back tears, Gina kept her gaze straight ahead as she was marched out of the Third Door and over to the paddy wagon waiting to take her to the Harrison Street station.

CHAPTER 19

Still numb thirty minutes later, Gina found herself being escorted by a grim-faced Nancy Doyle into the Harrison Street station. Throughout the short ride to the jail, she had pleaded with the policewoman to see reason. Nancy ignored her, other than a curt reminder to address her as "Officer Doyle" rather than "Nancy." Officer Dawson, who had driven the paddy wagon, walked behind them into the station without speaking.

Holding Gina's elbow, Nancy led her to a small room, furnished only with a heavy wooden table with a chair on either side. "Sit," she said. "The captain will be with you in a moment."

She shut the door behind her, leaving Gina alone. Sinking down into one of the hard wooden chairs, Gina blew on her icy hands, trying to muster some warmth. At least they had let her keep her coat.

She did not have to wait long. Captain O'Neill walked in and introduced himself. He was carrying a cup of water, which he placed in front of her. As he sat down, he looked at her more closely. "We've met before."

"Mm-hmm," Gina said, her throat feeling tight and scratchy. "When you came to the drugstore. You had pictures of—" Here, she faltered. "Marty Doyle."

"Ah, right." He watched her take a drink of water. "Tell me how long you've worked at the Signora's establishment."

Gina stiffened. "Not that long. A few weeks. I started just after New Year's."

"I see. How did you get the job?"

"Lulu, another girl, told me about it. Told me they needed to replace a girl to—" she broke off, biting her lip. She wasn't sure what she should disclose about the Third Door, even though it seemed to be a very open secret.

"Look, we all know about the Third Door. I'm not a Prohibition agent. What is sold or not sold there doesn't concern us. We *are* concerned about the death of Genevieve Beering, and the theft of her jewelry, specifically a piece she was believed to have been wearing shortly before or even at the time of her death. Frankly, I want to know how *that* necklace ended up in *your* bag."

"I don't know anything about it," she whispered, a bit of tension rising in her voice. Here was her chance. She could tell him about Marty, about the camera, about the photographs. About everything. Clearly she'd been framed. Surely he'd see that. Yet Marty's words about not trusting anyone clung to her mind. She remembered, too, how the Signora had left out the envelopes for the officers. How those envelopes had been tucked away, into their uniforms. So she kept her mouth shut.

Captain O'Neill returned to something she'd said earlier. "You said that you'd been hired to replace a girl who'd left. Who was that? Do you know why she left?"

"Her name was Dorrie. I heard some of the others talking about her," Gina said. "She was killed. Stabbed."

"Like Marty Doyle," the captain commented.

"Well, yes. On the L." Then she changed the subject. "What's going to happen to me?"

"Right now we're just asking some questions—"

"But am I going to be arrested? What happens if I'm arrested?"

"You could be released on bail, if you can afford it."

Her heart sank a bit, thinking about how little money she and her father still had to spare. Working at the Third Door had only helped in the short term; she hadn't been able to set much aside. She looked down at her hands where they rested on the table.

"You haven't been arrested yet, you understand. As I said, we're just holding you for questioning right now." There was a long pause. When she looked back up, she found Captain O'Neill studying her carefully.

"Miss Ricci," he said, "tell me, what was your mother's maiden name?"

"O'Brien."

He grinned. "I thought I saw an Irish lass in there. Your mother from the North Side?"

"Yes, by Fullerton and Clark."

"O'Banion's territory," he stated.

"I suppose. I didn't grow up there."

The captain nodded. "Keep your chin up, kid. I'll make sure you have a blanket in your holding area. We may have some more questions for you in the morning."

"I have to stay here all night?"

"For a little while longer, at least." He opened the door. "Doyle!"

The holding area looked a lot like a cell, and Gina almost started to cry at the sight of the iron bars and hard, unadorned benches.

"In you go," Nancy said, practically shoving the blanket into her arms. Gina was forced to take a step back, and the guard clanged the iron gate behind her.

"Wait, I'm being locked in?" she exclaimed. "Please don't leave me here! Nancy! Officer Doyle! I'm happy to answer more questions! My papa will be so worried if I'm not home in the morning when he wakes up. What else do you want to know?"

"Hush!" Nancy hissed. "There are canaries everywhere." She looked intentionally toward the cell's other occupant, a young-looking woman huddled on one of the long benches. Her low-cut bodice and overly made-up face suggested she might be a prostitute.

Gina followed her gaze, then turned back to find that Nancy had walked away.

"Bad night, toots?" The other inhabitant of the cell had a raspy voice and turned out to be older than she first appeared. There was a gleam in her eye that made Gina feel suspicious. Canaries, Nancy had said.

Ignoring her, Gina sat on the other bench, contemplating her plight. The numbness was wearing off, and questions swayed over her. How had the heiress's necklace gotten in her bag? Who had put it there? How could she defend herself? What if they arrested her, as the officer had suggested they might? Her mind flashed to Mr. Darrow. Could she ask him for help? She sighed. Not in a million years could she afford a high-priced attorney like him.

She sat down gingerly on the bench and pulled the blanket around her. It smelled clean, at least, and she couldn't help but be grateful for the small kindness from Captain O'Neill. As her cellmate continued to ramble on, Gina curled up in a ball, pulling the blanket over her head, bewildered by the evening's strange turn of events.

Gina didn't know how long she'd been lying there when she heard a disturbance in the corridor and then a man's booming voice that she recognized. "Let me through."

It was Roark. With a groan she asked, "What are you doing here?"

"Tsk, tsk," he said, looking at her from the other side of the bars with mocking concern. "Got yourself in a bit of a pickle, didn't you?"

"Mind your own beeswax," she said, turning away from him.

"Hey, Roark," the other woman simpered, walking over to the cell door.

"Hey, Sally," he replied. "How's tricks?"

Sally ran a painted finger along the iron bars. "Fair. How about you bust me out of this joint and I'll show you a real good time?"

"No thanks," he replied. "I'm here for *her*." He nodded at Gina, who scowled at his innuendo. She was too tired for jokes.

With a disappointed twist of her lips, Sally flounced back to her bench and sat down, still watching Roark.

"What do you want?" Gina asked.

"I heard about the necklace," Roark said, watching her. "How do you explain that?"

"I didn't take it."

"Assuming that's true—"

"It is true!"

He held up his hand with exaggerated patience. "Why would someone hide it in *your* bag?"

"I'm being framed," she said, sullenly picking at a tiny hole in the blanket.

"So it would seem."

Gina blinked. He actually sounded sincere. "You sound like you believe me."

"I believe that you would be smart enough not to keep an expensive copy of a three-thousand-dollar necklace on your person. Particularly not one recently owned by a deceased woman now presumed to have been murdered. One that she'd been wearing at the time of her death. You seem a *little* smarter than that."

"Thanks a bunch."

Roark moved on, ignoring her sarcasm. "When was it placed in your bag, I wonder? How about you walk me through your steps."

"I already thought about it," she said. "All of our bags were in the dressing room, and it had to have happened when I was on the floor. I imagine a lot of people could have handled it when no one was looking."

Roark nodded. "Now, the question is, who has it in for you? Who called in the tip?"

Gina's thoughts leapt to the policewoman, who seemed delighted by her comeuppance. "Nancy?"

Roark looked skeptical. "She wouldn't have done that."

He looked down at Gina through the bars. "You were flashing those pictures around the other day. Rather stupidly, I might add."

"Yeah, I got the message." She touched her knuckles.

"You got someone scared. Enough to want to deflect attention from themselves and onto you. Maybe that's the same reason why you were attacked last night."

"I don't know. The man who attacked me wanted something. Looking for more photographs, I think. I think the Signora sent him after me. Why would she also frame me with the necklace? She wouldn't want police to come to the Third Door."

"You think the Signora had a man attack you? That doesn't seem her style." His words echoed those of Madame Laupin. Lowering his voice, he added, "Those photographs. The ones that you had in your handbag. Where *did* you find them?"

Gina glanced at Sally. Nancy had called her a canary. Could she be listening? Right now, the woman was just humming to herself and regarding her red lacquered nails. She didn't want to chance it. Besides, Gina thought Roark could give her something in return. "Get me out of here and I'll tell you everything," she whispered. "Just don't let them arrest me."

Roark raised an eyebrow. "Done."

Soon after, Gina and Roark left the police station to where Roark's Model T was waiting on the street. He took her arm as she walked, a gesture which, she guessed, was not born out of concern for safety, but rather to ensure she would not run away from him.

He unlocked the passenger door. "Get in," he said. "I'll get you a cup of coffee."

"At this hour?" She knew it had to be around eleven o'clock.

"I know a place."

He didn't seem to have any trouble maneuvering the car, despite his limp and war-torn hand. As he was driving down the quiet street, he glanced at her. "Look, I got a tip from the station. That the necklace had been stolen, and that one of you girls had done it. They said it was you, but I didn't believe it. I didn't expect that the necklace would turn up in your bag, or that they would take you in."

"Thanks a bunch," Gina muttered.

They pulled up in front of a late-night coffeehouse, the kind that had popped up all over Chicago with the advent of Prohibition.

A platinum blonde pushing forty greeted them at the door. "Roark," she said, giving Gina the once-over. "Long time no see."

"How you doin', Josie," he said. "Bring us two coffees and some pie, would you? Apple if you have it."

"Sure thing, hon," she replied. "Be back in a jif. Just seat yourselves."

Very few people were there, and no one looked up as Roark led her to a table in the back corner. They sat in silence until Josie placed the food in front of them. He pushed her slice of pie toward her. "Eat."

She picked up her fork without hesitation. The apple pie, golden and warm in its soft sugary crust, could not be resisted. She slid her fork through the pie and took an enormous bite.

"Now. No more screwing around," Roark said, watching

her chew. "Where did you get those pictures? You found Marty's missing camera, didn't you?"

After swallowing, she spoke carefully. "Yeah. I developed the photographs." She took a swig of the coffee.

He didn't seem wholly surprised. "I figured. You weren't as subtle as you thought."

Gina took another bite of the pie, waiting for him to go on.

"What I can't figure out, though, is how exactly you came by the camera. Did you find it in his flat?" Before she could answer, he continued to muse. "Marty must've hidden it. We both know that the Signora's men would have searched his flat when they found out he died."

Gina shrugged, letting him work it out. She'd had the same thought about Marty's flat when she'd seen it, that someone had searched it before she'd gotten there. But she certainly wasn't going to tell him what Marty had actually done with the camera.

"That camera was an extension of himself. It was always with him." He took a bite and chewed absentmindedly. "When would he have had time to hide it? Did he meet up with the people who murdered him? Was he suspicious?" He seemed more intent than before. "Did he die in the gangway? Are you the one who found him? I've been wondering this for some time now. Tell me the truth."

Gina took a deep breath. "I found Marty as he was dying. Right where you saw that bloodstain on the ground." She looked down at the coffee cup, swirling in some more sugar with her teaspoon. Tears welled in her eyes at the memory and at the relief of finally telling someone. "I saw it happen. It was awful."

"You saw it happen?" he said loudly, then, after a quick look around, forced himself to lower his voice. "You saw Marty get murdered?! Why in hell haven't you said anything? Why in hell didn't you say anything that night?! For God's sakes! Who did it? Who killed him?"

"I don't know! It was dark! I couldn't see. I didn't even realize at first what had h-happened. It was aw-awful. T-terrible!" Gulping back tears caused her to hiccup. "I wanted to tell someone, but I was afraid." She put her face into her hands and sobbed in earnest.

Roark came around to sit beside her then, and she leaned against him, sobbing. For a moment he held her while she cried, but then she pushed him away. She took a napkin and blew her nose, then used another to wipe her eyes. She was sure she was a streaky mess.

He returned to the other side of the table and faced her. "All right, tell me what happened. From the beginning."

Still hiccupping, she explained how she had wanted to talk to Marty and went looking for him. When she couldn't find him, she ended up taking a breather in the gangway. "Then I s-saw some shadowy figures, but I didn't think anything of it. Until I heard this s-sound," she gulped, "and one of them slumped to the ground. Only when I kneeled beside him did I realize it was Marty. He begged me to hide the camera, I swear it." She twisted the napkin in her hands. "Then he, you know. Died."

Roark tapped his fork on the plate. "You didn't ask who had stabbed him?"

"Of course I asked him," she said, her anguish giving way to irritation. "You gotta understand, he only had a few words left in him. He was just worried about the camera—about keeping it from the wrong hands." She stared down at the crumbs on her plate, trying not to be overcome by a sudden feeling of nausea. "I'm not sure he even knew who attacked him."

"Why didn't you tell anyone?"

"I didn't know who I *could* trust. Not really. I didn't know what he had taken pictures of, so I hid the camera and film until I could figure out what to do with it. You have no idea how hard this has been."

"Anything else?" he asked.

"Well, there was a key . . ." She explained about the key and about the photographs she had found under the floorboards, with pictures from the Third Door.

Roark pulled out his wallet and, after gesturing to the waitress, laid a few bills on the table. "All right, I want you to show me everything in Marty's flat. Everything you've been hiding. All the photographs you developed, Marty's notebook, everything. All right?" He looked wary then, as if he expected her to refuse.

Distantly she heard the bells of the St. Francis of Assisi Catholic Church toll twice. Two a.m. "That's fine," she said. "Tomorrow afternoon."

He frowned. "How about now?"

And what would your wife think about that? she wondered. "That's not possible," she said instead. "I need to get home. I need to check on my father."

"Then first thing in the morning. At eight a.m."

She shook her head. "No. I need to rest. I'm exhausted. We can meet in the afternoon."

"Fine. Let's go. I'll drive you home." Perhaps sensing her surprise, he asked, "You thought I would just leave you here?"

After Gina gave her address, she and Roark were silent as he drove through the dark Chicago streets. This time of the morning, very few people were out and about.

When he pulled up in front of the brownstone, she put her hand on the handle, preparing to jump out.

"Hold on," he said, turning off the engine. For a wild moment, she thought he was going to get out of the car and open the passenger door. What was he doing? Was he going to walk her to her front steps?

"I'll be fine," she said, suddenly tensing up. She opened the door.

He gave her a curious look. "Yeah, maybe. I'm not so sure. Someone has it in for you." He tapped his fingers on the steering wheel. "Let's meet at Marty's. At three p.m. I want to look at those pictures again. I want you to walk me through everything, step by step."

Then the question she'd had for a while surged up before she could stop it. "Hey! Won't *your wife* mind that you're helping me so much?"

He raised an eyebrow. "I doubt it. She left me over a year ago."

"Oh, I—" She stopped, a mortified flush rising in her cheeks.

"Forget it." He gestured impatiently toward the car door. "I'll see you at three."

Embarrassed, she jumped out of the car and hurried up the walk. When she reached the door, his car roared off, leaving her feeling exhausted and drained from the events of the evening.

CHAPTER 20

Hearing the clip-clop of the milk truck making its rounds outside, Gina burrowed deeper into her bed. She'd slept surprisingly well, but now her mind was starting to race as she remembered everything that had gone on the night before.

The necklace, being carted off to jail, and even those odd moments with Roark. Why had he helped her? Out of respect for Marty? *Maybe he's interested in you*, a little voice whispered inside her, before she hastily pushed the thought away. She had bigger things to worry about. Like reviewing the photographs later.

Then she sat bolt upright in her bed, a thought coming to her. What was it that Miss Van der Veer had said? *I'll never forget how I found her at the Drake Hotel* . . . Didn't some of Marty's last pictures have the Drake Hotel in the background?

She glanced at the clock. "I'm not waiting for Roark," she said out loud, slipping her legs over the side of the bed. "Maybe he got me out of jail, but it's not like I deserved to be there in the first place."

Within a few minutes she had already begun to fix her father's breakfast. Though she felt a little bad about doing it, she banged the pan against the stove a few times, in order to wake him up.

Her gambit worked. A short while later he emerged a bit bleary-eyed from his bedroom. "You're up early, sweetheart," he said. "I didn't even hear you come in last night."

"Oh, the Signora kept us a little later than usual," she said, feeling a pang at the lie. Sliding the scrambled eggs and bacon onto a plate, she placed it all in front of him. Luckily Mrs. Hayford had already dropped off the day's paper for her father. "Here's the news," she said, practically dancing in her impatience. "Is there anything else you need? Pepper? Salt?"

He looked at her, and for a moment she felt he could see through her, see through the lies. "You have somewhere to go? Something to do?"

"Yes, Papa."

"Then go!" he said, swatting her playfully with the newspaper. "Let me enjoy my breakfast in peace."

Turning the light on, Gina studied the prints as they dried on the line above the tub, feeling pleased by their appearance. She'd decided to make another set, so that the details were crisper. She'd used the enlarger more precisely and had left the prints a little longer in the developer.

Being careful not to touch the prints, Gina took a magnifying glass and, standing on her tiptoes, began to examine them in order, this time focusing on the male subject who appeared in the first five images of the roll. What was special about this man? What about him had caught Marty's attention?

Gina paid more attention to the man's stance, noticing how he was leaning against a streetlight, with a newspaper held open in front of him. Except she could now see that he was not reading the paper, as she had initially assumed. Rather, his eyes were looking above the paper, apparently in the direction of the hotel entrance.

She then looked at the photograph of the same man, this time lighting the cigarette of the woman wearing the long fur coat. The woman's face was turned away from the camera and obscured by her cloche hat.

Moving to the last of the prints featuring the same subject, Gina was struck by the man's positioning. He appeared to be looking straight at Marty's camera, an angry squint shading his expression. She drew her breath in sharply. Had he been aware that Marty was taking his photograph?

Turning back to the third photograph, Gina scrutinized the woman. Her fur coat and matching cloche appeared to be a bright, snowy white, with a spotted trim.

She began to breathe more rapidly, recognizing the markings on the fur coat. Angling the magnifying glass, she was sure now that this coat belonged to Genevieve Beering, the deceased heiress. Given that this image had been left undeveloped in the camera, Marty must have photographed her shortly before she died. The question was, why?

Gina was still pondering these questions several hours later as she stretched out on Marty's sofa, waiting for the prints to dry. A great pounding at the door to Marty's flat interrupted her reverie. Was it Roark arriving early? She wasn't sure if she felt more resentful or excited at the thought, particularly as the pounding grew more intense.

Looking through the peephole, however, she discovered that the impatient visitor was none other than Nancy Doyle.

An angry wave swept over Gina and she stepped back from the door, unsure what to do.

"Open up!" Nancy called with all her authority as a police matron. "I know you're in there."

Gina opened the door a few inches, keeping the chain in place. "What do *you* want?"

"I want to speak to you."

"I have nothing to say to you, *Officer Doyle.*"

"Gina, I know you're angry. Let me explain."

"I think you explained everything quite well last night. When you allowed me to be locked up for theft and *murder.*"

"Oh, Gina, I didn't really expect it to be *you.* I had to follow up on the tip. See how things would shake out."

"There's nothing to shake out here." Annoyed, Gina closed the door.

"I can wait here a long time," Nancy called.

"Fine. Do that," Gina called back through the door. "You can't arrest me. I answered their questions, and they released me. No thanks to you."

There was silence. "I'm the one who gave you back your radio. I left it on your porch."

Gina opened the door completely and regarded the policewoman, hands planted on her hips. "If you gave it back, then you're also the one who took it."

Nancy bowed her head but didn't seem particularly ashamed. "Just let me in. I'll explain everything."

Curiosity winning out over her sense of annoyance, Gina gestured for Nancy to follow her into Marty's living area.

To her surprise, the policewoman seemed uncharacteristically nervous. "You're right. I'm the one who broke into your flat."

"Why did you do that?"

"I'm not proud of it," she said. "I just had to know what you were hiding. I didn't even believe that you were really Molly's daughter. I had to check your identity before I let them give you access to Marty's things. I wasn't at all sure that you were on the up-and-up."

"I was."

"Yes. I see that now."

"Why'd you take the radio?"

Nancy actually grinned. "Well, I had to make it look good, didn't I? No offense, but it was the only thing of value that I could find. You know, I wasn't going to steal your mother's jewelry. I do have some scruples." She scratched her nose. "Besides, I gave it back, didn't I? Now. How about you tell me what you've been hiding, and maybe I can help you."

"Maybe I should have *you* arrested for theft. I wonder what Captain O'Neill will say when he learns that his very own police matron is a burglar."

"Gina, come on. Just tell me."

"Fine." For the second time in twenty-four hours, Gina found herself explaining how she had witnessed Marty's murder and how he had given her the camera.

"Show me the pictures," Nancy ordered. "This I've got to see for myself."

Gina shrugged. "All right, then. Come on."

Once in the darkroom, Nancy gave a low whistle when she saw the hanging prints. "So you learned how to develop the film," she commented, her voice holding a grudging admiration. "Good for you."

Gina pointed to the picture of the woman in the fur coat. "That's Genevieve Beering, I think. For some reason, Marty was taking photographs of her and that man. Perhaps they were having an affair." She continued to study the photographs. "He must be very tall. Look how much taller he is than her. I met Genevieve Beering once, and she towered over the other women. Particularly in heels. Stood eye to eye with the Signora, though."

Nancy looked where she was pointing. "Oh, I don't know. I'd guess he's average height. See where the top of his head comes to against the lamppost? Maybe five-ten or something in that range."

Gina frowned. "I remember how Miss Beering's coat swept around her legs when she walked. On this woman, the coat seems much longer, almost to her ankles . . ."

"Different coat," Nancy said with a shrug.

"No, I'm sure it's hers. I remember the markings." Gina snapped her fingers. "This is not the heiress. This is a much smaller woman who is wearing Miss Beering's coat." She began to speak out loud, musing more to herself than to Nancy. "Why was someone else wearing the heiress's fur coat on the day she died? What had that person been doing outside the Drake Hotel? Besides—why had Marty been taking pictures of this woman at all?"

Gina trained the magnifying glass on the woman's lower limbs, stopping cold when she began to examine the woman's shoes. They were unusual—a gently sloping heel with dark spots, a swirling pattern, and an elegant buckle. "It can't be!"

"What? What is it?"

"I know these shoes. I've seen them before." Not on the huge ungainly feet of the heiress, but on the petite feet of a dancer. A memory was telling her that the swirls had hues of rose and purple, with a few dabs of blue and gray. She remembered where she'd seen them, too—in a tousled heap on the floor of the ladies' dressing room at the Third Door.

Scooping up the photographs, she grabbed her handbag and darted to the door. "Those shoes are downstairs, I'm sure of it."

As she raced away she heard Nancy call after her, "I'll phone this in from Mrs. Lesky's apartment. Marty's isn't working."

"You do that!" As she rushed down the steps, she nearly collided with Roark on his way up. He put his arms on her shoulders as much to steady himself as to keep her in place. "Gina, I learned something today. Also I wanted to talk to you. About my wife. I—"

She cut him off. "Sorry, Roark! No time to explain. I have to figure something out. I'm heading to the Third Door."

"Wait, Gina!" she heard Roark call, but she kept going. She could hear him stomping furiously after her.

A few minutes later, she walked straight through the tea room and down into the Third Door, directly past a startled-looking Little Johnny. She'd probably been fired after her indecorous removal the night before, but she descended into the Third Door as if she were still employed.. At the foot of the stairs, she nearly collided with Donny, who had evidently just arrived for his game.

"Hey, doll, how's tricks?" he asked.

Gina paused, not wanting to ignore the ex-soldier. She quickly traded a few pleasantries with the man, trying not to breathe too loudly. Her mind was racing, and she wasn't sure what she'd said, but whatever it was made Donny laugh. That brief exchange allowed time for Roark to catch up with her as she walked toward the ladies' dressing area.

"Gina!" he demanded. "Tell me what's going on!"

"All right," she said. "There's something I need to tell you." Without thinking how it might look, she pulled him into the ladies' lounge. Luckily the room was empty.

"What is it?" he growled.

"Sit," she said, pointing to one of the stools at the makeup table. She began to lay the photographs on the wooden surface. "Look at these. These were the first images on Marty's last roll of film. He took them outside the Drake Hotel. I think that the Signora may have sent him to take pictures of Genevieve Beering."

Roark glanced at the pictures of the woman in the white fur coat. "Okay, so he took a picture of Miss Beering."

"So it would seem. But see here. This man"—she pointed to the man with the cap pulled low across his face—"appears here to be very tall because the heiress, as you know, is quite tall. However, I believe this man to be of regular height. Look at him against the streetlight."

Roark whistled. "So what you're saying—"

"This isn't Genevieve Beering. This is a shorter woman, *wearing* Genevieve Beering's fur coat. On the same day that Miss Beering was found dead. My guess is that this woman knows something about her death. This can't be a coincidence." She pulled the magnifying glass from her purse. "Now look at the woman's shoes."

He took the magnifying glass and frowned. "What am I looking at?"

"I know these shoes. They have this distinctive swirling pattern and spotted heels. Very unusual. I'm sure I've seen them. Here at the Third Door." She began to look through the piles of the entertainers' show shoes. "Will you help me? We have to find out who they belong to."

"It can't be," Roark said, still staring at the photographs.

"It makes sense that it's someone who works here," she insisted, feeling a bit annoyed. Then, triumphantly, she found the shoes at the bottom of the heap. "Here they are!"

He glanced at the shoes but then pointed to the photograph again. "No, I mean I know who this is." He pointed to the man who'd been featured in the first few photographs, the cap pulled down over his face. "He's one of the guys who plays cards in the back some nights. A vet, like the rest of us. I think his name is Milt Sweeney. What was he doing there?"

"Look at the way he's holding the newspaper," Gina replied. "It's open, but he's not reading it. Looks like he was waiting for something, or someone."

"He's here tonight!" Roark said. "I saw him when I walked in. I'm going to go grab him while I can."

Holding the photographs in one hand and the shoes in the other, Gina walked over to the speakeasy bar. "Billy," she said to the bartender, laying the shoes on the bar, "can you hang on to these for a moment? It's important."

Out of the corner of her eye, she saw Nancy, Captain O'Neill, and another copper descend the main staircase.

Billy noticed them, too. "Sure thing, doll," he said, throwing a towel over the shoes before tucking them away below the bar. She was grateful but not surprised when he didn't ask any questions.

At the sight of the police, the few patrons present began to slip away, downing their drinks and avoiding eye contact as they departed. Donny winked at her as he left. Only Mr. Darrow stayed seated upon his usual stool at the end of the bar. The other cocktail waitresses approached, taking in the sight.

"What's with the fuzz?" Faye asked, eying Gina with suspicion. "Steal another necklace?"

The other girls laughed, although Lulu looked sympathetic. Linking Gina's arm in her own, she whispered, "How you doin', hon? You doin' okay?"

Big Mike walked toward the police, rubbing his hands together. "Gentlemen, lady," he said, speaking grandly to the cops. "To what do we owe this unexpected visit?"

The Signora came to stand beside her husband. "Yes, Captain O'Neill," she said, her eyes stern and foreboding. "I thought we had an agreement."

"That was before I received an urgent call from Officer Doyle here, that new information related to the murder of Genevieve Beering had come to light," he replied.

Nancy stepped forward. "Gina, show them what you figured out."

Everyone swiveled around to face her, causing her mouth to go unexpectedly dry and her body to shake. Trying to steady herself, she leaned against the bar. She glanced at Mr. Darrow's glass of whiskey. *I sure could use a drink.*

As if reading her mind, Billy Bottles placed a shot glass in front of her and poured it full of gin. "Drink up," he whispered. Then he looked straight at Captain O'Neill and shrugged. "I didn't charge her for it."

Not caring that everyone was watching, Gina tossed back the shot, ignoring the burning sensation as the gin tore through her throat and stomach.

"Perhaps we should all go back to my salon," the Signora suggested.

"No, we'll stay here," Captain O'Neill said. "Start talking."

Coughing a bit, Gina set the empty shot glass aside and began to lay out the photographs on the bar as if she were dealing a hand of blackjack. "These photographs were all taken by Marty Doyle, on the last day of his life. Some, you can see, were taken here. And some were taken outside the Drake Hotel, where the heiress Genevieve Beering was killed, that very same day."

Everyone peered at the photographs.

"Hey, that's Milt Sweeney!" Lulu cried, pointing to the man in the photographs.

"This Milt Sweeney?" Roark pushed the man in, keeping Milt's arm tightly behind his back.

Seeing him, Gina felt a little queasy. "That's the man who attacked me the other night," she declared, noting the bruising on the man's lower jaw with some satisfaction. Her wallop had left its mark, the bruise a sharp contrast to his pallid, uneasy face. "He probably wanted these photographs. He must have known Marty had seen him outside the Drake the same day Genevieve Beering was murdered inside."

"I don't know what you're talking about. I never laid a hand on her," Milt said, a pained expression crossing his face as Roark pushed his arm up behind his back.

"And I never laid a hand on you either," Roark muttered, giving him another painful push.

"Roark!" Captain O'Neill said. "Enough of that!" He gestured to the other cop to take Milt from Roark. "Now, Sweeney, explain what you were doing in these here photographs."

"These pictures don't mean nothing," Milt replied, struggling now against the cop. "So I was in front of a hotel. What's it to you?"

"How can you know when the pictures were taken?" Big Mike asked, having looked them over. "There aren't any dates."

"Marty didn't use an autographic camera," Gina replied, remembering what Roark had explained about the film up in Marty's flat. "Usually he'd write information on the prints after they were developed."

"So this is just on your say-so that these photographs were taken that day," Faye commented, flicking a stray feather from her dress.

Mr. Darrow spoke up then. "I believe that I can help you with that point. The man in the photograph, Mr. Sweeney, is holding a newspaper, on which the layout, headlines, columns, pictures, and so forth, are clearly visible. It should not be difficult to find a copy of that day's *Tribune* and match it. That could easily help confirm the date when the photograph was taken."

"What was Marty doing taking pictures at the Drake anyway?" Big Mike broke in, beads of sweat forming on his forehead. He glowered at his wife. "Do you know?"

"Of course, *darling.*" The Signora's glance was frigid. "I sent him."

"You sent him?" Big Mike said, his face reddening. "Why?"

"I know you were having an affair," the Signora replied, her voice icy. "I suspected it might be with *that woman.* Genevieve Beering. So I told him to wait outside the Drake in case you came to visit."

"No, I . . . I wasn't having an affair with her," Big Mike protested weakly. But the guilt was written all over his face.

"Then why did you pay off the coroner?" Roark asked, looking rueful as he caught Gina's eye. "I tried to tell you

earlier," he said in a low tone, "but you'd already rushed off."
Speaking louder, Roark added, "I had assumed her family had
paid him off, but when I spoke to the coroner, he admitted—
with some more greasing on my part—that it had been Big
Mike who wanted to keep Miss Beering's murder out of the
news."

"If she was having an affair with anyone, it was with that
man," Big Mike said, jerking his head toward Milt Sweeney.
"That's him in the photograph with Genevieve. Look at the
way he's lighting her cigarette."

"That's not Genevieve Beering," Gina said. "That's a different woman. A woman wearing Genevieve's white fur coat
and cloche hat. A woman who works at the Third Door." She
signaled to Billy to hand her the shoes he'd stashed behind
the bar. "I know, because *these* are her shoes."

Simultaneously Lulu and Jade gasped, turning to stare at
Faye.

"Those are your shoes, Faye!" Lulu exclaimed, popping
her hand over her mouth.

"Check out the photograph," Gina said, grabbing one of
the shoes and holding it against the picture. "I'm telling you,
these are the shoes that the woman in this photograph is wearing. That woman is Faye!"

The Signora picked up the other shoe and held it against
the image. "They appear the same." She gave her employee a
chilling stare, and dropped the shoe back on the bar in distaste.

"I didn't have anything to do with that woman's death,"
Faye declared, lifting up her chin. "Just a coincidence that I
own a similar pair of shoes." She glared at everyone in the
room, her chest rising and falling quickly.

Captain O'Neill coughed, and Nancy stared at Gina. *Fix this*, she could almost hear the policewoman saying. Gina felt deflated. This was not how this was supposed to go.

After a long moment, the captain spoke. "All right, I'm tired of this," he said. "Milt Sweeney, I'm taking you in for questioning about the murder of Genevieve Beering and—"

"Hey, you can't lay that rap on me!" Milt interrupted. "Faye, tell him!"

"Shut your trap!" Faye hissed. "I've got nothing to say."

"Let's take him away," Captain O'Neill said to the other cop, who started to pull the man's elbow.

"No, wait!" Milt shouted. "Faye, come on, tell them I didn't have anything to do with that woman's murder."

"I don't know what you're talking about," Faye shouted. "I wasn't there! That's not me! And you're just a backroom cheat! How many times has Gooch thrown you out of here? I don't get on with the likes of you!"

"Faye!" Milt said, looking deeply hurt. "I thought you loved me. You said you would do anything for me! Like I would do anything for you—"

Faye tossed her head in disgust, and Milt's pathetic confusion started to turn to a deeper, darker anger.

"All right, gentlemen," Big Mike said smoothly. "Why don't you go ahead and take Mr. Sweeney in."

"Hey, wait a minute," Milt cried, his eyes getting wider. "I didn't know Faye was gonna kill that Beering woman! She came out of the Drake in that fancy fur coat and hat, just needed her cigarette lit. I swear I didn't know till later, when I saw the blood on her dress. That's when she told me."

"Shut up!" Faye shouted, trying to speak over him. "He's lying!"

"Told you what?" Captain O'Neill asked Milt, ignoring Faye's outburst.

"That she'd bashed in the woman's head. That's when she told me to pawn the necklace and the fur coat, and she'd pay me my cut from there. That's why Big Mike hushed it up."

"So she *did* kill Miss Beering," Gina said. "I imagine Faye put on her fur coat to hide the blood on her own clothes, and the hat to keep from being noticed. But the heiress's feet were too big, so Faye had to wear her own shoes when she left the hotel."

"Oh, you think you're so smart," Faye said, a harsh flush staining her cheeks. "You can't even serve drinks without spilling them. Isn't that right, girls?"

Lulu and Jade, wearing similar expressions of horror, edged away from Faye.

Ignoring her, Gina continued to speak to Captain O'Neill. "Miss Beering had been gambling at the Third Door," she said slowly, remembering what she had overheard. "Losing a lot of money. She must have been deep in debt."

"How much did Genevieve Beering owe you, dear?" the Signora asked her husband, her voice sounding like poisoned honey. "Were you tired of accepting her *favors*? Is that why you went after her?"

Again, the guilt on his face was easily read, even though he tried to demur.

But Milt confirmed her guess. "That's exactly it, Signora. Big Mike sent us to collect on her debt. Faye's been helping him out. Told her that he'd make her the new Signora at the new joint he was setting up. Faye asked for my help, too. Thought there might be a spot for me in the new place. Like Gooch." He faltered when he glanced at Faye, who was breathing harder now. "Faye told me she'd handle it, so I waited outside the hotel. I didn't expect Faye to *kill* her, just to take something valuable to, you know, pay down the debt. That's what we usually do, right, Big Mike?"

"Dead men can't pay debts," Big Mike muttered, glaring at Faye. "You're such a moron! Couldn't grasp a thing like that. And you wanted to work in my new place? Couldn't even get a simple collection right. As dumb as Dorrie."

Suddenly Faye's rising rage seemed to explode within her. She grabbed the shoe from the bar and flung it furiously at Big Mike, hitting him square in his forehead. "That flimflam debutante laughed at me! Called me stupid to believe that I could be anything other than a two-bit hoofer at a gin joint. Me! Said that Big Mike was just using me, stringing me along to keep me doing his dirty work!"

Her hysteria began to rise as Nancy grabbed her by the arms and pinned them around her back. "She said you were never gonna recognize my loyalty, no matter what I've done for you!" she screamed at Big Mike. "So yeah, I slammed her against a wall and then I smashed her perfect mouth in to stop those lies! I did everything you asked of me, and this is my reward! I even slept with this buffoon to make sure he would do what I asked! I even had him—"

Big Mike struck her across the mouth, and the violence of the act shocked them all into silence. Without being asked, Gooch and Little Johnny stepped forward and grasped their boss's arms. Faye slumped back against Nancy, holding her cheek, making little moaning sounds.

"Kill Marty," Gina said dully, finishing Faye's sentence. "You even had Milt Sweeney kill Marty. Later that night." She barely noticed the tears slipping down her cheeks until

Roark gently wiped them away. She crossed her arms as she stared at Milt.

"They killed Marty Doyle, too?" Captain O'Neill asked quietly. He seemed stunned by the revelations, like everyone else, but was trying to maintain a sense of authority. "Explain, please, Miss Ricci."

"It makes sense, right?" Gina said, working it out as she went. "At first, Milt didn't know that Faye had killed Miss Beering. So it didn't occur to him that Marty being on the scene, taking some photographs, could be a problem. But he tells her about seeing Marty, later. Must have spooked her, not knowing what he'd seen, or what he'd say when news of Miss Beering's murder got out."

Nancy made an odd sound, as if she might have been biting back a wailing cry.

Gina looked away. "Faye must have realized then that she had to find out what Marty knew, and if he had told anybody anything." She closed her eyes as she remembered the scene, and how Marty couldn't identify his attacker. "She must have sent Milt to confront him. Then Milt killed him, and left him for dead."

"Hey, dummy," Milt called out. "He *was* dead, I made sure of that." At the sound of Roark's mirthless chuckle, Milt's eyes grew wide as he realized he had just confessed to Marty's murder. Faye and Mike threw up their hands in disgust.

Billy Bottles reached across the counter and grabbed Milt by the throat. "I'd do you in right now, if I could," he said menacingly. "Marty was my pal!"

"Ahem," Captain O'Neill coughed. Billy let go.

"Yeah, well, you didn't finish him like you thought," Gina

said, smirking at Milt. "He was still alive when I found him. Barely."

There was collective shock in the room, even from Faye.

"Yeah, I was in the gangway when you killed him." Seeing Captain O'Neill frown, she added hastily, "But I didn't realize what had happened at the time. I saw two men talking, and then all of a sudden one of them had slumped to the ground and the other man had run off. When I went to check on the poor sot, I discovered that it was Marty, and that he had been stabbed. He was fading fast." She bit back a sob. "Marty's only concern was that I hide the camera, which I did."

She gazed coldly at Milt. "Yeah, I guess Faye didn't tell you to look for his camera, but it was right there, on him. With all the pictures." She gulped. "He begged me not to trust anyone, not even the police. Or you, Signora." She looked at them both apologetically before staring down at her hands. "And then he died."

She leaned against the back of a bar stool for support. Brushing a tear from her eye, she continued. "I went back to work then, even though I scarcely knew what I was doing."

"I remember the blood on your forehead," Ned muttered.

"And you brought me the same drink order twice," Roark said, giving her the faintest of smiles. "I wondered why you'd be so nice to me."

Gina continued her narrative. "When I came back to the gangway at the end of the night, Marty's body was gone."

"Milt must have come back later," Roark replied. "To dump the body under the Harrison Street Bridge."

"A favorite spot for the mob," Mr. Darrow mused. "A perfect cover-up."

"And what about Dorrie?" Ned cried out. "Did you kill her, too?"

"*She* did that, too," Milt said, pointing at Faye. "Because *Big Mike* told her to."

"Why?" Ned asked, his voice cracking. "Why'd you have to kill her?"

"Dorrie was trying to get in on the act," Milt said. "She'd been one of Big Mike's messengers, delivering *reminders* to customers who owed him money."

"Just small-timers," Big Mike said, a bit resentfully. "I never sent her to anyone who might hurt her. I care about my employees." Gina bit back a laugh.

"Until they cross you," Faye said spitefully. "Dorrie, our own dumb Dora, started cutting in as the middleman, blackmailing *our* customers. Saying she'd tell other things she'd witnessed at the Third Door."

"Is that what she told Genevieve Beering?" Gina asked, remembering what Miss Van der Veer had recounted about the conversation with Dorrie she'd overheard.

Faye sniffed. "The perfect heiress, who'd never worked a day in her life. Guess she didn't want her family to know that she'd been gambling away her fortune. That she'd been sleeping with Big Mike when she couldn't pay him back."

"So Dorrie tried to blackmail her," Milt continued, despite Faye's glare. "'Course it never occurred to her that Miss Beering would just rat her out, tell Big Mike what she was planning. Rubbed him the wrong way."

Big Mike glowered at him. "Dorrie would've ruined everything! Everything I've built here."

"Everything *you've* built here? You know how many of *your* scrapes I've had to clean up over the years?" the Signora asked, her voice rising. "You killed Dorrie!"

"Of course not," Big Mike replied.

"*Scusami,*" the Signora said, without any sincerity. "So one of your lackeys did the hit for you. Same thing."

"Big Mike told Faye to end her," Milt said, not holding anything back now. "So she did. Just followed her onto the L, and slammo-bammo, that was all there was to it."

"I've heard enough," Captain O'Neill said. "Officers, please arrest these three individuals for the murders of Dorrie Edwards, Genevieve Beering, and Martin Doyle."

After Big Mike, Faye, and Milt had been led away in hand-cuffs, and the last of the patrons, including Mr. Darrow, had exited the building, the Signora turned to the rest of the Third Door staff. They all appeared to be in shock. Billy Bottles poured out shots of gin for everyone, which they all silently downed in one go.

"We're closing down for the evening. But tomorrow we're back in business." Her words were pure steel, as if her husband had not just been arrested for murder, alongside two of her employees. "Jade, you're taking on all of Faye's roles from here on. I assume you'll be staying? No more auditions."

Jade's eyes glinted in the light, and she smiled like a satisfied cat. "Thank you, Signora."

As the staff began their closing duties, the Signora moved to the balcony, where she stood silently, like a porcelain art deco statue.

Gina moved to stand beside her, and for a moment they looked over the speakeasy together. For the first time, Gina could see cracks on the ceiling and the walls. She could see sparkles here and there on the floor as well, probably sequins broken off from glitzy costumes. Something dark had happened here, but the chandeliers still shone brightly, as did the flutes and gin glasses above the bar, catching gleams of light and color.

Glancing at the Signora, Gina noticed a few strands of her sleek black hair were out of place, making her seem more vulnerable than ever before. Perhaps this was finally the moment to ask the question that had been puzzling her for weeks.

"Signora," she ventured carefully. "Why *did* you have Lulu tell me about the position? Why did you want me to work here?"

The proprietress's expression softened as she turned to look down at Gina. "Oh, I had heard about your father's troubles. I asked her if she knew you—I thought there was a good chance she would, given you'd grown up just a few blocks apart. I told her to tell you about the job, make it sound good. But let it seem like your idea."

"Thank you, but *why*? Why give me the job? Lots of people have hard lives, need work."

To Gina's great surprise, the Signora touched her face. "You look so much like your papa," she said. With that gesture, Gina saw her as she might have looked thirty years before, in love with a young boxer from the old neighborhood, before he went and married an Irish girl from the North Side. Then the Signora smoothed her hair, and the tender moment passed. "You'll be here at six p.m. sharp tomorrow night?"

"Yes Signora." Then, before she could overthink her next

words, she pressed on. "You know, I've learned a lot about photography these last few weeks. Just in case, you know, you're looking to, uh, fill Marty's place."

The Signora gave the smallest of smiles. "I'll keep that in mind."

Two weeks later, Gina and Lulu huddled over the *Tribune* in fear and amazement, reading the front-page news again and again. MASSACRE 7 OF MORAN GANG, the headline read. The North Side hit had occurred the day before, on Valentine's Day, and had left everyone in Chicago reeling. That such a thing could occur in broad daylight was unthinkable, and that the deed had been carried out by men dressed as cops had been even more shocking. Though no one said it outright, the name Capone was on everyone's lips.

When they pored over the newspapers, looking at the victims' photos, they had been stunned to discover that the man they'd called Jack had been one of the victims. A member of the Moran gang. There were pictures of some of their wives, too, including Jack's, who had been on the receiving end of Mimi's cocktail, and Maxine, the woman Gina had met in the ladies' room shortly after. Collectively the women were called "the Bullet Widows," a term that made Gina shudder.

Given that it was a slow night, the Signora told Gina she could leave around ten. Taking a deep breath, she walked into the back room, her coat and hat already on. Roark looked up at her. "You leaving already?"

"Yeah, I——" She hesitated. Things had been friendly between them, but she had definitely held herself back. She knew he'd been wanting to talk to her, and she wasn't sure if she wanted to hear what he had to say.

"Hang on," he said, downing his gin and tonic. "Let me join you. I'll drive you home."

Ignoring the whistles and hoots that came from the other ex-soldiers, they walked out together. Briefly she felt his hand on her lower back as they maneuvered among some drunkards toward the stairs. When she passed Ned, he gave her a little mock salute, which she hoped Roark hadn't noticed.

Crossing the landing, she brought up the St. Valentine's Day Massacre, as the terrible event was already being called by the newspapers. "It's awful. I didn't much care for Jack, but no one deserves to be mowed down like that."

"That's for sure," Roark replied. "I've heard that there's going to be a new forensic unit opening up. I may start taking photographs for them. I'll be returning to the force soon anyway."

Little Johnny nodded at her as he opened the door into the alley. At the gesture, Gina smiled to herself, feeling like she might finally have been accepted by the others. Her actions two weeks before had all been understood as loyalty to the Signora, and that seemed the only thing that mattered to everyone else at the Third Door.

Roark pointed to the end of the alley. "My car's just over on Halsted."

As they passed by the gangway where Marty had been killed, Gina paused. "Give me a second," she said. From her purse, she pulled out several prints that she had made earlier. She'd gone to the flower shop and taken photographs of some beautiful blooms.

Silently she placed the photographs in the spot where

Marty had been murdered. "Good-bye, Marty," she whispered. "And thanks . . . for everything."

Roark touched her shoulder. "Gina, I—"

She smiled up at him. "Wanna grab that cup of coffee? I
know a great place."

ACKNOWLEDGMENTS

Though Gina could find her way into the Third Door with a few quick knocks and a password, for me, finding that speakeasy required many years of research, with many friends and experts helping and guiding me along the way. The first stirrings of the story began when I was co-teaching "The History and Philosophy of American Higher Education," a graduate course at Northwestern, with my wonderful colleague Eugene Lowe, Jr. I had come across some intriguing stories about college life during Prohibition and intrigued, I began toying with the idea of writing a mystery set on a campus, much like where I worked, in the shadows of the Great Depression. This quest led me to Northwestern's archives and Kevin Leonard, the University's tremendously knowledgeable archivist, who showed me fascinating yearbooks, scrapbooks, college papers, letters, and other artifacts from the period.

Yet when Minotaur picked up my other series, I thought this book might end up in the proverbial drawer. In some ways, a version of it did. But, several years later, I reimagined the series with the help of my wonderful editor, Kelley Ragland, moving it away from a campus and into a Chicago speakeasy, and pushing it from 1930 to 1929 (which is a much more dramatic and exciting year). Most important, I got rid of all the characters but one, a gum-cracking amateur photographer and general sidekick named Gina Ricci, who of course became the story's lead.

From that point, I've been so fortunate to work with many terrific people at Minotaur, including April Osborn, who provided great insights into pesky plot problems and character issues, and Sarah Grill and India Cooper who helped smooth away inaccuracies and odd things. (But of course, any lingering mistakes are mine!) I thank you all for bringing my story to light.

I'd like to thank too, several terrific friends—Nadine Nettman, Erica Neubauer, and Maggie Dalrymple, all excellent writers themselves—for serving as beta readers and providing me with helpful thoughts and advice. Thanks too, to Christy Snider, my old friend from grad school and current professor of U.S. history at Berry College, for reading the manuscript with a historian's critical lens, and offering invaluable insights into historical issues and developments during this time period. More generally, I'm so grateful to good friends Lisa Bagadia, Gretchen Beetner, Terry Bischoff, Jamie Freveletti, Alexia Gordon, July Hyzy, Jess Lourey, Clare O'Donohue, Lori Rader-Day, and Lynne Raimondo for always being willing to help with my 'cocktail research.' You dolls rock!

Lastly, I thank my family for their support, especially my children, Alex and Quentin Kelley, who inspire me every day. And once again, I'm dedicating this book to my husband, Matt Kelley. Someone said to me "You know, this will be the fifth book you've dedicated to him. You *can* dedicate the book to someone else." And yet, no one else is as dedicated to my writing, or to my books, as him. So once again, I thank my dear husband for being my Executive Plot Consultant, my Alpha Reader, my personal publicist, and above all, my Defender Against Dark Moments. You're the bees knees!

ABOUT THE AUTHOR

Lisa Bagadia

SUSANNA CALKINS, author of the award-winning Lucy Campion series, holds a Ph.D. in history and teaches at the college level. Her historical mysteries have been nominated for the Mary Higgins Clark and Agatha awards, among many others, and *The Masque of a Murderer* received a Macavity. Originally from Philadelphia, Calkins now lives in the Chicago area with her husband and two sons.